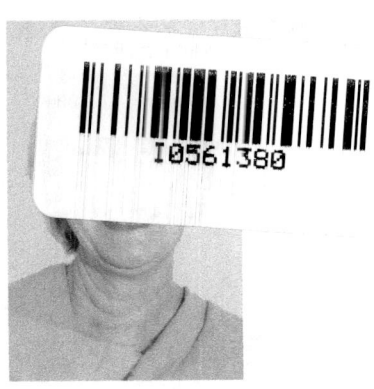

Karen grew up in a small country town in north-eastern Victoria, Australia. She spent her childhood riding horses through beautiful scenery of eucalypts, lakes, and snow-capped mountains and her love of landscape deeply affects her writing. She worked in a range of educational settings and holds a Ph.D. and M.Ed. (Hons) in the areas of fantasy. She is particularly interested in the power of the hero's inner journey which she explores through Deep Fantasy. Karen has travelled extensively overseas but enjoys nothing more than camping in the Australian Outback. She lives in Melbourne and now writes full-time. You can find out more about Karen and her books on her website.

Connect with K. S. Nikakis

Amazon: https://www.amazon.com/author/ksnikakis
Twitter: https://twitter.com/KSNikakis
Facebook: www.facebook.com/ksnikakis
Goodreads: www.goodreads.com
Website: www.ksnikakis.com
Email: author@ksnikakis.com

WORKS BY K S NIKAKIS

Non Fiction

Journey: Seeking the Sacred, Spirit and Soul in the Australian Wilderness

Fantasy Novels
Series

Angel Caste series:
Angel Blood
Angel Breath
Angel Bone
Angel Bound
Angel Blessed
Angel Caste – Complete 5 Book Series

The Kira Chronicles trilogy:*
The Whisper of Leaves
The Song of the Silvercades
The Cry of the Marwing
remnant hard copies only

The Kira Chronicles series:
The Whisper of Leaves
The Silence of Stone
The Secrets of Stars
The Thunder of Hoofs
The Crying of Birds
The Music of Home
The Kira Chronicles – Complete 6 Book Series

Fantasy Novels

The Emerald Serpent
Heart Hunter
The Third Moon
Messenger
I Heard the Wolf Call My Name
Finalist Best YA Novel Aurealis Awards, 2019

Fantasy Short Stories

The Gift
The Tale of Prince Anura
Dragon Sprite
Glass-Heart
Finalist Best YA Short Story Aurealis Awards, 2019

Angel Caste Book 5
Angel Blessed

K.S.Nikakis

Angel Caste – Book 5 Angel Blessed

First published by SOV Media Australia 2017
Amazon: www.amazon.com.au

Publisher: SOV Media
Melbourne, Australia.

Cover by AS Nikakis: http://asnikakis.com
Shutterstock.com/ schankz
DaFont.com/Abdullah Alkhafaji – Ghost Theory 2

National Library of Australia
Cataloguing-in-Publication entry:
Nikakis, Karen Simpson
The Angel Caste series – Book 5 Angel Blessed
ISBN 978-0-6489797-8-4

Learn more about KS Nikakis and her deep fantasy
books at: http://www.ksnikakis.com

For Anne and Wayne, Flynn and Hannah

Glossary of the Rynth

ANGEL CASTE

Crystal Fold
Principae (*prin-sip-pay*)
Nearest to ultimate transcendence. Manifest mainly as aqua light, with white wings and group consciousness. The Principae transcend from Crystal Fold into the Great Beyond.

Ezam Fold
Archae (*ar-kay*)
Five levels: angels ascend from Quin-archae through Quar-archae, Tri-archae, Du-archae, Prime-archae to Archae. The Archae transcend Ezam Fold to Crystal Fold to become Principae, then transcend into the Great Beyond.

Members of the Archae
Archae Kald
Archae Dejon (*day-jon*)

Members of Prime-archae
Prime-archae Mirek
Prime- archae Serith

Dane
Lowest in the hierarchy and newest angels to Ezam. Ascend from Dane to Quin-archae, and then through the hierarchy to Archae to eventually transcend to Crystal Fold as Principae, and then into the Great Beyond.
Members of Dane

Thrisdane
Kydane (*kie-dane*)
Ashdane

Erath Fold
Iahhel – female-aspected angels. Three ascending levels:
Non, Sai, and Hoth. The Iahhel seek oneness with Erath,
and the levels indicate the degree of oneness attained.

Members of Sai
Syatha

Members of Non
Essera
Firah
Orsia

DAIMON CASTE
Reside in any fold where angel caste has joined with
other castes and produced offspring. The term is also
used for those who have *any* angel caste heritage.

Moonsun Fold
Violet (Lettie) Wright – Viv's mother
Viv Wright
Viv's maternal ancestors from Ireland and the USA (also
in Moonsun Fold)

Wheel Fold
Females - elddra; males - elddric

Elddra
Anfarena – most senior (*an-far-reena*)
Anetherey (*a-neth-er-ray*)

Elddric
Ataghan – Syld, band leader, lein to Sehereden (*ata-gan*)
Baraghan – surgeon/healer (*bara-gan*)
Orthagh

Archae Thero - Syld of the Council in Astraal
Meresh – member of the Council in Astraal

HUMAN CASTE

Moonsun Fold

Members of Human Caste
Jimmy (Ronald James) Wright – Lettie Wright's husband
Rim (Rimmon) – gang leader

Wheel Fold
Scharii – travelling musicians (*shar-ree*)

Members of the Scharii
Tarchen en-Scharii (*tar-chen*)
Darch en-Scharii

About Wheel Fold: The eight sectors or Vales of Wheel
Fold are: Eshavale, Ascavale, Warinavale, Genessavale,
Beshavale, Terissavale, Sonoravale and Morvavale.
These run north-south or cloudwise-starwise from the
hub/peak: Astraal. The lake and city are also called
Astraal.

Each Vale has countless smaller valleys or vals. Each Vale has a main river eg Eshavale has the Eshacade; Ascavale has the Ascacade etc. Settlements near the river take their name from the river. eg Esh-embrin; Esh-accom. The tributaries that flow from the vals are rills. Smaller settlements (setts) take their name from the rills eg Scinta-ril (on the Scinta Rill). Inhabitants of these setts are identified by their sett eg Ataghan en-Scinta-ril; Sehereden en-Scinta-ril.

Directions
Cloudwise – north
Starwise – south
Nightwise – west
Sunwise - east

Time Divisions
Zadicans (years) are divided by zadics of 45 days that include a period of recalibration in between (Vorash). Zadics are marked by constellations which appear and disappear in the night sky. Each has a particular meaning. The zadics are: Pool, Cascade, Fire, Ice, Lirium, Glimwing, Cadestone and Horse. Other brief zadics (Call Zadics), are meaningful to individuals and indicate the individual should visit the sacred city.

Eshavale – Vale of Wheel Fold

Members of the Eshadi
Sehereden en-Scinta-ril – lein to Ataghan, member of Ataghan's band (*se-hera-den*)
Fariye – choose-daughter of Ataghan (*far-ree-ay*)
Brithergen – member of Ataghan's band

4

Jethren – member of Ataghan's band
Anthran – member of Ataghan's band
Daran – member of Ataghan's band
Sandagh – member of Ataghan's band (*san-da*)
Inaghan – member of Ataghan's band (*in-a-gan*)
Tormis – server in Ataghan's compound in Esh-accom
Mereya - server in Ataghan's compound in Esh-accom
Sirenya – Fariye's mother (deceased)

Caibel – unacknowledged son of Baraghan (*kay-bel*)
Galian – choose brother of Ithreya

Eshadi Sylds (acknowledged leaders)
Ataghan en-Scinta-ril
Darthen en-Within-ril
Mathian en-Fessen-ril
Garath en-Moss-ril
Kurnen en-Vara-ril

Valen Setts (communities)

Tahsin's Sett (later Gothral's)
Tahsin – sett leader (*tar-sin*)
Enesha – harvester (*ee-nesh-a*)
Prenya – cook (*pren-ya*)
Borash – cook
Fahan – harvester – twin brother of Merhen (*fay-han*)
Merhen – harvester – twin brother of Fahan (*mer-han*)
Doran – guard, kitchen helper
Cazir – harvester, guard (*kaz-eer*)
Jered – harvester, guard
Gothral – Tahsin's choose-brother and new leader of
Tahsin's sett – formerly of the Bracken Rill

Orthagh – harvester (formerly of the Bracken Rill)
Pitren – harvester (formerly of the Bracken Rill)
Norsen – harvester (formerly of the Bracken Rill)

Amethen's Sett
Amethen – sett leader (am-a-then)
Drasen – band leader
Ithreya – sett member (*ith-ray-a*)

Baraghan's compound in Esh-accom
Mishia – female server
Derisi – female server
Verena – female server
Ershen en-Esh-accom – male server and guard

Caibel's mother's compound in Esh-accom
Morvin – elderly server

Stonash – a small people with hooded eyes, flattened
faces, and leathery skin - urrut traders
Long-arms – long-armed kin of the Stonash

LEFER CASTE

Wheel Fold
Lefer Caste are bird/bat-like beings with human caste-
like intelligence

Members of Lefer Caste
Roaith en-Leferen – blue crest (*ro-aith*)
Garian en-Leferen – red crest – alpha of the Rookery

BEASTMAN CASTE

Beastman Fold
Beastmen are puma-human mix creatures with human caste-like intelligence

IDIOMATIC EXPRESSIONS COMMON IN AUSTRALIA

Viv is Australian and uses a range of idiomatic expressions.

Keep tabs on – check on; monitor
Didn't wash/did wash – didn't/did sound true; wasn't/ was acceptable
On the line – to take a risk/be at risk
Knocked-up – made pregnant; being pregnant
Get out of jail free card – from a board game where a special card grants the player advantages
Second chance draw – another ticket is picked out from the losing tickets in a lottery
Sticks the boots in – attacks physically or verbally
Dodged the honesty bullet – to 'dodge a bullet' is to escape something bad
Brownie points – points awarded by doing good deeds that will eventually grant a reward (from the junior group in the Girl Guides movement)
Take the cake – win the prize
Druggies – drug addicts
Sh*t hits the fan - something bad happening with widespread effects

Angel Caste Book 5
Angel Blessed

Chapter 1

Viv stared at Ithreya in horror. Of all the things she had feared in her time in Esh-accom, it had not been this. Fariye had been taken! God in Heaven. Viv had thought the places beyond Esh-accom's walls were hazardous, but the real danger had been right here in the arsehole's compound, and yet none of it made sense.

'But who took her? And why?'

'We were at the festivities but the Syld brought Fariye back early and put her to bed,' said Ithreya thickly. 'She was crying for you. Sehereden told me later you might have gone with Baraghan but we didn't get back here until after midnight. I thought Fariye might still be fretting so I went to her room to tell her but she was gone and a message cylinder left on the bed.'

'What was in it?' asked Viv hoarsely.

Ithreya shrugged helplessly. 'The Syld hasn't said but he's pulled in his band. All Sehereden's said is the traders who lost Lefer to you and Baraghan want compensation.'

'But they *know* the Syld will come after them!' cried Viv.

'Yes. They're not stupid.'

Viv brought a shaking hand to her mouth. They would have worked out a way to collect the *compensation* and be long gone before Poss's whereabouts were known, except it would all be too late by then. Kidnappers killed their victims, not released them.

Viv's legs threatened to give way and Ithreya caught her arm. 'You need to rest. You're not long from your sickbed.'

'No! I *have* to find out what's going on!'

The hall was packed with grim-faced men and Sehereden was there too, but she headed for the arsehole. The hall hushed but she was almost to him before he turned. Heat radiated from him like a furnace and his expression was murderous. 'Tell me what's happened,' she demanded.

'It's no concern of yours, elddra,' he ground out.

'It is! Fariye's *my* lein! Tell me what's happened,' she insisted.

'What's happened is a result of your thefts!'

'And your lack of care! I told you to post—' The blow caught her on the side of the face and sent her sprawling. Her vision blacked then cleared in time to see him stride towards her, fists clenched, but then Sehereden was suddenly between them. 'Get her out of my sight!' the arsehole grated.

Viv's head swam and she tasted blood as Sehereden half-carried her down the passageway to Fariye's room and locked the door behind them. 'Viv ... let me see to your face.'

'Stay away from me,' she panted as she wiped her mouth. The arsehole had split her lip and her head pounded so sickeningly she gripped a chair to stay upright. 'Tell me what the message said,' she choked.

'We're to give coin to certain traders, over twenty in fact, then we'll be told of Fariye's whereabouts.'

9

'Twenty?' she repeated, struggling to make sense of his words.

'None of whom, I'm guessing, know where Fariye is *or* who's responsible,' went on Sehereden grimly. 'Her captors will collect the coin over the next zadics from different vals and compensate those *we* pay for their trouble. The coin will be dispersed quickly. The traders' have their own networks.'

'You won't get Fariye back,' muttered Viv. 'They won't risk her identifying them.'

'They would have blindfolded her.'

Viv turned on him. 'She would have heard their voices! Where I'm from, kidnappers murder their victims!'

Sehereden's face hardened. 'And where *are* you from, Viv? Where *is* this place where kidnapping's so commonplace you're an expert on it? The place that Thrisdane returned to? The *man* with wings? The place you took Baraghan? That was the bargain, wasn't it? The price for freeing *your* lover, the Angellus?' He smiled bitterly. 'I've trusted you when even the most deluded Valen would have walked away, but this is different. I *won't* tolerate your secrecy risking Fariye!'

'*You* won't tolerate *my* secrecy risking Fariye?' retorted Viv furiously. 'I could have saved my stinking skin a dozen times since I've been in this shit-hole! I could have left her in that cave or taken her with me, but I refused to rob her of those she loved, like her arsehole of a father who *should* have protected her! I *told* him to post guards, but he was too arrogant, and now she's gone.'

Viv collapsed onto the chair and cradled her head in her hands. 'There's always a way to hurt people you despise, Sehereden,' she choked. 'Oh, I've no doubt the traders want coin but those who sleep on muddy ground *always* want to cut down those who sleep in feather beds. And there's *always* something to use against them, something that makes them vulnerable, something called love.'

She took a shuddering breath. 'I stayed because Fariye gave me unconditional love and that made *me* vulnerable, just like the arsehole's love for Fariye makes *him* vulnerable, just as your love for *him* makes *you* vulnerable.'

'And my love for you?'

'The act of a fool, as you've more or less said. But don't worry, Sehereden. It will pass, along with Fire Zadic.' She dragged in a breath. 'Doesn't this conversation prove it? *And* the locked door?'

'No. It proves Fariye's welfare takes precedence over all else.'

'Then let me out! I have to find her!'

'For her sake *and* yours, you'll stay here, out of the way, until my lein decides otherwise.'

Viv struggled upright. 'Don't you understand? The arsehole will kill her if he sends in his men. You can't retrieve her by force!'

'How do you know that?'

'Because the traders aren't fools, Sehereden! If you get *anywhere* near her, they'll kill her, out of spite, if nothing else, though I'm sure they would enjoy showing the *powerful* Syld just how *powerless* he really is.' Viv slumped back onto the chair and dashed the tears from her eyes.

'We'll get her back, Viv,' said Sehereden gently.

'No, you won't! At least tell the arsehole what I've said and that I want to speak to him.'

Sehereden nodded, then bolted the shutters, and left, locking the door behind him. Which was exactly what the arsehole should have done to protect his daughter, concluded Viv savagely.

The arsehole failed to appear but her lip blew up to match her throbbing face. Thugs like him always found it easier to beat people than listen to them, she fumed as she paced. The gloomy room added to her foreboding and made it hard to keep despair at bay. She had to believe Thris had escaped but she knew for sure that Poss had not. God, how frightened she must be!

Viv seized a chair by the legs and strode to the window but at that moment, the arsehole's men came out into the yard and she pressed her ear against the shutters instead. Even had they been stupid enough to discuss their plans, the shutters muffled their words and all she heard was the lilt common amongst his men.

Viv froze. The voices she heard at Stelin Ridge had been missing the lilt. Her heart thundered. They had to be traders! But surely the timing was all wrong? The traders had snatched Poss while she and Caibel were on their way back, but they would have had to sort a place to hold Poss *first*, and Stelin Ridge was a really good choice.

Viv's mind raced. It was not far from Esh-accom and they would be unlikely to be intercepted once they reached the trees because travellers stuck to the flatter land near the Eshacade. But Stelin Ridge's main advantage was its tangled tunnels and sinkholes. *Break-neck Ridge*, Baraghan had called it. The fractured stone made sneaking up hazardous, not just because of the risk of plunging down holes, but because the stone carried sound.

Poss *had* to be at Stelin Ridge, there was no other reason for traders to be there. If they were late to the festivities, they would have camped near the Eshacade or more likely pushed on to start earning their precious coin.

Viv's breath sifted between her teeth. One group would have organised the camp while the other had snatched Poss. It would have been easy too. The arsehole was pretty bloody obvious wherever he went, including leaving the dances early with his daughter. They would have seen the lamp in Poss's room as the arsehole had put her to bed and listened under the colonnades to make sure it *was* her room and not his. But why had the arsehole's horse not warned him? Maybe it did not differentiate between good guys and bad guys.

There were still voices in the yard and she bashed on the shutters and shouted, and when the bang of the compound gate told her the men had gone, beat on her door instead. Her knuckles bled and she grabbed the chair again and smashed it against the shutters. The shutters did not budge but bits of the chair went flying. So much for the arsehole's carving!

She stormed around the room. Shit! Shit! Shit! Ithreya, Tormis, and Mereya should still be here and even Sehereden, given his arm was in a sling, but no one came. She had nothing remotely useful for lock-picking either and there was no man-hole in the ceiling, which left the chimney.

The broken chairback was about the same width as her shoulders and she pushed it into the sooty space and got a face full of grit for her troubles. It fitted but climbing up a chimney with a dud arm was not high on her list of fun things to do. She knew from Oliver Twist that chimney-sweeps got stuck in chimneys and died there and she doubted Wheel Fold had Emergency Services.

There had to be another way. Tormis was old but she did not fancy her chances of over-powering him, or Mereya, or Ithreya, for that matter, and the idea of fighting any of them was abhorrent. When she had been in jail, people had stabbed themselves or swallowed things to get to the Infirmary because it was easier to break out of. She needed to con Tormis, who was most likely in charge, into relocating her, hopefully to somewhere less secure.

It must be close to midday and, at some point, someone would show up with food, and she needed to be ready. She did not have long to wait long before she heard footsteps and clawed her way into the chimney. 'Elddra?' Good, it was Tormis. She heaved herself higher, scrabbling noisily, and Tormis's hand fastened on her ankle. 'That's a dangerous thing to do, elddra,' he said, and tugged her down.

Viv cradled her injured arm and winced to give the impression she was in no shape to escape. 'Fariye's my lein, Tormis. I can't just sit here while she's in danger!'

'The Syld orders you remain here.'

'The Syld doesn't know I was at Stelin Ridge yesterday with Baraghan and heard voices that I'm sure were traders. There's no reason for traders to be there *unless* they have Fariye. I need to get to Stelin Ridge before they hurt her.'

'The Syld orders you remain here.'

'I'm not abandoning my lein!'

His brows bristled as he considered his options. 'I'm sorry, elddra, but I must take you somewhere less comfortable.'

Viv did not struggle as he marched her down the passageway, his grip on her good arm, but nor was she willing. She liked Tormis, although the *just obeying orders* excuse had not washed in WW 2's war-crimes trials. They

14

came out into the sunshine and he escorted her to the stables, empty of horses, and then into a room off one of the stalls. It looked like a feed-store, with sacks of grain and bundles of hay, and the only light came from a broken-shuttered window, high above her head. Tormis went out and the bolts slide into place behind her. 'I'll bring your food, a blanket, and a lamp, elddra,' he said, from the far side of the door.

Viv made no reply, her gaze on the window. 'Bingo,' she whispered, and grinned.

Chapter 2

Tormis was as good as his word and she soon had urrut-sa, gorash, a blanket, and a lamp. The blanket and lamp told her Tormis did not expect the arsehole's return before nightfall, but she could not leave before dark anyway given the risk of witnesses to her escape. But she *did* want Tormis to tell the arsehole where she had gone *and* why.

Knowing Poss was at Stelin Ridge was one thing, rescuing her something else entirely. She would have to fly Poss out but the tunnels and Poss's weight would stop her flying high and fast and give the traders plenty of time to kill them both. She and Poss would need the arsehole's knife skills, *and* those of his men, to survive.

She wondered where they were now. The arsehole had only called in the men closest to him because he trusted only those he knew. Rim had preferred to act alone too, or with a select few, and like the arsehole, dismissed those with different opinions as liars, which was fine with her, except when Poss's life was at stake.

Viv paced around the small, dusty space. Why the hell did she end up keeping company with the same sort of men, although *keeping company* was a pretty fancy way of describing her lowly status. Jimmy Wright, Rim, and now the arsehole. Sehereden might be different, but he would always choose the arsehole over her, as Thris had chosen Ky, although in Thris's case, the Great Beyond trumped them both.

Thris's presence in The Wheel had changed things between her and Sehereden, she conceded. The arsehole had obviously shared with his lein what he had seen at

16

the entertainments, and in his terms, Thris *was* Angellus, although no one seemed bothered about the Angellus except the elddra *and* elddric like Baraghan, who wanted out, *and* the arsehole who hated everything Angellus and wanted *her* out.

Sehereden had been distracted by Poss's abduction but he would soon ask her directly where she came from and, given her reaction at the *entertainments*, it would be stupid to deny the bleedingly obvious even *if* she were capable of lying. But how was she to describe a world of cars and planes and bombs; and music that was plucked from the air; or the Rynth and rifts, for that matter. She had coped with The Wheel because it held lots of familiar things but her old life would seem so bizarre to him, and she so strange, he would want her gone too.

'Viv?' Viv started. It was Ithreya, her voice tentative but concerned. 'Viv? Are you all right?'

'I'm fine. My lein's going to be murdered and her father has locked me up.'

'I'm sorry, Viv. Sehereden said it's for the best.'

'Sehereden is wrong.'

'Is there anything you need?'

'I need to get out of here, Ithreya, but failing that, I need to know when the arsehole's coming back so I can talk to him.'

'I don't know their plans. If anyone asks, I'm to say I'm unaware of the Syld's whereabouts, or of his men's. I'm sorry, Viv,' she repeated thickly.

Viv's throat unexpectedly tightened. '*None* of this is your fault, Ithreya. Not Sehereden, or your feelings about me, or me being locked up, and *nothing* of what might come is your fault either. Remember that.'

'He wants you.'

Viv shut her eyes. Ithreya loved Sehereden and deserved so much better. 'He wants what he *thinks* I am, but there's a gap between what he *thinks* I am and what I *really* am. There's no gap with you, and he'll see that in the end.'

'I don't understand,' came Ithreya's puzzled voice. 'Have you lied to him?'

'I can't lie.'

'Because of your Angellus blood?'

'Because of my blood, but . . . there are things I can't tell him that would change his feelings about me. I'm not a good person, Ithreya.' Viv was taken aback by her confession, and wondered whether it was triggered by knowing she was unlikely to survive Poss's rescue and wanted Ithreya to know the truth.

'I think you *are* a good person, Viv.'

Viv swallowed several times. Hell! She was going to cry in a minute. 'I have everything I need in here, thank you, Ithreya,' she managed to say. 'Please don't concern yourself about me.'

Night took a long time to come and it seemed to Viv she spent her life waiting for darkness to arrive or waiting for it to end. She worried the arsehole would return and scupper her plans but the stables remained quiet. The yard gate remained quiet too which meant Tormis, Ithreya, and most likely Mereya, were still in the compound.

They would be enjoying Mereya's urrut-sa and probably her tocki too. They would be enjoying the fire and each other's company. *Poor Vivi, been left out the party again, eh?* Yes, Rim, I have, but I have not been left out of their kindness. She would miss Poss and Sehereden when she left, and Tahsin, Ithreya, Tormis and Mereya as well.

18

She missed only her mother from Moonsun and only Thris from Ezam. Wheel Fold was already more like a home except her usual luck meant she had arrived during a war looking like an Angellus and befriended the child of a man who hated the Angellus with a passion.

She tried to use her waiting time to plan. Only two traders had held Thris captive and she guessed only a small group would guard Poss. A large group would need more fires to warm themselves and cook their food, making the smoke more obvious, *and* they would need more supplies which would have to be traded in Esh-accom and carted back. It risked attracting attention especially if the traders headed off towards the Ristavals.

And it only needed one man to guard a child who was probably bound, blind-folded and gagged. Viv struggled to steady. It would be safest to approach from the air and search for smoke and voices, and if luck were on her side, she could fly down a shaft, snatch Poss, and be gone before they knew what had happened. The trouble was, luck had never fancied being anywhere near her, let alone on her side.

Viv forced herself on. *If* the traders had set a fire outside, Poss would be close otherwise they would have to fumble about in the tunnels to take her food, and *if* they had set a fire *inside* a tunnel, it would have to be near a shaft or else they would be smoked out. She tried not to think of the possibility that Poss was already dead.

The traders must know the arsehole would be ruthless in retrieving his daughter alive and be *very* careful he never got anywhere near her *or* them, which pointed to Poss being *deep* in a tunnel and the traders guarding the ridge-top *and* shafts, or at least the climbable shafts.

The light finally dimmed and she donned her shirt halter

neck style and slid the amè casque into her jacket pocket with the bracelet, tribute-charm, and chain, then tossed the jacket onto a grain sack. The jacket would hamper her and she doubted whether death would be improved by wearing an amè!

There was a real possibility that she *would* be killed and her stomach clenched. Fast reactions had saved her in the past but this time Poss's life was at stake too. *Get ya arse into gear, Vivi. If ya gunna die, best get it over with.* Yeah, thanks for the vote of confidence, Rim.

She unbedded her wings and beat them hard in celebration of the despised angel-half she was forced to hide then leapt upwards and slid between the broken shutters. She would have liked to keep flying but the risk was too great, and she landed in the street outside, rearranged her shirt again and set off

Lamps glowed from the surrounding compounds, but the street was quiet, and she kept to the shadows and saw no one until she neared the gate. The streets were usually crowded here as people headed towards Axian's enjoyments and she kept her head down, aware her bruised face and bloodied lip made her even more conspicuous, and she was within sight of the wall before she realised the traders would have set watchers.

They would obviously want to know the arsehole's movements, and his men's, and if they knew she was Poss's lein, her movements too. Viv swore under her breath. She should have flown from the stable roof after all, and now she would have to find some dark hole to wait until Fire Zadic passed and Esh-accom's citizens were more intent on dancing than staring skywards.

She turned down a side-street but had not gone far before she noticed she was being followed. Whoever it was made no attempt to disguise their pursuit and then figures stepped from an alley ahead and blocked the street. Baraghan had cut her off the same way but he was long gone and as her pursuer closed the distance between them, Viv feared that Poss's abductors wanted to add to their haul *or* even the score.

Chapter 3

Ash sat motionless in Haven, his gaze on Thris, his dreams elsewhere. He saw folds with air as red as blood, folds with creatures toothed and clawed, and folds with wraiths akin to the trapped dead of human caste folds. He saw angelic folds too which revealed that angel caste could be as lethal as human caste, and that transcendence was not unique to the Host.

The understanding humbled him, as did the folds troubled by war, and he perceived that war ranged from petty jealousies to the total annihilation of the other. He felt the acrid fumes of it as if he were there and pulled the roaming strands of himself back to Haven, and was shocked to recognise the same taint in Ezam.

It had accumulated over the eons as mist did in some human caste folds, but unlike human caste folds, Ezam lacked the gales to disperse it and so it lingered, a sour stagnation, at odds with a hierarchy that outlined a clear pathway to transcendence, first as Dane, then as Quin-, Quar-, Tri-, Du- and Prime-archae, then Archae, and finally Principae.

Ash sighed, rose and flexed his wings. He wondered whether Senquar-archae had dreamed too and whether, despite the angel bones in the Green Helixai, he had transcended. Ash's dreams had taught him how amorphous the seemingly solid was and that the things *he* perceived, might not be perceived by others, not even those closest to him like Thris and Ky. And again he wondered at the fate of Senquar-archae's companions.

Ky searched the scrolls for answers to Ash's questions, as did Prime-archaes Serith and Mirek, but the Bokos's empty heart might be a reminder that angelic understanding would be forever incomplete *or* that some angelic understanding so perilous, it must be destroyed. And if so, Ash feared it might be due to the nature of his blue angel predecessor and his friends, a trinity replicated by him, Ky and Thris.

Thris at least posed no threat to Ezam's tranquility, for he had yet to rouse and Ash went to the bed and kissed his forehead. His unblemished body did not mean he had suffered no injuries for unlike physical wounds that healed quickly, spiritual wounds might never heal. Thris had suffered both since accepting the Guideship and Ash did not know what else he had endured before his return.

Baraghan followed the green-robed Angellus through the trees *if* they were trees. He had no idea how things that looked like metal could grow. He was also troubled by the Angellus being content to have an armed stranger walk behind him. It meant he was dangerously unaware.

The Angellus had said little beyond his first odd words and they had not gone far before a domed building emerged from the trees and Baraghan followed him in. He wondered whether the Angellus lived in setts rather than larger settlements like Astraal and then stumbled to a stop as he grappled with the sight of scroll-crammed shelves stretching away into a distance far vaster than the building that housed them.

The Angellus had all but disappeared down a gloomy passageway and Baraghan hastened after him, gripping his knives as he heard others, and then emerged into an open space near a window. There was another Angellus there, more like Thrisdane, examining a scroll and as he did not immediately look up, Baraghan had time to appraise his glossy auburn curls, and the superb musculature of his shoulders and flank.

'Kydane,' said the robed Angellus, in the same dreamy tones. Kydane glanced up and his purple eyes widened in fright. 'As you have recently spent time in human caste folds, I thought you might be interested in meeting Baraghan en-Esh-accom.'

'That was Thris, Prime-archae Serith,' choked Kydane.

'The same thing,' said the Prime-archae.

'Do you mean Thrisdane?' asked Baraghan, careful to keep his voice soft. Kydane nodded jerkily. 'He came from here?' asked Baraghan, relieved he was in the right place.

'Yes.'

'And the female Angellus?'

'Angellus?' Kydane glanced at Prime-archae Serith in confusion, but the robed Angellus was intent on the scroll.

'Violet Iris Vacia, otherwise known as Viv,' explained Baraghan.

'She is a shekinah. Her father is Archae Kald, her mother is human caste.'

'She's from here too?' pursued Baraghan

Kydane shook his head. 'From Moonsun. The Host are male-aspected. We have no human or daimon caste here. Ezam cannot meet the needs of—'

'So, Paendane disappeared too,' murmured Prime-archae Serith and straightened. 'Many will delight in the obvious being confirmed, though fail to see its significance. You should take Baraghan en-Esh-accom to visit Thrisdane, Kydane.'

'Thris is yet to rouse, Prime-archae,' said Kydane.

'He's ill?' asked Baraghan sharply.

24

'Disease is a human caste flaw not an angelic one,' said Kydane tightly, 'but since Thris accepted the shekinah's Guideship, he has suffered greatly. It is not the first time he has been injured.'

Baraghan bowed. 'I'm part Angellus, and the Angellus were, I believe, like you. I'm also aware of what Thrisdane endured before he returned.'

'You were in the same fold?' asked Ky eagerly.

'Yes, if *folds* are what you call different worlds. I helped Thrisdane escape and have healing skills. I also carry a healer's kit. I would like to see him.'

Kydane nodded and Baraghan turned back to Prime-archae Serith. 'I thank you for your welcome,' he said with another bow, but the robed angel's attention remained on the scroll, and Baraghan followed Kydane out.

The trees had lost none of their strangeness but there were more familiar plants like creepers among them, and the enormous spent blooms from something higher in the canopy. It was quiet, the only sound the musical crunch of leaf-fall under their feet. 'Do you have birds in Ezam?' he asked, peering about.

'We are blessed the Great Beyond fashioned our fold without them.'

Add birds to the list of things Kydane disliked, noted Baraghan. The sky held the same sunset colours as his arrival and he realised it should have been dark. 'Your days are long,' he said.

'Days?'

'When it's light.'

'Ezam does not have the darkness that blights other folds. The Great Beyond bequeathed us cycles of glorious orange, umber, and peach, gentle warmth, and an absence of things harmful.'

'Yet you choose to visit dangerous places.'

'Most do not. I transited because Thris did, and he because his mentor appointed him the shekinah's Guide.'

'What of visitors from other folds?'

'The shekinah was the first visitor to Ezam for eons, and Archae Kald brought her, and now there is you.' Kydane glanced at him, his violet eyes intense under the trees. 'Did you find yourself falling inside an iridescent tunnel?'

'Yes, but Violet Iris Vacia directed me to it.'

'That was wrong of her!'

'She warned me of the dangers, but it was part of a bargain she made with me to free Thrisdane.'

Kydane jerked to a stop. '*Free*, Thris?'

'I knew Violet Iris Vacia searched for someone called Thris and when I discovered he had been captured, I devised a way to release him. Violet Iris Vacia wanted him freed, and I wanted to visit the Angellus, so I offered a trade.'

'We are angels not *Angellus*,' said Kydane, going on.

'You don't call yourself *Angellus* but the words are similar, don't you think, and you match what I know of the Angellus. I'm from a place called The Wheel where the Angellus appeared, seeded children, and left. Is it possible they came from here?'

'The possibilities of the Rynth are uncountable.'

'The Rynth?'

'Ezam, where you are now, Moonsun, where the shekinah is from, and The Wheel where you are from, are three of the uncountable folds that make up the Rynth. The Rynth's immensity makes all things possible, including what you suggest.'

26

'Violet Iris Vacia told me there were many different places but my interest lies in the Angellus. The building where we met was full of scrolls. Is it possible they hold what I seek?'

'It is possible but searching them all would take eons. The store is also incomplete. Ash might be able to tell you more. He cares for Thris.'

Baraghan struggled not to stare when they reached the building Kydane called Haven. Its columns and pitched roof were the same as Astraal Hall, but Haven gleamed brilliant white, making Astraal's white stone seem dull. Even more extraordinary were the angels gathered under its portico, their naked perfection more astonishing because they were coloured grey, yellow, green, black, and red as well as normally like Kydane.

The angels stared as he passed, but Kydane led him on through endless passageways and stairs of glittering stone to a door identical to the dozens they passed. The room was sumptuous but Baraghan was riveted by the sight of the blue angel and his exquisite snowy wings. The angels under the portico had been magnificent but this one was luminous. The angel's gaze was curious, not fearful like Kydane's, but Baraghan's attention swung to the motionless form on the bed.

The elusive Thrisdane. Baraghan had last seen him painted and masked in a night full of smoke, but it was definitely him. His black curls gleamed and his magnificent black wings shone blue-green. Violet Iris Vacia's longing for him was understandable but the angel was unnaturally still and Baraghan barely nodded to the blue angel as Kydane introduced them, his attention on Thrisdane.

'What have you given him?' he asked urgently.

'Given him?' the blue angel, *Ashdane*, repeated.

'He was drugged. Do you have something like hareesh here? It's a stimulant.'

'The Host needs only ambrosia to refresh ourselves.'

'Is that what Violet Iris Vacia lived on?' asked Baraghan, rummaging in his pack.

'When she first came, Thris retrieved human caste food for her, and again when she was injured,' said Kydane. 'But her angelic part allowed her to function like us.'

Baraghan located his flask of hareesh and unscrewed the top. 'I'll give him a little of this *if* I may. It will aid his recovery.' Kydane was clearly uneasy but Ashdane nodded, and the two angels supported Thrisdane while Baraghan coaxed the liquid down his throat.

They lowered him back and Baraghan was pleased to see his breathing quicken. Hareesh had a powerful effect on the Valen and it seemed to on the Angellus as well. Kydane gripped the angel's hand and leaned closer. 'Thris?'

Thrisdane's eye-lids fluttered open and Kydane cried out in delight and hugged him. Ashdane hugged him too and the angels' love for their friend woke an intense longing in Baraghan. Ezam was not going to be the home he hoped for, and not just because it lacked food. It lacked women too, which oddly, was not the main impediment to him staying. It was the understanding that his Valen blood would forever deny him belonging.

He had felt the same in The Wheel, where his Angellus blood had been the problem, but The Wheel held other elddric, whether they acknowledged it or not, and he had made a home for himself in Esh-accom. He knew he would be better off in The Wheel but it would advantage him to learn as much as possible about the Angellus before he returned home.

Chapter 4

Viv braced herself as she recognised her pursuer but knowing it was Anfarena was hardly reassuring given men still blocked the way ahead. 'Violet Iris Vacia,' said Anfarena, pleasantly. 'I've been looking for you.'

'You told me I'd be watched so I find that surprising,' said Viv coldly.

'I've been looking for Anetherey too,' said Anfarena, ignoring the jibe. 'You both left Esh-accom yet only you returned. I'm hoping you can solve the puzzle.'

'Your spies know I left on the back of Caibel en-Esh-accom's horse and probably know his relationship to Baraghan en-Esh-accom. They won't know I made a bargain with Baraghan en-Esh-accom to free what you call the *Angellus* from the wagoners.'

'And your part of the bargain?' demanded Anfarena, the polite mask gone.

'To find Baraghan what you call a door.'

'And did you?' she hissed.

'Yes and warned him not to use it for the same reason I've warned you not to use *doors*. They can lead anywhere including death.'

'Baraghan is of the Astraali and shares their violent arrogance,' she said dismissively. 'Is he responsible for the injuries to your face?'

'No.'

'Another of his kind then,' said Anfarena obscurely. 'So Baraghan ignored your warning?'

'Yes, but I was unaware Anetherey had followed us.'

Anfarena stiffened. 'She left too?'

'She rushed after him into the rift before I could stop her.'

'And you have *no* idea where they ended up?'

'No.'

'There might be safety in them being together,' muttered Anfarena.

'There's no guarantee of that either,' said Viv bluntly. 'Some rifts split. They might have gone to different lands.'

Anfarena was rigid. 'Is there *any* chance *either* of them will find their way back?' she whispered.

Viv shrugged. 'I had to be trained to find rifts and it wasn't easy to learn, even as a half-angel. There's a chance they might stumble into a rift, and it might exit here, but I was told only angels can return to the same land more than once because, unlike us, their bodies are airy. The time differences complicate things too.'

Anfarena paused as if she mulled over Viv's news. 'When we last spoke, I said I would seek advice,' she said. 'It may be some time in coming, given the dangers of travel, but if the advice is to proceed, you will guide us.'

'I've *told* you I have no idea where rifts lead,' said Viv in exasperation.

'But you know where the doors are, which is why you *will* remain in The Wheel.'

Viv decided not to waste her breath describing the dangers of elddra trooping en mass into another fold. They and their Du-Daimon masters had waited a long time for the key to the magic door and were not about to let it slip through their fingers. 'I pledged my lein not to leave here permanently without farewelling her, and I am willing to pledge *you* that I'll speak with you first if I intend to leave. But in the meantime, I need to come and go within The Wheel without constraint.'

31

'And where is it you need to go *within* The Wheel tonight, Violet Iris Vacia? Obviously not to the festivities.'

'No. Obviously *not* to the festivities.'

There was a long pause while Anfarena eyed her. 'Very well, you may go on your way, to do whatever it is you feel you need to do. But you will be watched, and if we feel you've been less than honest, you *will* be restrained.'

Anfarena gestured to the men and they followed her back up the street, their eyes sliding sideways as they passed. Viv glared back, making no effort to hide her antagonism. Anfarena had accused Baraghan of violent arrogance, but she was no better.

Viv went on but had not gone far when Fire Zadic burst into the sky and she stopped, entranced by its beauty. Pool, Cascade, Fire, and the brief one she had dubbed the Owl Zadic thrilled her and she wanted to see Lirium and Glimwing that Sehereden had spoken of before she left, but first she had to ensure Poss was safe.

She waited until the zadic's splendour was replaced by the stars' dull glitter, re-arranged her shirt again, and launched skywards, flying straight upwards until she was beyond even the keenest eyes then sped off cloudwise.

Baraghan was surprised Kydane did not linger after Thrisdane woke. His love for Thrisdane was obvious but he spoke of his need to resume his search of the Bokos and left. Thrisdane said little before he slipped into a doze but his wings disappeared which Baraghan found astonishing.

He and Ashdane shifted their chairs close to the window so as not to disturb Thrisdane, and Thrisdane's ability to hide his wings was the first topic Baraghan raised. He learned that Dane kept their wings bedded *inside* their backs most of the time and the Archae all of the time. He also learned the *Host* consisted of a rigid hierarchy with the lowest angels or *Dane* at the bottom and the Archae at the top, and that Archae transcended Ezam to become Principae, translucent aqua angels who inhabited Crystal Fold.

The number of angels in Ezam and Crystal Folds neither grew nor diminished, Ashdane explained, because when new angels appeared in Ezam, the same number transcended from Crystal Fold into the *Great Beyond*.

'So, when *you* appeared in Ezam, an Archae went to Crystal Fold, and a Principae *left* for the Great Beyond,' said Baraghan thoughtfully, and wondered if the phenomenon had somehow triggered the Angellus's arrival in The Wheel.

'Three,' said Ashdane.

'Three?' repeated Baraghan startled.

'Thris, Ky, and I appeared simultaneously, so three Archae transcended to Crystal Fold, and three Principae to the Great Beyond.'

'Do Dane usually appear in groups?'

'The scrolls tell us it has happened once before, and one of the angels was blue.' Ashdane's voice remained even but Baraghan sensed his tension rise. 'The scrolls also tell us there is only one blue angel in Ezam at any time. The previous blue angel we know of was Senquar-archae who appeared with Paendane and Anasdane. We know Paendane transited the Rynth at the request of his mentor but little else, and Ky searches the Bokos to discover more of the threesome, as do Prime-archaes Mirek and Serith.'

'I found Prime-archae Serith difficult to understand,' admitted Baraghan.

'As do most of the Host,' said Ashdane. 'The Prime-archae was changed by the Black Obsidian Stele which Archae Kald summoned after the Prime-archae sought the shekinah's death.'

Baraghan's brows drew. 'Prime-archae Serith tried to murder Violet Iris Vacia?'

Ashdane's snowy wings fluttered 'Of course not. Angels are impelled by love, not hate, and are prohibited from taking life.' He paused. 'There are scrolls that suggest female daimon are a threat to the Rynth. Prime-archae Serith simply allowed the *circumstances* of her destruction. The shekinah was terribly hurt but Ky transited her to Crystal Fold where she was healed.

'Archae Kald was *concerned* by his daughter's injuries and *encouraged* the Black Obsidian Stele to take up position near the Bokos,' continued Ashdane. 'Prime-archae Serith was one of many angels caught in its thrall. His insights were deeper afterwards but his ability to communicate them less.'

'What *is* the Black Obsidian Stele?' asked Baraghan fingering his knife.

'One of many steles sent to aid the Host's journey to transcendence. Visitors describe them as giant, faceted, shards of crystal, and see them as beautiful. They test aspects of an angel's being, some steles less gently than others. The Black Obsidian is the most violent. Steles can be fatal to other castes and are best avoided.'

'Anything else I should avoid?' asked Baraghan dryly.

Ashdane shook his head. 'The Great Beyond created a place of safety for the Host.'

It did not sound like it, thought Baraghan, as he considered Kald's vindictiveness and Serith's murderous tendencies. 'What sorts of things must the Host do to transcend?' he asked.

'Once I could have answered that question but not anymore,' said Ashdane with an exquisite smile. 'Dane endure physical testing which changes to spiritual testing once we ascend to the Archae's lowest ranks. But physical testing might be augmented. Thris and Ky had mentors, senior angels whose guidance promised quicker ascension. Thris's mentor was Archae Kald, who seeded the shekinah.

'He assigned Thris the perilous task of guiding his shekinah through the Rynth to her mother. Placing the shekinah in a fold suited to her daimon state would have aided Archae Kald's transcendence too. Thris had proved his strength, resonant sensitivity, and self-discipline many times in the trials, and the task should have been within his capabilities, and yet ...' Ashdane's troubled gaze went to the bed. 'He has suffered terribly in the Rynth and come close to death more than once. Nothing is as it seems, including perhaps, the journey to transcendence.'

'Violet Iris Vacia remains in The Wheel,' said Baraghan. 'She showed me the door that brought me here, so has the skills to leave, but stays because she has love for others, including Thrisdane. Yet when I discovered he had been captured, she wanted him as far away as possible. To wish someone safe, at the cost of losing them, is a sign of love's deepness.' He paused. 'You're Thrisdane's friend, Ashdane. Does he return her love?'

'Angels are impelled by love, but you speak of the human caste love that includes sexual congress. Ky told me Thris joined with the shekinah and that feeds Kydane's dislike of her, for sexual congress is believed to inhibit transcendence. It also risks the creation of daimon.'

'Which is to be avoided,' said Baraghan sourly.

'Daimon are one of the uncountable possibilities of the Rynth *and* one of the reasons I find it hard to answer your question about transcendence. Thris was all but destroyed protecting the shekinah in Beastman Fold and while the Principae healed him physically, he was not fully healed until *after* he joined with the shekinah. I have come to believe that love gifted with a pure heart aids transcendence, whether it is spiritual love, the love of friends, the protective love gifted to the young and old, or sexual love.'

Baraghan nodded. 'Violet Iris Vacia remains in The Wheel because she loves a child there, but it isn't an easy place for her. Daimon are disliked and the child's father is antagonistic.' Baraghan smiled ruefully. 'There's still much about Violet Iris Vacia that I don't understand.'

'You probably understand more than the Host. Ezam is home to male-aspected angels whereas the shekinah is a *female* daimon. The female-aspected angels of Erath Fold are more like her kind.'

'Could she find a home with them?'

'Erath Fold is closed to the Host. Whether it is also closed to daimon caste is unknown.'

'Have the Host ever called themselves by another name?'

'Not that I am aware of, but given the Rynth's immensity, angel caste likely inhabit more than Ezam, Crystal, and Erath Folds.' Ashdane looked at him curiously. 'You have said you are a daimon from The Wheel and so obviously angel caste exists there.'

'They *did*,' acknowledged Baraghan,' but departed many zadicans ago. They called themselves Angellus and came from somewhere else. Once in The Wheel, they coupled with human caste to create Daimon, who coupled with human caste to create Du-Daimon, which is what I am. Many who carry their blood want to join them in whatever fold they came from and presumably returned to.'

'Is that why you asked the shekinah to show you a rift?'

'Yes. I hoped it would take me to the Angellus, and maybe it has, *if* you once called yourselves the Angellus. The words are very similar.'

'I cannot answer your question or aid your search beyond directing you to those who explore the Bokos. Prime-archae Serith is the wisest but Ky's wisdom might surpass his in the end, though he has yet to realise it.'

'And then he will enter the Archae,' said Baraghan lightly.

'He should have done so already. Any white plumage is a marker of ascension, while full white marks transcendence.' Ashdane smiled. 'Given my wings, I see you wonder why I remain a lowly Dane? So do I *and* why Ky is not Kyquin-archae. I wonder too why Thris's wings remain black, given all he has endured. But mostly I wonder what became of my predecessor and his friends, and if we three will suffer the same fate.'

'You make it sound as if someone or *something* controls these things. Isn't it up to you what happens?'

'Perhaps or perhaps not. Why does a rift admit one angel and refuse the next; exit into one fold, one moment, and then another? Why do rifts allow angel caste the freedom to transit the Rynth but not other castes?'

'*I* came here,' pointed out Baraghan.

'Yes, but you cannot go back.'

Baraghan stiffened. 'Why not?' he demanded.

'The time differences make it too risky. You are still where you were before you entered the rift. The shekinah cannot return to her original fold for the same reason.'

'I'm used to taking risks.'

'I do not want to be responsible for your death.'

Baraghan grinned. 'Violet Iris Vacia was also concerned, but things turned out well, as they usually do for me. Just show me a rift that will take me back, preferably close to when I left, and I'll take responsibility for the rest.'

Chapter 5

Tormis was waiting in the yard when Ataghan rode in with Sehereden and Drasen, and clearly wanted speech alone. More ill news, no doubt, concluded Ataghan grimly, and the burn of his body escalated. 'Tormis will stable Fara and Jal,' he said to Sehereden. 'I'll join you inside.'

Tormis waited until Sehereden and Drasen had disappeared into the building before he spoke. 'I've secured the elddra in the feed-store, Syld, after she sought escape from Fariye's room. She believes Fariye's at Stelin Ridge. She requests speech with you.'

Ataghan grimaced and added Taris to Sehereden and Drasen's mounts. Tormis led them into the stables but Ataghan stayed where he was. Drasen had proved surprisingly useful, as had his kin who kept compounds in Esh-accom and setts in the surrounding vals. They had lost children to Waradi and Ascadi knives and needed to know nothing more than a child's life was at stake to send out word and set watchers.

They had drawn on their networks of urrut herders and wrights too, simply because the Scinta-ril's Syld requested it. Some had ridden Soaich Spine with him, others shared the hard gallop to Esh-telin and many of them would make their home with him at the Scinta-ril, *after* he and Quen en-Sar-ril had cleaned out the Perin-ril's filth.

Those who had taken Fariye must keep their lives a little longer to ensure his daughter kept hers but once she was safe, those who had even the smallest part in her abduction would be grateful to enter death even without their amès.

The fume of his blood was scarcely bearable and his hand went to his knife but then Tormis emerged from the stables. 'The elddra has food, Syld, and a blanket and lamp. Ithreya spoke to her too. She has all she needs.'

Tormis obviously confused him with Sehereden if he thought Ataghan cared about the elddra's comfort! 'We'll speak further inside, Tormis,' he said briefly, and waited for Tormis's boots to grit away. Taris moved restlessly in his stall as he sensed Ataghan's turmoil and Ataghan went to the feed-store and wrenched back the bolts.

The room was empty and he glanced up at the broken-shuttered window. The food was untouched too and the blanket still folded but the elddra's jacket was there and he picked it up and checked the pockets. The Waradi tryst-bracelet, chain, tribute-charm, and gold amè casque Sehereden had traded for her. It seemed ominous she had abandoned everything she valued or perhaps she valued nothing.

The elddra created a dangerous complication whatever her motivations. The icestone country around Stelin Ridge *would* make a good hiding place for Fariye, but so would a dozen other places and the traders had ensured their accomplices had travelled in many directions from Esh-accom over the previous days.

Something glimmered on the floor and he picked it up. A glossy feather the same colour as the elddra's hair and of unusual softness. It held her scent and he thrust it deep into his pocket, bolted the feed-store doors, and strode into his compound.

Ithreya was with Sehereden, Drasen, and Tormis in the hall and he tossed the elddra's jacket on a chair and deposited the jewelry on the table. 'The elddra's gone but she's left her possessions behind.'

Ithreya gasped as she took in the amè. 'Gone?' said Tormis. 'But that's impossible.'

'Not if she were released Ithreya?'

'I understood the reasons for your orders, Syld, and respected them,' she said steadily. 'I spoke to Viv from *outside* the feed-store door, that's all.'

'She's gone to Stelin Ridge and doesn't expect to survive,' said Sehereden slowly, his gaze on the amè.

'*If* Fariye's there, *neither* of them will survive,' gritted Ataghan as he prowled up and down.

'Why Stelin Ridge?' asked Drasen.

'She said she had been there with Baraghan and heard *trader* voices,' said Tormis.

'When?' asked Ataghan sharply.

'I think it was the night of Fariye's disappearance,' said Ithreya. 'She had come from there this morning.'

'They couldn't get Fariye to Stelin Ridge in that time,' said Drasen.

'They would have prepared a hiding-place first,' said Sehereden. His eyes flashed to Ataghan. 'It fits.'

'But why was Viv at Stelin Ridge?' asked Drasen.

Ataghan's lip curled but Sehereden spoke first. 'She told me she made a bargain with Baraghan en-Esh-accom and might be absent for a time.'

'A bargain?' asked Drasen.

'Baraghan arranged the release of one of the trader's *entertainments*, who Viv confirmed this morning was Thrisdane,' said Sehereden. 'Baraghan's good deeds always come at a price,' he added dourly.

'Galian said it was a winged-man,' said Drasen. 'Is Thrisdane Angellus, Sehereden?'

'She refused to say, but it seems so.'

'Thrisdane's status is unimportant,' snapped Ataghan.

41

'What did you discuss with her, Ithreya?'

'Nothing of relevance.'

Ataghan strode back to the table. 'I'll be the judge of that.'

'I asked her whether she was all right,' said Ithreya.

'And?'

'She said her lein was going to be murdered and her lein's father had locked her up, so things were just fine.'

'What else?' pursued Ataghan, ignoring her tone.

'She said I wasn't to blame myself for anything that had happened or that might happen in the future. And then we discussed Sehereden,' said Ithreya reluctantly.

'Go on.'

'When I said Sehereden wanted her, she said she wasn't what Sehereden thought she was. I asked whether she had lied to him, and she said she couldn't lie but there were things she couldn't tell him. She said she wasn't a good person.'

'And what did *you* say, Ithreya?' asked Sehereden softly.

'That she *was* a good person. I think she prepared me for her death.'

'*And* Fariye's *if* the traders are at Stelin Ridge, and she tackles them on her own!' snarled Ataghan.

'How much of a start does she have on us?' asked Drasen urgently.

'Not much but if she were seen leaving in the direction of Stelin Ridge and we follow, the traders' spies will try to warn Fariye's captors.'

'And will they succeed?' asked Drasen.

'They have the advantage of having put their spies in place first. If they know we're coming, they will kill Fariye and leave, and even if we reach them undetected, they will cut her throat before we can cut theirs.' There was a brittle silence and Ithreya brushed away tears.

'What we do now depends on whether we believe Viv is right about Fariye's whereabouts and whether we believe she is honest,' said Sehereden evenly. 'If we believe she is a liar, we wait as planned but if we believe Fariye *is* being held at Stelin Ridge, and Viv's gone there, we must act, for Fariye's sake, if not for Viv's.'

'Easier said than done,' ground out Ataghan as he continued his prowl.

'Do you think Fariye *is* at Stelin Ridge, Syld?' asked Drasen directly.

Ataghan stopped and there was a tingling hiatus. 'It's likely.'

'And that Viv's lied?'

'She admitted omissions to Ithreya, and omissions can be as deceitful as outright falsehoods.'

'If we believe Fariye's there and Viv has gone there too, we *must* act,' repeated Sehereden.

'The traders' disguised the *direction* of their movement around the time of Fariye's abduction, not their *actual* movement,' said Drasen quickly. 'We could do the same.'

Ataghan swung back to him. 'Send horsemen from all four gates?'

Drasen nodded. 'Not at the same time nor in the same numbers nor with the same urgency. Let them think we've heard something but make it unclear what. Add to the confusion by disguising who goes where. They would be most interested in where *you* headed, Syld, and in the dark, would judge your direction more by your mount than your face.'

Ataghan's eyes flashed. '*And* by my companions, particularly if one had his arm in a sling.'

43

Sehereden half rose from the table. 'I *must* be in the party that goes to Stelin Ridge.'

'But won't be,' said Ataghan. 'I need men with *two* good throwing hands.'

'At …'

Ataghan touched him briefly on the shoulder. 'Your injury could mean the difference between Fariye's life and death, or yours, or the elddra's. Trust me in this, lein,' he added softly.

'If we *are* going, we must go now,' said Drasen.

'Yes,' said Ataghan. 'The zadic has passed and even if we take the route I envisage, it will be hard to reach Stelin Ridge before dawn.'

Viv slowed her descent to search for landmarks, listen for voices, and sense for smoke. She had taken a lot of care in her approach, having learned from Esh-telin how hard it was to match the view from the air with the view from the ground. She was sure it was the right place but not whether it was the right place to rescue Poss.

The tree-tops were close enough to touch but she could hear nothing except the pound of her heart. It kept time with the throb in her lip but she did not need the arsehole's violence to know her time in the fold was up. There was no way Thris would return here even *if* he had escaped, and no way Sehereden would ever defy his lein. Yet there were things about the fold she loved, all of which she would trade for Poss's safety.

Ya already know Lady Luck doesn't do bargains, Vivi. She took a steadying breath and managed to land in a tree but her wings made such a racket in the leaves she had to force herself not to flee. She crouched shaking in the branches but there was no sound of someone clambering up and no scent of smoke. The traders might have eaten, quenched their fire, and gone to bed, *or not be here at all* but looking like a fool was the least of her worries.

Tormis should have passed on her message by now *if* the arsehole and Sehereden had returned. Shit! She had not even considered they might spend the night elsewhere, and even if they did not, the arsehole might dismiss her message as lies.

He had hated her from the moment he had clapped eyes on her, initially because of the Waradi, but for other reasons since. Maybe he had fallen foul of an elddra and held a grudge. Maybe he simply hated red hair. Carrot-top, ranga, blood-nut, rust-knob; none of the names she had been called were complimentary. Few people had red hair at home or here so maybe it was just the old hate-the-minority thing.

Forget it, Viv, and find some effing smoke! Or some voices! It was safe in the trees but being safe was not going to save Poss. She pulled her wings close and descended, then crouched in the shadows to listen. Not even an owl's cry and she suddenly longed to hear one. *Before ya die, eh, Vivi? How sweet and sad.*

She half shook her head. She must think only of how to find Poss and get her away. She started up the slope, mindful of hidden shafts, and reached the grove where Baraghan and Anetherey had transited. There was no longer the tell-tale hum of a rift and she swallowed dryly. It would have been a comfort to know that if all else failed, she could transit, because despite the complications of getting back, it would keep Poss alive and that was all that mattered.

Chapter 6

Ataghan rode hard with Drasen and Brithergen, but they were all hampered by mounts that lacked the close mental links of their own. Taris and Fara had left earlier by Esh-accom's sunwise gate, ridden by Sehereden and a band member. Galian had gone with them too on his own mount. Drasen and Brithergen's mounts would leave by the same gate, as if they were reinforcements and more band members would leave at dawn, one with his arm in a sling, from the nightwise gate.

Ataghan's hope lay in speed, presuming Fariye *was* at Stelin Ridge, and confusion bought time. He planned to cut across to the ridge's far side to avoid the Ristaval Forests, a longer but quicker route, and cross the ridge on foot. It was too treacherous for horses and even on foot, men risked broken necks.

They reached the starwise sprawl of the icestone and as they galloped on, Ataghan hoped his mount was as agile as Taris. Then, as the stars dulled, he smelled smoke and signaled Drasen and Brithergen to halt. The smoke was spicy and his thoughts swung to the sidari stands.

He had camped there on his first visit to Esh-accom and had not forgotten them or the nearby tunnels. He signaled to dismount and shared his thoughts, then they instructed their horses to wait and set off on foot, using sticks to probe the ground where the bushes grew.

Heat boiled in his veins as he considered the need for speed *and* stealth. *If* Fariye were here, they would need to kill the traders fast *before* they killed her. He had fought with Brithergen many times and Drasen had proved himself as skilled as Sehereden. He would need to be. Ataghan had no idea how many traders they would confront.

No smoke issued from shafts or cracks and Ataghan hoped it meant the traders' fires were in the open and Fariye not hidden deep in a tunnel. It would be even better if the traders had saved themselves the trouble of hauling firewood and set camp near the sidari stands.

Viv smelled the smoke too and crept on, fear keeping her wings clamped to her back. Dawn was close and daylight increased the risk of being brought down by a dart if she must fly. The ridge fell away in front and her caution increased. She could see the smoke now but still not hear any voices, but if those near the fire slept, they would have posted guards.

Viv forced herself on. There was a shaft to her left large enough to fly down, *if* she were careful, and it was not far from the end of the ridge. The shaft might even open into the tunnel that led to Poss. *That simple, ya reckon, Vivi? In ya dreams.*

Viv dropped to her knees. crawled forward, and peered over the edge. The fire was below but her view was blocked by a shelf of rock. Directly in front, a sweep of silvery grass ended at stand of dark trees that looked like pines. God in Heaven! There was someone in the trees! It was not a trader collecting firewood but someone intent on staying hidden. One of arsehole's men!

Viv's heart thundered. Poss was not safe by a long shot but the arsehole was no fool and she prayed he had a *really* good plan in place. And then light exploded in the trees. Shit! A rift had just spat somebody out! And then all hell broke loose.

There were shouts and running feet, and Viv launched into the air, and dropped down the shaft. Her wings hit the sides and she landed with a jarring thud. The sounds of fighting were all around her, carried by the stone, as well as the sound of running feet.. Viv whirled. Which way? Which way? A shadow flashed along the wall in front and Viv gave chase.

The man unsheathed his knife as he ran, and his final few strides took him into a cavern and a huddled shape. Viv launched herself at him as his knife hand swept back but he barely faltered as he threw her off, hard against the wall. Her wings bedded and she leapt again, onto Poss this time, and locked her close to form a shield, and then the knife plunged into her back. It knocked the air from her lungs and white-hot pain exploded as the man wrenched the knife free and plunged it in again.

'Poss,' she choked, as she waited for the final strike. It never came. There was a thud, then a crushing weight as the trader collapsed on top of her, and then he was gone and Viv managed to turn her head.

It was the arsehole, his face contorted with the blackest hatred she had ever seen, as he twisted his knife in the trader's back. She rolled clear, clawed her way upright, and stumbled back down the tunnel.

Cool air told her she had reached the outside and grunts told her fights still raged, but she fixed her eyes on the trees. She coughed as she staggered on, her chin wet with blood, but desperate to reach the rift with its promise of ending her days anywhere but here.

She had no awareness of falling, only that the leaf-litter smelled of pine as it pressed against her cheek. She liked the smell. There might be owls in the trees too. Owls would be good, or rifts. *Make-up ya effing mind, Vivi. Ya*

don't have much time. Night's coming. Owls, Rim. I'll
have owls to sing me to sleep.

Ataghan slashed Fariye's bonds and wrenched open her
jacket. She was drenched in blood and he examined her
urgently. 'Are you hurt? Did he stab you?'

Her screams had given way to sobs but she managed
to shake her head. 'Viv,' she sobbed. 'Viv.'

He swept her up and ran back along the tunnel, knife
in hand. The elddra had lost so much blood he slipped in
it as he reached the open. Five traders dead, soon to be six
as Baraghan finished off the last, though Enda only knew
where he had sprang from. 'The elddra?' he asked Drasen
hurriedly.

'In the sidari,' panted Drasen.

'Take Fariye,' he ordered and thrust her into Drasen's
arms. 'And set guards!'

'Da!' shrieked Fariye, but Ataghan sprinted off. The
blood-trail was easy to follow but he did not need to go far.
She lay with her battered face turned towards him, blood
seeping from her mouth, and with a stillness that told him
she was dead.

There was a flash and Ataghan dropped into a crouch.
He had only glimpsed the Angellus at the entertainments,
but it was the same one. His chest heaved like bellows and
his massive black wings scythed the air so powerfully they
swept Ataghan's hair forward. The Angellus scooped her
up and his face suffused with such tenderness Ataghan's
heart missed, and then he was gone leaving Ataghan
staring at the air.

'Magnificent, isn't he?' said Baraghan behind him.
'The angel Thrisdane, from the fold of Ezam, home to the

male-aspected angels of the Host, including Violet Iris Vacia's father who, I'm led to believe, is far less charming than she is.'

'Can he save her?' asked Ataghan as he sheathed his knives.

'Not if he takes her to Ezam. They have little in the way of healing. I'm hoping he'll take her to one of the other *uncountable* folds in the *Rynth* where they *do* have healing.'

Ataghan stared back towards the ridge where Brithergen collected wood for the pyres but Drasen still held Fariye, and his hatred for the traders surged anew. There would be many more pyres to be built before he was done!

'You seem singularly lacking in curiosity about the *elddra* who just saved your daughter for the second time,' said Baraghan, as they made their way back.

'It would have been unnecessary had you not raised the alarm.'

'I doubt even you believe that Syld. Three against five, plus the man who guarded your daughter in the tunnels? Not good odds when it takes but an instant to cut a child's throat, which I've no doubt they intended, had Violet Iris Vacia not intervened. So they turned their knives on her instead,' he added grimly.

Ataghan stopped. 'How do you know, what you know, Baraghan?'

'I wondered when you would ask that. When I organised Thrisdane's release from the entertainments, I requested a little favour from Violet Iris Vacia, namely to show me a door, or what is more properly known as a *rift*, to the Angellus. She did, although she warned me against using it. She told me there were thousands of different places and the Angellus could be anywhere.'

'*If* her father's an angel in a place called Ezam, why is she here?'

'Her father is indeed an angel, but he seeded her in another world or *fold*. Her mother appears to have been like a Valen but from Moonsun Fold, where Violet Iris Vacia grew up. At some point recently, her father brought his *shekinah*, which is what they call a female daimon, to Ezam and appointed Thrisdane to guide her through the rifts, like the one I just used and you saw Thrisdane use, to her mother's fold.'

'That doesn't explain why she's here, *unless* her mother's here too.'

'Her mother might indeed be here. She's the type our friends the Astraali would favour, but Violet Iris Vacia still searches. In answer to your original question, she's *here* by accident.' Baraghan smiled. 'Our magnificent friend Thrisdane hasn't enjoyed much good fortune in his job as guide. They got separated and she ended up here. I didn't stay in Ezam long enough to have extended discussions on the matter.'

'If you found the Angellus, I'm surprised you came back,' said Ataghan.

'*If* being the key word,' said Baraghan dryly. '*If* the Host were once the Angellus, I can see why they came here. Their life in Ezam is *very* limited,' he added with a smile.

'And yet they left again.'

'Yes. They didn't like the mess they made.' Baraghan's easy smile faded. 'The Host aren't keen on daimon either, especially female ones. There's no home for Violet Iris

Vacia there, which is why, Syld, if she returns, I'll lein-tryst with her.'

Ataghan's eyebrows rose. 'We both know you're *particularly* unsuited to that arrangement.'

'She'll be the little bit of Angellus-life I can never reclaim,' said Baraghan, as they came out of the trees. 'And we're a good fit. Her enhanced life-span means she'll still be young when your lein's an old man, and that leaves only two contenders worthy of her. Given your hatred of all things Angellus *and* the bruising to her face, that only leaves me.'

Ataghan grunted and Baraghan's hand fastened on his arm. 'I'm serious, Ataghan. If she comes back, she's mine.'

Chapter 7

Ataghan charged Drasen with Fariye's care, despite her shrill pleadings to stay with him, and sent them back to Esh-accom with Brithergen. They rode a single horse and when they neared the wall, would put Fariye between them and cover her with Brithergen's cape.

Drasen would loll forward and coupled with his absent mount, suggest a riding accident, but there would still be enough suspicion from the traders' spies to come looking. They would be cautious but discover the pyres, howl and curse, and swear revenge, and angry *grieving* men were easy to kill.

It unfolded more or less as Ataghan predicted although the spies used a direct route and left their horses some distance away but in the end, all four were gathered around the charred bones. Baraghan's knife took one in the back and Ataghan's knives the other three before Baraghan could throw again. Ataghan wrenched off their amès and he and Baraghan heaved their bodies atop the bones of their comrades, set the fire, then rode back the way the spies had come.

Ataghan stopped now and then to whistle, testing different harmonic combinations, until one by one the spies' horses appeared. He cupped their muzzles and reassured them before, with a single knife slash, severed the tendons in their front legs. They would be lame for zadics, *if* they ever recovered, and the loss to their owners great.

'I sometimes wonder whether Soaich had a share in your fathering,' said Baraghan, as they rode on.

'Do you have children, Baraghan?'

'Not that I've acknowledged, but Fariye's *safe*, Ataghan. The blood-letting can end.'

'Nothing is *ever* safe, Baraghan. Ten, I've found, but there's double that number involved and I'll hunt every last one of them down. It will be a long time before *any* trader decides that murdering children is a good way to raise coin.'

It was past midday before Ataghan reached Esh-accom, and he kept his hood up and took the backstreets to his compound. Baraghan took no such precautions, but as no one had seen him leave, his arrival simply added to the confusion.

Fariye would remain unseen and Ataghan and his men continue their tactics of swapping horses and leaving by different gates to draw out the rest of the traders. Some would load their wagons and head back to their vals, sacrificing the festivities' coin for their lives, but they would never reach home, even if they swapped their slow-moving urruti for the swiftest of horses.

Others would lay low in the hope the storm would pass them by but would be taken, one by one. Ataghan would let them wonder when the blade would find *their* flesh as they had forced Fariye to wonder when their blades would find hers.

The horses in the stable told him Sehereden and his other band members were back, but he went straight to his room, where Fariye had be taken. His band would shift to his compound, as would those who had ridden with them *if* they chose. Shutters would be bolted, and guards set. From now on, no one would enter or leave his compound without his permission.

Fariye lay on the bed in Sehereden's arms but scrambled up and flung herself at Ataghan as soon as he appeared and sobbed afresh. He paced the room with her, soothing her as he had since she was barely from her mother, and when she had quietened, cleaned her face with a cloth. 'They killed her, didn't they, da?' she asked, her voice catching. 'They killed my lein.'

Sehereden stilled but Ataghan kept his attention of Fariye. 'She was badly hurt, Fari. Thrisdane took her.'

Fariye's mouth formed a circle. 'Thrisdane was there?'

'She ran into the sidari and then he came.'

'I knew she would come for me, da, I knew it. And I knew you would come. But the bad men stabbed her ...' Fariye sobbed again and Ataghan's eyes met Sehereden's above her head. His lein said nothing, simply kissed Fariye and left, but Ataghan did not join those in the hall until late that night, when Fariye finally slept.

There was an air of celebration in the hall muted by a grim determination to exact revenge that Ataghan skilfully harnessed. He briefly outlined the happenings at Stelin Ridge, which the men already knew from Drasen and Brithergen, and simply said the elddra had been injured, and another of her kind had arrived to aid her.

It begged the question why she had been there in the first place but the men were more interested in pleasing him and he described his plans to eliminate the remainder of those involved. The men finished their meal and left soon afterwards so that only he and Sehereden remained sprawled at the table drinking semna. 'So, the blood on Fari was Viv's,' said Sehereden heavily.

'Yes, thanks to Baraghan, who spoiled our attack.'

'Why was *he* there?'

Ataghan took a long draught of his drink. 'Baraghan shares the elddras' keenness to discover where Astraal's *beloved* Angellus went. Apparently my daughter's lein showed him how to leave The Wheel in return for Thrisdane's liberation, but Baraghan didn't like his new home and returned *just* before our attack.'

'And Thrisdane? Is he Angellus?'

'Baraghan said they call themselves angels in the place he visited.'

'So, Viv is Angellus or *angel* too?'

'If Baraghan's to be believed, her father was an angel but not her mother. Thrisdane's job was to guide her to her mother but they became separated.'

'Which is what she told me,' said Sehereden slowly. 'And she told me *and* Fariye she wasn't from the Vales *or* from Astraal, but I was blind to what it meant. She told me the truth,' he added grimly and for a while only the hiss of the kitchen fire disturbed the silence.

'There must be some link between her and Thrisdane for him to appear when she was injured,' said Sehereden after a while. 'Did Baraghan learn anything new about her?'

Ataghan poured himself another mug of semna and topped up Sehereden's. 'It's hard to tell with Baraghan given his inclination to boast.'

There was a long pause. 'Do you think she will come back?'

'No.'

'She promised not to leave Fariye without a final farewell,' Sehereden reminded him.

Ataghan considered him steadily. 'She wasn't breathing when Thrisdane appeared, lein. It's hard for the dead to keep their pledges.'

Thris staggered from the rift and struggled to orientate himself. He was covered in blood, which proved he had retrieved Viv, but she was no longer with him and he had no memory of where he had taken her.

The urgency of the summons still gripped him as did the horror of returning to the fold that had reduced him to a dumb thing driven only by fear and pain and then, as he gazed about, he realised his present fold was just as perilous. It was here he had been torn apart, but it was quiet now, which might give him time to find a rift out.

He dismissed any thoughts of flying because canopies blocked a rift's resonance and set off on foot. He sensed he had been to this part of the fold before and had just found a pool when Ash's urgent call had come to aid Ky.

After the Principae had healed him, Thris had wondered whether angels might be granted a second chance at ascension. The notion had seemed so at odds with everything he believed, he had dismissed it as a cowardly attempt to justify his failures, but now as he heard running water and knew where it led, he wondered whether he had indeed been granted a second chance.

The pool was unchanged from his first visit, with clear water that revealed a pebbled bed and with crimson blossoms that swirled on its surface and astonishingly, Viv's resonance was there too. Ash's summons had stopped him searching for her last time and he would not search for her now. He sensed she was beyond him, at least for a time, but he did need to wash away her blood and consider why he was back at the pool.

He swam out into the centre and floated as he had before. The beastmen of this fold seemed a mix of castes and Thris had visited enough human caste folds to know mixed parentage attracted suspicion. And yet no caste was wholly one thing or another, nor static, but with attributes that changed over time.

Viv's arrival in Ezam had changed him and though the changes had all but cost his life, he was glad of them. Her arrival had changed Ky too, who now pursued the same learning path as Prime-archae Serith, but Thris was less clear whether she had changed Ash. Certainly, Ash's wondrous *abilities* seemed to have been heightened by her presence, or maybe their development had been accelerated by the events she triggered.

The insights comforted him and he swam back to shore and was unsurprised to sense a rift. It exited him into Ezam, as he knew it would, and he took to the air and headed to the Blue Helixai where he guessed Ash would be. Unusually, Ky was there too and they embraced him, their relief obvious, but there was something in their expressions that puzzled him.

'You returned to the fold where you were held captive and barely escaped with your life?' asked Ky.

'Yes. How did you know?'

'By your wings,' said Ky and embraced him again. 'You have white plumage, Thris. You have the marks of ascension.'

Chapter 8

There was brightness beyond Viv's lids, the sound of birdsong, and the warm smell of a summer's day. Grass pricked her back and she wondered if she were under the gums behind her childhood home and had dreamed a life yet to come. Or maybe she was dead and this was heaven. She had read it was always summer in the meadows beyond the light-filled tunnel, but there had been no tunnel, just blood filling her lungs.

She opened her eyes. She *was* under a tree but it was not a gum, and for all its brightness, the sky was a dusty pink. Someone leaned over her, the light transforming their red curls into a fiery halo. 'Hello,' said a female voice, low and husky.

'Hello,' croaked Viv.

'It is good that you have woken. Now we can welcome you.' Viv was mortified to realise she was naked and the voice softened. 'You are safe here, *exenda*. Erath cannot heal what it cannot touch and you had need of great healing. I am Essera. Syatha asked me to watch. You have slept a long time, as Erath decreed, and I wondered whether you would wake at all. Do you still suffer pain?'

Viv took a careful breath. She felt normal but the world swayed when she tried to sit up and Essera pushed her back. 'Stay in Erath's embrace a little longer. Her work is not yet done.'

Viv had heard the word *erath* before but could not remember where. Footsteps passed nearby and Essera's head turned. 'Firah,' she called. 'Tell Syatha the exenda has woken.'

'My name's Viv,' said Viv.

'Viv,' repeated Essera. 'That is a strange name, although we get so few exenda here, perhaps it is not strange at all.' The bright light kept Essera's face in shadow but she gripped Viv's hand reassuringly.

'Where am I?' asked Viv.

'In Erath's care.'

'Erath?'

'The name of our fold,' said another voice, in tones as musical as a flute. 'You may return to the erathi now, Essera.'

There was no mistaking the speaker's authority and another shape took Essera's place. 'I am Syatha, a *Sai* of Erath. Would you like to sit?'

'Yes.'

Syatha's muscular hand eased her up and Viv hugged her knees to hide her breasts. A female angel knelt in front of Viv, her face lined, the red of her long curly hair streaked with silver. Both leant her a majesty Kald lacked despite his smooth skin. She wore a robe of sheer material that left her as naked as Viv, but Viv would have been grateful for even its flimsy cover.

'Erath does not harm,' said Syatha. 'There is no need to be uneasy.'

'Do you have my clothes?' asked Viv, having trouble looking at her. She had got used to naked male angels, but naked female ones were another matter.

'All things need Erath's touch but none more so than the injured. Erath is mighty, but I feared even Her strength might be insufficient to bring you back to us. Why did others seek to quench your spirit?'

A strange way to describe attempted murder, thought Viv. 'I was trying to save someone I loved.'

'And did you?'

60

'Yes.'

'Perhaps that is why Erath saved *you*. She repays in kind.'

'It's a pity more folds don't work like that,' muttered Viv.

Syatha helped her up and kept hold of her arm, even after Viv had steadied. 'Let us walk,' said Syatha, and shifted her grip to Viv's hand. It was odd to be led like a child but Viv was soon distracted by her surroundings. Erath was forested like Ezam, but its trees looked normal, despite their pinkish hues, and there was a lot more variety.

Smooth trunks mixed with rough ones, and slender boles with those that were bottle-shaped. Delicate trails of pink, white, and purple flowers tendrilled over the leaf-fall, and their lacy fronds flicked with tiny birds. The trees' branches were alive with birds too.

'Erath has healed your flesh but your wounds are deeper than I suspected,' said Syatha thoughtfully. 'Perhaps it is why Erath allowed you entry. It will be some time, I believe, before your healing is complete, and then only if you allow it.'

'How did I get here?' asked Viv.

'An exenda from Ezam brought you.'

'Ash, probably,' she murmured. 'Was he blue?'

'His skin was coloured as yours, but his hair and wings were black.'

'Thris!' gasped Viv. He *had* come back but her joy was tempered by the risk he had taken. 'Did he say anything?' *Like he loved me and would wait for me?*

'His visit was brief. Erath is closed to exenda,' said Syatha as she drew Viv on.

'It let me in,' pointed out Viv.

'Erath accepted you as Iahhel, which you mainly are.'

'I'm daimon,' corrected Viv. 'My mother was human caste.'

'She was not human caste,' said Syatha in the same musical tones.

Viv gaped at her but Syatha's attention was on the angels ahead. 'She *was* human caste,' insisted Viv, 'and my father was Archae Kald of Ezam Fold.'

'I am not disputing your male parentage.'

Viv stumbled at the wild idea she was adopted and Syatha stopped. 'I am *Sai*, Viv, which means I have attained a certain level of harmony with Erath. I feel Erath's thrum, not in its totality, but more fully than *Non*, like Essera. And all Iahhel are attuned to each other, regardless of their Oneness with Erath. There is discord within you, but the discord generated by exenda blood is too small for your female parent to be human caste.'

'I don't understand.'

Syatha ran her fingers down Viv's cheek. Her fingers were roughened by work but gentle. 'Do you resemble your mother?'

'Yes,' said Viv thickly.

'And *her* mother?'

'So I'm told.'

'And her mother,' pursued Syatha.

'Are you saying they had angel blood?'

'Yes, and for you to be as you are, they joined with angels.'

Viv brought a shaking hand to her mouth. 'So what percentage angel am I?'

'*Percentage*? That is an exenda word.'

'Am I nearly all angel, or nine tenths, or eight tenths or seven tenths ...'

'Erath accepted you, which should answer your question. Come, it is time for you to see the erathi.'

Viv was in turmoil. If she *were* almost all angel, she might have a future with Thris after all and if not, her angel blood *should* allow her to transit home, *if* she chose to, or make her home here, with the Iahhel, *if* they allowed it. There were likely other angel folds too, where she could live without fear.

Syatha came to a stop and Viv blinked at the change. The trees here grew at odd angles and the undergrowth was so dense in places it all but obliterated them. The delicate creepers she had noticed earlier were sinewy and their flowers had been replaced by thorns. Angels like Essera moved between the trees, stroking things as they passed, and Viv watched them in mystification.

'This is the erathi,' said Syatha gesturing at the trees. 'Stay close and try not to touch the things that grow.'

Easier said than done, concluded Viv, as thorns scratched her legs and snagged Syatha's diaphanous robe. Viv peered about uneasily. Her surroundings were silent as if the birds had fled. 'Is the forest sick?' she asked.

'There is no illness in Erath Fold.'

'Then why is it so different here?'

Syatha came to a stop near a younger angel. 'Watch,' she told Viv softly.

The angel looked like she practiced harmonising, her eyes shut and her breathing deep, but then her eyes opened and she caressed the yellowed leaves in front of her. Her breathing quickened until she panted and then, astonishingly, the leaves suffused with green. The yellow had not entirely disappeared, but the change was obvious, and the young angel staggered sideways.

'You have done well, Firah,' said Syatha. 'Rest now.'

Firah moved away and Syatha turned to Viv. 'Erath bequeaths us the erathi to aid our journey to Oneness with Her.'

'So, the fold has things you have to heal to transcend?'

'Transcend?'

'In Ezam, the angels have to complete tasks to move up the angel hierarchy and transcend out to the Great Beyond. Thris, who brought me here, agreed to be my guide to help him transcend and my father appointed him as guide to help *him* transcend.'

'We seek to become One with Erath, not leave Her.'

'But how ...' began Viv and stopped, as she wondered whether *all* the female angels who had ever existed were still here. Maybe the bent branches and razor-sharp thorns actually harboured the female equivalents of Kald and Dejon.

'We are the Iahhel,' said Syatha, as if it were an explanation.

'It must be nice to know *exactly* what you are,' muttered Viv, rattled by her thoughts.

'*No one* knows *exactly* what they are,' said Syatha. 'That is what we seek to discover.'

'I thought you sought to be One with Erath,' said Viv, irritated by Syatha's certainty.

'It is the same thing. Come, it is time you rested.' Viv followed her out of the twisted trees, surprised that the sky had darkened to amethyst. At least the birds still sang. 'You like birds, I see,' said Syatha. 'Why is that?'

'They're pretty,' said Viv, 'and they can fly.' Shit! She sounded like a simpleton. Syatha took her hand again and they walked in silence. Younger angels smiled as they passed, and after a while, Viv forgot she was naked, and that they were too. Despite Erath's strangeness and Syatha's, she felt safe.

'Tell me of yourself,' said Syatha.

'There's not much to tell.' said Viv. 'I grew up in a fold Ezam's angels call Moonsun and didn't know I had angel blood until my angel father visited me at eighteen. I thought my mother had died when I was ten, but he told me she was living in another fold. He took me to Ezam and appointed Thris to guide me to her, but lots of things have gone wrong since we left Ezam. Being almost killed is the latest.'

'You carry deeper wounds than those inflicted by knives. What caused them?'

'The usual things of living in a human caste fold,' said Viv uncomfortably.

Syatha stopped and laid her palm over Viv's heart and Viv had to resist the urge to swat it away. Syatha's eyes had closed and she half expected Syatha to recoil, march her to the nearest rift, and hurl her in, but she simply looked at Viv thoughtfully. 'You have a strong heart.'

Viv guessed it was true, given how many times she had survived murder attempts, but she hoped Syatha meant she had a *good* heart. *Foolin' ya self again, are we, Vivi? Strong ain't the same as honest.*

A glow appeared ahead and Viv gaped. The trees arched towards each other to form a living hall and the light spilled from its entrance 'This is where you live?' asked Viv in amazement.

'We live on Erath,' said Syatha. 'She provides all.'

It seemed to be Syatha's stock answer and Viv bit back questions as she followed Syatha in. The hall's sides were partitioned into alcoves with beds, although the raised, leafy platforms looked more like nests. Angels curled in them asleep, many of whom looked like children which was strange given Ezam's angels appeared there fully grown. There was no reason for Erath to be like Ezam or any other angel fold, she reminded herself, but she wondered how Erath's angels were created given there were no males.

The alcoves ended, to be replaced by an immense table that ran lengthwise up the hall. It was crowded with younger angels like Essera and Firah, who rose and bowed at their approach. They accorded Syatha respect, but Viv hoped it was not the same mindless respect Dane accorded Archae.

Older angels sat further up the table, their faces as lined as Syatha's, and Viv struggled with her expectations of angelic beauty as she passed them. Her arsehole of a father had a glorious agelessness, despite his crappy heart, whereas the Iahhel *looked* old. Perhaps they *were* old even in angelic terms, given they did not transcend, whereas Kald, for all his eons, was comparatively young.

Syatha continued to the head of the table where five angels sat, snow-haired and bone-shouldered. They looked as frail as human caste in their flimsy robes, but their eyes burned with purple fire. Syatha bowed to each in turn and Viv awkwardly followed suit. 'These are the *Hoth* who expended their strength in your healing,' said Syatha.

'Thank you,' said Viv, and bowed again.

'Erath has a gentle heart,' said one in a gravelly voice, as if it explained why they had saved a complete stranger. Viv bowed her thanks a third time and was relieved when Syatha led her away.

Chapter 9

Syatha settled her with Essera and the other younger angels and moved away to join the Sai. The younger angels all seemed to know her name but Viv soon lost track of theirs, not that they seemed to mind. They kept up a steady stream of questions, mostly about the angels in Ezam, and passed along platters of food and jugs of drink. There were nuts, all subtly different; a variety of berries, both dried and fresh; and a drink that tasted like cider, but Viv ate only to be polite.

'Our food is unpleasant to you?' said Essera after a while.

'It's very nice,' said Viv. 'It's just that in Ezam, angels are in perfect balance and have no need to eat. I had no need to eat there either or much since *unless* I've been hurt.'

'Which you were before you came here.'

'Yes,' said Viv, taken aback she was *not* ravenous. Maybe it had to do with the Hoth who had saved her.

Essera's hand closed over hers. 'Things will be clearer to you after you sleep,' she said.

'I don't sleep much either,' said Viv apologetically.

'Erath gifts us a time to dream. The birds roost and the trees slumber. Share my bower, Viv, and let my heart soothe yours.'

Essera's smile was luminous but Viv did not know what the invitation meant. 'Who do you usually share your bower with?' she asked. 'I don't want to cause upset.'

'Orsia or Firah, but they know you are in need of comfort; all Iahhel know it, Erath tells us. Would you prefer to sleep with one of the other Non?' she asked, when Viv still hesitated.

Viv was not sure she wanted to sleep with anyone, but that did not appear to be an option. The younger angels drifted away and she did not resist when Essera took her hand and led her back to the alcoves. She hoped Erath's dark cycle was short so she would not have to lie quietly for hours to avoid disturbing Essera or those who slept nearby.

The bed felt more like feathers than leaves and cradled her in a delicious softness. It smelled nice too, as if it were full of aromatic herbs. Essera lay behind her and brought her arms around her so that her hands rested over Viv's heart, but Viv was rigid, hammered by memories of other encounters.

'The birds are going to their rest,' said Essera softly. 'The last will be the olin. You can hear their song now. The higher songs are those of uris and chiar who share the olins' reluctance to roost. The Sai can hear the trees' song too and the Hoth Erath's music in its totality.' Essera sighed. 'I long for the time when I will hear it too.'

'What happens to the Hoth in the end?'

'There is no end. Their song becomes Erath's. Your coming enriched Erath's symphony.'

Viv's heart missed. 'Do you mean some of the Hoth died *because of me*?'

'They joined Erath's song to allow *your* music to continue. What is given, must be returned, or Erath would cease. *All* things would cease.' There was a pause. 'Be at peace, Viv. Let sleep come.'

Viv quieted but she was far from *at peace*. Some of the oldest angels had given their lives to save hers and she was as sure as hell their lives were worth a lot more. She would have thought the Iahhel would resent her intrusion, and what it cost them, but she had never felt more welcome in her life.

Nothing made sense, and every question seemed to be answered with a variation of *Erath's will*. She would have to demand clearer answers from Syatha tomorrow. The Hoth's lives might not be the only cost of her presence and if there were more to be paid, it was best she went on her way.

'Only the olins sing now,' murmured Essera.

Essera was right. The birdsong had reduced to a single resonant note, sometimes like the drawn-out cry of an owl, sometimes like a flute. Viv was reminded of the Leferen with its background chorus of Lefer. Neither The Wheel nor Erath's birdsong were like the magpies and currawongs of home, but at least there *was* birdsong, unlike Ezam. If she did end up with Thris, they would have to find a fold to live in that had birds.

Essera's breathing told Viv she slept and Viv was surprised to feel herself drift and then she was dreaming. She was back in the old wooden house with the gums at the back, and the magpies *were* singing, and then she was inside, with her mother and Jimmy Wright. There was the familiar musty odour of the carpet, the smell of booze on Jimmy Wright's breath, and the stench of fear. And then her perspective shifted and she was looking down on the scene as a violent drunk beat a helpless woman, and a petrified child cowered in the corner.

Viv jerked awake and Essera woke too, and stroked Viv's hair. 'Sleep, dear one,' she murmured.

'I don't want to,' said Viv shakily and sat up.

'Erath sends what you need to see.'

'I've seen it hundreds of times before. I don't *need* to see it again!'

Essera sat too. 'Would you like me to fetch Syatha?'

'What bloody use will she be? I've lived with these shitty memories every single day of my life! I don't want to dream about them too!'

'Syatha is more skilled at soothing than I am,' said Essera sadly. 'I am failing you.'

'You're not responsible for me!'

'*Responsible*?'

'You don't have to worry about me.'

'But I do,' said Essera in confusion. 'You are part of Erath.'

'I'm an exenda, remember. I just launched in on you by chance. The rift Thris used could have taken us *anywhere*.'

'Chance?'

Viv sighed. 'Don't fret about me, Essera. Just go back to sleep.'

'You lie down too, Viv. At least you will get *some* rest that way.'

Viv lay down to appease Essera but felt in no danger of sleeping again. The angels here believed everything stemmed from the ground beneath their feet, *the mighty Erath*, but if Erath were going to send Viv horrible dreams every night, she would make her farewells sooner rather than later.

Viv's eyelids drooped but she forced herself to stay awake. She had not slept normally since leaving home and she wondered if there were soporific herbs in her bedding. The birdsong started again just before the darkness faded and she eased away from Essera and sat up. The lightest of cymbal-like chirps were followed by those that sounded like harps, pipes, and flutes, then the deeper woody notes of bassoons. The music built to a crescendo, as it had in the Leferen, then dissipated, as if the birds had flown in different directions and sang randomly from a distance.

Viv wiped her eyes, barely aware she had cried. 'It is good you love birds,' said Essera, smiling up at her as she stroked Viv's arm. Viv sourly presumed the reason it was good had something to do with Erath. 'I can show you more birds if you wish or take you to other parts of Erath to help you better understand Her.'

'Don't you have to work?'

'Work?'

'Do whatever you were doing yesterday. Sort of make the leaves in the erathi green again.'

'The Non seek to know Erath as the Sai do, and the Sai as the Hoth, but I can also learn of Her by learning of you. It would give me pleasure to show you things that might give you pleasure.'

By the time the light dwindled again, Viv had concluded Erath had a lot in common with her favorite places. There were rocky valleys with rushing streams, shady clefts filled with dripping ferns, vales of dappled light strewn with fragrant flowers, and everywhere the call of birds, some thrilling, and others so sad Viv's throat grew too tight to speak.

Not that Essera demanded much speech. She seemed content, like Viv, to walk in silence, but her love of the fold was clear in the way she caressed the things they passed. Erath was beautiful and as Essera took her further afield, Viv began to wonder if she could make her home there.

The days flowed together, if *days* they were, and Viv eventually abandoned trying to track them. She and Essera wandered Erath's rosy landscape, ate with the other angels in the evening, and slept together in the leaf-filled alcove. And thankfully, Viv did not dream again.

'It would be easier to fly,' she said one morning, as they scrambled over rocks at the head of a steep valley.

'Fly?'

'Use our wings.' Viv had not seen the Iahhel fly and wondered if there were rules about it.

'To fly would be to lose connection with Erath's music,' said Essera. 'We do not fly.'

'But you have wings,' said Viv, taken aback.

'We do not have wings. To have wings would be to lose connection with Erath's music.'

'I have wings,' said Viv, feeling obliged to confess, as if she carried some deadly disease.

'That is an exenda trait, not an Iahhel one.'

'It's an angelic trait,' corrected Viv. 'All of Ezam's angels are winged including my father.'

'It is an exenda trait,' repeated Essera.

They continued to climb, Essera naming what they passed as usual, but something had changed. Viv had thought the impediment to making a life with the Iahhel might be her tiny percentage of human blood; she had never imagined it would be her angelic blood.

Viv dreamed again that night. She was back in the old weatherboard house but she was older now and her mother long gone. The musty smell was the same, and the staleness of her sheets as she climbed into bed. The noise of her drunken father's card game was audible down the hall, but she drifted, and then there was a hand over her mouth and the terror of being pinned to the bed. Then her viewpoint changed as it had before, and she watched a man maul a terrified girl, the girl break free and run. And then she was awake, dragging in air as she struggled not to vomit.

'You are safe here, Viv,' came Essera's soothing voice.

But Viv knew she was not safe anywhere since sleep had returned to liberate the rats of memory. 'I need some air,' she said and scrambled from the nest. The hall was lit with a pinkish glow and the trees outside glimmered pink too. She stared up, hoping for stars, but the sky's deep amethyst was empty. There was no moon either.

It might be the wrong cycle for both, she comforted herself, but Essera had not mentioned any cycles. The Wheel lacked a moon but its constellations more than compensated, and its valleys and streams were similar enough to home to ease her homesickness. And Fariye was there.

'This is Erath's time of rest,' said Syatha behind her, making her jump. The Sai glided closer and Viv's skin pricked at how ethereal she looked. 'You have slept since you have been in Erath's care,' continued Syatha. 'Why do you not sleep now?'

Viv was tempted to tell Syatha to ask Erath. 'I'm having bad dreams.'

Syatha smoothed Viv's curls from her eyes as a mother might. 'Erath sends what She must.'

'That's kind of Her,' said Viv sarcastically.

'It *is* a kindness though it causes you pain. Essera will bring you to the erathi when light comes. I think it is time. Go back and rest now, Viv. You will not dream.' Viv said nothing and Syatha kissed her on the forehead and glided away.

Chapter 10

Viv stayed awake to ensure, that in fact, she did *not* dream and was rewarded for the tedious hours of darkness by the birds' dawn symphony. It lifted her spirits more than anything Essera could have said *or* Syatha, but dread surged back when Essera led her towards the erathi.

Syatha waited there and dismissed Essera with a nod. 'There is much about you that makes you Iahhel and much about you that does not,' she said.

'My ten percent of human caste blood?' asked Viv, suspecting Syatha's words were a preamble to expulsion.

'Your human caste blood is less important than you imagine. I refer to the life you have lived.'

'Not everything was my fault,' muttered Viv.

'That is both true and untrue.' Viv stared down at the leaf-fall knowing arguing would not prevent her being thrown out. She was just sorry she would not have the chance to farewell Essera. 'You have been in pain a long time,' continued Syatha. 'To rid yourself of it, you must endure more. Do you choose to?'

Viv looked up startled. Syatha's *deal* reminded Viv of other deals she had been offered. *Ya want me to hurt ya, Vivi? Do as ya told, and ya will be just fine. Your choice.* 'What do I have to do?' she asked grudgingly.

'You do not *have* to do anything, but you might choose to test yourself in the erathi.'

'You mean, make yellow leaves turn green?' Syatha nodded. 'Okay,' she said, despite knowing success was unlikely, and followed Syatha into the tangle.

Syatha halted by a branch of jagged thorns, and when she did not speak, Viv stepped forward. Firah had stroked leaves to bring them back to health but these were thorns, long dead *and* vicious. Best get it over with, she decided, and carefully extended her hand, then jumped back as she was sliced.

The thorns moved! She recalled the flowers at the Keeper's house in Hearth Fold, but they had seemed merely curious while these thorns were hostile. She changed her angle of attack with the same painful result, and sucked the blood from her hand. Firah had caressed *leaves* and Viv wondered whether Syatha set her up to fail.

Then again, Firah's face had held intense concentration, so maybe the trick was mental. Viv shut her eyes, braced herself, and extended both hands. The thorns attacked immediately and as the pain escalated, she searched for something, *anything*, to concentrate on. Healthy thorns? Glossy leaves that went with thorns? Roses? Her hands throbbed and she was sure they were shredded. Red roses! Think of red roses! Of their velvety petals, of their heavy scent, of their thorns. No! Not thorns! But perversely, her attention focused on thorns.

She was on the ground, drenched in sweat, her hands bloodied. Syatha knelt beside her but Viv's gaze jerked back to the thorns. They were unchanged. Tears spilled down her face and she was so tired all she wanted was to crawl away and sleep. 'You have made a good beginning,' said Syatha as she raised her, then gently took her hands.

Warmth pulsed through them and Viv saw the wounds close over. 'You healed me!' she exclaimed in astonishment.

'*Erath* healed you because you allowed it.' Viv was too weary to decipher Syatha's meaning and she heard her summon Firah. 'Take Viv to her rest and stay with her until she is well again,' instructed Syatha.

A smaller hand replaced Syatha's grip and Firah's arm came around her as Viv lurched sideways. 'I'm sorry to inconvenience you, Firah,' mumbled Viv, as she stumbled along.

'There is no sorrow in Erath, Viv. Do not bring it with you.'

They must have reached the hall but Viv was only aware of the delicious softness of the bower and made no effort to fight sleep, a decision she regretted as she plunged into another dream.

She was back in the derelict squat with its shouts and brawls, and then Rim lurched out of the shadows and she was above the scene, as Rim choked and slashed a skinny, red-headed girl into submission. Firah was there when Viv woke and stroked Viv's hair as she sobbed. 'I can't stay here,' choked Viv, unsure whether she meant the bower or Erath.

'Where would you like to go?' asked Firah.

'Somewhere I don't dream.'

'Erath's higher places bring you pleasure. I shall take you there.'

Firah's warm hand guided Viv through the trees, and steadied her as the land steepened, but Viv walked in a daze. She had fought to confine the rats of memory all her life but Erath had set them free.

Firah stopped when they reached a place where a stream broke white over river-stones, the cool air was full of spicy fragrance, and the trees rang with chimes like bellbirds. 'How did you know?' whispered Viv.

'Erath gifts sharing.'

'Of my thoughts and dreams?'

'I feel your thoughts as happiness or sadness. Erath does not share dreams but I *feel* the distress your dreams cause Essera and the concern they wake in the Sai.'

'Do you dream, Firah?' she asked, her gaze on the water.

'Yes.'

'Are they happy dreams?'

'They are what Erath sends.'

It did not answer the question, but Viv did not pry. 'Why do you try to heal the plants in the erathi?'

'Nothing in Erath needs healing, Viv. Erath aids our journeys and the erathi is part of Her aid.'

'But you made the yellow leaves green again.'

'It is Erath who determines such things. You did not see what *I* saw.'

'I don't understand *any* of this,' muttered Viv in frustration.

'There are thorns in the erathi,' said Firah.

'Yes and they're bloody sharp.'

'Is that what you saw?'

'Of course, it's what …' Viv stopped. She had seen roses as well and Firah had probably seen something other than yellow leaves but Firah had green leaves to show for her efforts and Viv still had thorns.

'I have been to the erathi many times,' said Firah as if she guessed Viv's thoughts. And presumably had lots of practice doing whatever the mighty Erath wanted, deduced Viv.

'Do you need to visit the erathi to become Sai?' she asked.

'It helps.'

The erathi sounded like the tests Ezam's angels endured to ascend. 'Do all the Non visit the erathi?'

'When they are ready.'

'Can't they just stay Non?'

Firah looked at her. 'Do you wish to stay as you are, Viv?'

'No, but … what I felt in the erathi …' she shuddered. 'It was painful.'

Firah smiled. 'I have never been beyond Erath's blessed bounds. Is change easier there?'

'No,' said Viv slowly. 'It's hard everywhere.'

Viv knew her dreams were part of what she must endure but she dreaded sleep that night. The dreams followed a sequence and the next in line was the crash that killed the child, or Thris's attack on her in Moth Fold, or the Waradi rape.

Essera curled about Viv and kissed Viv's hair, but this dream was a slide-show instead of a single, violent incident, and every slide included the arsehole. His knife poised above her heart after the rape; his burning of Thris's feather; his tethering of her to the urrut to disfigure her in the Grey Fire; his poisoning of her welcome at Tahsin's sett; his verbal and physical abuse in Esh-accom. There was no shift that made her simply an observer either, and as the violence continued, her fear gave way to hatred. She had pledged to see the arsehole dead and she held to that pledge.

She was panting when she woke and Essera caressed her face. 'Syatha says you are to come to the erathi,' she said softly.

'Great,' muttered Viv as she struggled to unclench her fists.

'You do not need to go immediately if you desire more rest.'

'I probably *do* need to go immediately,' said Viv. The dream had brought her up to date which meant things were coming to a head. Essera led her back to the erathi but Viv stopped before they reached Syatha. 'I want to thank you, Essera,' she said, and embraced her. 'You've been more than a friend to me.'

'*Friend*?'

'Someone who is kind,' said Viv then hastened towards Syatha before the burn in her eyes grew worse. Syatha led her back through the crooked trees and Viv's heart sank as Syatha halted at the thorns again. If there were any justice, they would be coated with her blood and flesh 'Why am I doing this, Syatha?' she demanded.

'Because you choose to.'

'And if I choose not to?'

'Then you will not do it.'

'And then?'

'That is a question only you can answer, Viv.'

'I've spent my whole life doing stupid things, so I guess there's no reason to stop now,' she tossed off. She shut her eyes and conjured roses, but as the pain increased, thought only of thorns. Not thorns! Not effing thorns! Then she was on the ground again, knowing she had failed. She felt Syatha heal her hands but was too miserable to raise her head. 'I can't do this,' she choked.

Syatha knelt beside her. 'What do you love most of all?'

'What do you mean?'

'It is a simple question.'

'Fariye.'

'The person you were injured saving?' Viv nodded.

'And what do you hate most of all?'

Viv's answer was quicker this time. 'The arsehole—Fariye's father.'

'You have love and you have hate, Viv. Which is stronger?' Viv stared at her blankly. 'Do you love the daughter more than you hate the father, or do you hate the father more than you love the daughter?'

'It's not like that.'

'Is the father with the daughter?' asked Syatha. 'Are the thorns with the roses? Your early dreams were full of fear but this last one was full of hate. Erath felt it, and the Hoth, and the Sai. It even disturbed the Non. The erathi gives you only thorns, Viv, for thorns are all you give Erath. You have great love within you but also great hate. Which do you choose?'

'The arsehole did terrible things to me.'

'Yes.'

'He hates me.'

'Yes.'

'Are you saying I have to go back and face him? That I can't stay here?'

Syatha's roughened fingers caressed Viv's cheek. 'Every Iahhel who enters the erathi, whether Non, Sai, or Hoth, faces their version of thorns. It is Erath's gift to show us what we are and give us the opportunity to change. You can stay as you are in Erath, or as you are in the fold you came from, or as you are in some other fold. Erath insists on nothing.

'But I do not think you will choose to do that. You faced the thorns again, despite knowing their pain, and you allowed sleep and endured its dreams. I do not think you will choose to remain as you are.'

80

Chapter 11

Sehereden rested back against the new sett's wall to ease his aching muscles. The long days of building had gifted him friendships with the new members of his lein's sett as well exhaustion, but no cure for his frustration. Cadestone held the night skies, the dullest of the zadics but the most anticipated after Fire. Its heavy star-clusters marked the men's last chance to be named seed- or choose-fathers, before the long wait to Fire Zadic began again.

Sehereden's frustration was shared by the men who gathered with him around the fire. His lein's followers had grown to over forty and their loyalty was already strong. Once the sett was finished and the celebrations of Cadestone complete, they would bring their si- and lein-trysts, their children, and their old, to live here on the Scinta Rill. But in the meantime, they waited, like him.

Lirium and Glimwing gave men a sense of whether they would be gifted children come Cadestone, but none of them had been in Esh-accom to receive the longed for news. As soon as Fire Zadic ended, they had crossed the crest into Warinavale and with the Genessi bands led by Quen en-Sar-ril, had destroyed Perin-ril's murderers.

The fighting had forged unbreakable bonds, not just within their own bands, but with Quen en-Saril's, but the victory had come at a cost. They had left the bones of over a dozen of their own on the pyres, and even more of the Genessi. Scouring the Perin-ril had also sent a powerful message to the Ascadi, and given there had been no further Ascadi attacks, it seemed the message had been heeded.

Ataghan sat opposite in conversation with Brithergen, but even as Sehereden glanced in his direction, Ataghan

81

tossed his urrut-sa into the flames and strode away. His lein had rarely been at peace, even before the fighting, but Fariye's abduction had damaged him as much as when he believed her lost.

His lethal pursuit of those with even the slightest involvement had seen the festivities empty of traders, and Sehereden summoned by Esh-accom's Sylds to discuss his lein. But Sehereden's description of Fariye's abduction had been so shocking they had not pursued the matter. They had not wanted to lose the coin Ataghan generated either, not that many wagered against him in the end.

Ataghan's intensity had become an aggression so intimidating that even the most boastful adversaries were reluctant to face him in the rink. The crowds seemed relieved to see him don the champion's wreath too, so they could turn their attentions to more enjoyable activities.

Cadestone faded and as the fire burned low, the men went to their rest. Sehereden remained where he was, his thoughts on Viv, as they so often were. The sett's rebuilding meant he had a home to offer her and an incentive to accept a lein-tryst *if* she returned. Viv's trust in him had grown enough to gift herself and from what Baraghan said, she had no other home, even in Thrisdane's world, and that gave him hope, despite his lein's antagonism.

Ataghan had requested he not mention Viv in Fariye's presence, and he had complied, but Fari spoke of nothing else, and when they had left her in Brithergen's compound and set out for the Scinta Rill, she had convinced herself Viv would be with them when they returned.

They left the Scinta Rill a few days later, despite the sett being unfinished. Cadestone was drawing to an end and the men's frustrations could be contained no longer. There were twenty-six in their party as they came down into the Dart-val and turned starwise. Those who had no chance of fathering this zad-can had remained behind to complete the sett and then head deep into the cloudwise vals to reclaim the horses and urrut herds. When the men returned from Esh-accom after Cadestone with their lein-trysts and promised children, the stores would be full of urrut-sa, cheese, and cured meats to welcome them home.

Tension robbed the party of conversation and Sehereden was silent too as he rode with Ataghan at the head of the group. Dart rose squawking at their approach, butter-yellow against the sun, and he knew it was here that Viv had been taken.

'What is it?' hissed Ataghan, reaching for his knife.

'Just my thoughts,' said Sehereden. Fara had passed his disquiet onto Taris and Sehereden struggled to lighten his mood. 'It's where the Waradi captured Viv.'

'So she claims.'

'It was Fariye who told me. Viv hid her and drew them away.'

'To reunite with them in private.'

Sehereden glanced at him. 'Do you still believe that after everything she's done to keep Fariye safe?'

'What I believe is irrelevant since she's unlikely to return.'

'It will be relevant *if* she does return and grants me a lein-tryst. And even if she refuses me, Fariye will want her lein.'

'I've told you before the elddra wasn't breathing when the Angellus reclaimed her. If Fariye persists in believing she's coming back, I will have to tell her *exactly* what I saw.' Ataghan glanced back at the following men and lowered his voice. 'If Ithreya carries, she'll gift you the child, a certainty few Valen enjoy, and yet you would risk it all for an elddra who doesn't know the meaning of truth.'

'Viv's secrecy is understandable given she and Thrisdane are from beyond The Wheel,' said Sehereden softly.

'I have a request of you, lein. In the unlikely event the elddra does return, speak with me *before* you offer her a lein-tryst.'

Sehereden gave a small bow. 'Of course, if that is what you wish.'

'It is what I wish. I thank you, lein.'

Ataghan sensed the air of expectation in Esh-accom as soon as they passed through the gates and his own blood quickened. The crowds may have gone but the stalls of devotional tokens and tryst-bracelets were still busy, as were the semna-firi tents, which now provided private places to gift children rather than seed them.

When he had first come to Esh-accom, he had believed winning tournaments would be enough to win a child, and then that accumulating coin would be, but come Glimwing and Cadestone each zadican, women had gifted their children elsewhere. Perhaps they sensed what he was and that was one adversary he could not defeat.

Taris tossed his head and Ataghan sent him soothing thoughts as he led his men across Axian. He could have taken the back streets but he wanted to announce his return to any women who still considered him, and to any man tempted to persuade them to change their minds.

The majellus's familiar perfume welcomed him back to his compound and he noted the bolted shutters with satisfaction. He would rotate his men through guarding duties, both here and wherever Fariye went, even if she were with Sehereden, and when Cadestone gave way to the undulations of Horse Zadic, he would take her back to the Scinta-ril.

If Sita could not be reclaimed, he would let her choose another mare, and they would journey together to the deepest clefts where parien feathers might still be found. His sett would be a happy place for her again, with many playmates, and if Ithreya came as Sehereden's si- or lein-tryst, his lein's child would be akin to a brother or sister for her. Fariye's memories of the fighting and the elddra would fade, to become no more than a bad dream, obliterated by the bright light of a new day.

Viv leapt from the rift and darted behind a tree. She was in the pine-like forest at Stelin Ridge, as she knew she would be, and it was dark. This was where she had drowned in her own blood, where Thris had snatched her back, where Baraghan had returned from Ezam. She remembered her last moments in the trees, and the rift's resonant prints confirmed the rest.

Erath had heightened her sensitivity, and while she had no idea how long she had been gone from The Wheel, she hoped it was long enough to explain her long hair. Her absence had certainly been long enough for the seasons to change and she was cold. *Ya goin' to need more than long hair to deal with the arsehole, Vivi.*

She did not know what choosing love over hate entailed but calling Poss's father *arsehole* probably was not part of it. She was not ready to call him *Ataghan* so *Syld* would have to do. Viv grimaced. Staying on the side of love had been easier in Erath where the only things to hate were thorns, and she had been welcomed there, but Poss was here and so that was that.

At least Erath had shown her what it was to have a home and, if luck ran her way for once, her mother would be in Astraal and she could live with her there. Then, *if* the Syld were civil, or at least did not try to kill her, she could see Poss at Esh-accom's festivities once a zadican, or visit her at his sett. It would have to be enough. He certainly would not let her live with Poss full-time.

It was scary to think of making a home for herself, but Sehereden was right; she *was* tired of wandering. Elddra were accepted here, if not welcomed, and if her mother *had* come here, she might have stayed for that reason alone. And if she had not? Viv no longer knew if she could spend the rest of her very long life looking for her.

The forest remained quiet and she crept to the edge of the trees. Darker blotches marked the tunnel entrances where Poss had been held, but new mounds loomed from the night. Bones glimmered and she realised they were pyres. Six or seven, she counted grimly. When the arsehole took revenge, he did a *very* thorough job.

Chapter 12

She set off keeping to the trees' margin where the going was easier, and hugged herself to stay warm. Her shirt was halter neck and her jacket and spare clothes were all at the *Syld's* compound, along with her pack. They were the first things she would reclaim. It would be quicker to fly but she wanted to reacquaint herself with the *feel* of The Wheel or maybe keeping her feet on *Erath* was her Iahhel blood coming out!

Essera had wept when Viv had left and Viv had wept too. Essera was all the best friends Viv had never had, and it was going to be hard to sleep without her comfort, assuming sleep did not desert her again now she was back.

Esh-accom's walls came into sight as the sun cleared the horizon and she tucked her hair under her shirt collar. She wore the shirt normally now and her confined wings added to her tension. She was not in Erath's safety anymore and Esh-accom held irate traders, elddra intent on hijacking her rift skills, and the man formerly known as the arsehole.

The gates swung open and Viv strolled in and across the yard, despite every instinct screaming at her to sprint for the side streets. There were few people about, but it was early, or maybe it was because the festivities had finished. Viv faltered. She had not considered that the Syld and his daughter might be long gone.

She chewed her lip as she trawled through everything Sehereden had told her about their movements. They came to Esh-accom at Fire Zadic, and again at Glimwing and Lirium, but what bloody zadic was it now? Viv mulled over her options as she turned up the street to the

87

compound. If the Syld and Poss were *not* here, they would be back at their sett, *if* there had been time to rebuild it, *if* enough zadics had passed.

Poss might be happily settled with her new friends and Viv's reappearance dredge up a past best forgotten. Viv took a steadying breath. She had pledged Poss to farewell her before leaving permanently but she was not yet leaving permanently.

Viv no closer to resolving the dilemma when she reached the compound and was annoyed to see it still unguarded. It seemed the Syld had learned *nothing* from his daughter's abduction unless the compound was deserted. She pushed the gate open, pleased to see horses in the stable, at least *someone* was home, and right on cue, a man stepped from the lee of the compound wall. 'Your business?' he demanded.

Viv did not recognise him and he gave no sign of recognising her, and she wondered whether she had mistaken the gate. 'I've come to see my lein, the Syld's daughter. I'm Viv,' she added, as the man's hard expression remained unchanged.

'The Syld orders that no one enters his compound without his permission.'

'Well, can you tell him I'm here?'

'The Syld isn't within.'

'Is Sehereden here, then?'

'The Syld orders that those of his compound not be discussed.'

'Fine,' said Viv. 'When the *Syld* comes back, can you tell him the elddra would like to see her lein, unless of course, your orders are *not* to discuss his *former* guests.' The man nodded, and Viv strode out, only to collide with Caibel.

'Welcome back to Esh-accom, Violet Iris Vacia,' he said, steadying her.

'Why are you here?' she demanded, angered by her exchange with the guard.

'Baraghan en-Esh-accom asked me to watch for your return and extend his invitation to you.'

Viv gaped at him. Of course Baraghan was here; his resonance had been strong in the rift. Caibel waited and Viv collected her wits. 'How long has Baraghan been back in Esh-accom?'

'Since late Fire Zadic.'

'Which zadics have passed since then?' asked Viv, not caring if Caibel thought it suspicious she did not know. Caibel was not going to kill her.

'Ice, Lirium, and Glimwing. We're in Cadestone now, Violet Iris Vacia,' he added politely.

'Call me, Viv,' she muttered as she calculated the possible consequences of being away so long.

'Baraghan en-Esh-accom instructs us to use your full name.'

'Us?'

'Those of his compound.'

'Weren't you living with your mother?'

'I'm living with Baraghan en-Esh-accom now,' said Caibel proudly. 'He's teaching me his surgeon's skills.' There was a pause. 'Do you accept his invitation, Violet Iris Vacia?'

'What invitation?'

Caibel blushed. 'Forgive me. Baraghan en-Esh-accom invites you to be his guest during your stay in Esh-accom.'

'Why would he do that?'

'He didn't think you would want to stay *here*,' said Caibel, and blushed again.

Perhaps, but that did not mean she wanted to stay with him either. Apart from sharing the arse—*Syld's* arrogance, she had a feeling he wanted to best the Syld in some way. But she did not have a lot of choice. She had no trade for accommodation and did not fancy knocking on Anfarena's door.

Viv nodded and followed Caibel back towards Axian. The square was busier than the yard near the gate and she kept her head down and quickened her steps until Caibel took the hint and increased his pace too. If Anfarena's watchers were out and about, they would be here, and she wanted to avoid their demands as long as possible. She did not want to bump into Sehereden either, her feelings for him harder to deny now she was back. Same with Thris, but she was hardly likely to bump into *him*.

Baraghan's compound turned out to be even grander than the Syld's. A fountain sat in the middle of the yard, where a tree would have usually been planted, and the building's colonnades were heavily carved. There was an internal courtyard, like the other compounds she had visited, but in places the passageway's windows opened directly into it, and Viv stared out in delight.

There was a second, larger fountain, and ceramic tubs filled with flowering shrubs. The air was full of their sweet scents, the sound of fountain's tinkling, and the flutter of red-breasted birds as they used the fountain as a bath.

'It's lovely,' she breathed.

Caibel nodded. 'It's an enormous achievement. The courtyard was bare before Fire Zadic.' Viv looked at him at astonishment. 'Baraghan's changed the inside of the building too. Those,' he said, gesturing to embroidered banners on the wall, 'were only traded recently.'

Viv wondered if Baraghan's visit to Ezam had prompted the change, *presuming* he had gone to Ezam, and then Caibel stopped at one of the carved doors that lined the passageway. 'Baraghan en-Esh-accom instructed me to offer you this room and ensure your needs are met, should he not be here to welcome you himself.'

Baraghan really *was* a man who planned ahead, concluded Viv, as she stepped inside. 'It's bloody luxurious,' she muttered. A sumptuous cover topped a carved bed of the same honey-coloured wood as the chairs, table and clothing chest, and vases of silvery leaves adorned the mantlepiece.

'*Bloodyluxurious*?'

'It has a lot of comforts,' said Viv as she finished her inspection. 'Whose room was it?'

'No one's. Baraghan en-Esh-accom's compound has never held many people. There are a lot more of us now.'

'Since Fire Zadic?'

'Yes. Do you like the bed cover? It took the cloth-wright over a zadic to weave.'

Viv could see why. It was adorned with angels outlined in gold against a silver background of trees. 'Angels,' she muttered as her heart began an uncomfortable beat.

'Angellus,' corrected Caibel. 'They came to the sacred lake of Astraal zadicans ago and seeded the Astraali ...' He stopped and dipped his head. 'Of course, you know that Violet Iris Vacia.' He stroked the cover reverentially. 'Obviously, the Angellus weren't these colours. Baraghan en-Esh-accom asked the cloth-wright to make them prettier for you.'

Grey, yellow, and green angels hovered around the cover's border but the centre was devoted to a white-winged blue angel, a black-winged gold angel, and a pale gold-winged gold angel. Baraghan had sent her a message only she would understand.

'Do you like it?' repeated Caibel.

'It's very beautiful,' said Viv distractedly.

'But not as beautiful as its new owner,' said a voice behind her, and Viv turned as Baraghan strolled into the room. He wore his usual easy smile but there was no mistaking the intensity of his gaze. 'Welcome back to Wheel Fold, Violet Iris Vacia, and more specifically, welcome to my compound which I hope you will treat as yours.'

Chapter 13

Thris perched on the Blue Helixai's airy heights, closed his eyes, and let his thoughts drift. Ash's music pulsed around him and he saw again Beast Fold's jungles, Hearth Fold's emerald uplands, and Sand Fold's deserts. He even saw, without raising his head, the Thorny Mountains' crests and the Red, White, and Green Helixai's glimmering peaks.

Ezam was one of the Rynth's uncountable folds and he was one of its uncountable manifestations, no more important than the Beastmen of Beast Fold, or the flowers that had turned at his passing in Hearth Fold. Transiting had gifted him an understanding of his smallness but that even the most inconsequential of things had consequence.

Angel caste, human caste, plant caste, animal caste, and all the castes beyond his comprehension were important, not because they served a greater purpose, though they might, but because the Great Beyond had brought them into being.

But nothing existed in isolation. Ezam's vines must have the glis for their journey skywards, and mantises must have the scarabs to survive. Yet while vines caused the glis no harm, mantises killed scarabs. He considered the effects of the Host's hierarchy on Dane and Archae and recognised the hurt the powerful could inflict on the powerless. It might be accidental, but it might also be deliberate.

The music stopped, and Ash's honeyed breath dusted down on him. 'What is it you fear, Thris?'

'That I have hurt others and am *still* hurting others. I abandoned Viv in a violent fold.'

'She is safe with the Iahhel now.'

'*If* she is with the Iahhel,' said Thris. He had only managed to claw back fragmentary memories of a pink sky, trees and birds. 'I pledged to take her to her mother yet I linger here.'

'A lot has happened since that pledge. *We* are changed, perhaps more than our wings show.'

'Viv changed me when I joined with her,' murmured Thris.

'The consequences of joining are unknown,' said Ash, and settled beside him.

'Not entirely. Archaes Kald and Dejon joined with human caste females and suffered no consequences.'

'We do not know that,' said Ash gently.

'I do not sense the Archaes loved the human caste they joined with,' continued Thris.

'The Host is impelled by love, but you speak of sexual love. That is the preserve of human caste.'

'Human caste? My joining with Viv was a star-storm of beauty, a glimpse of what I imagine the Great Beyond to be. I felt no shame, Ash, nor that my chances of ascension were lessened. I felt healed and whole, and now she is gone, I feel incomplete again.'

Ash's hand closed over his. 'The Great Beyond keeps the Host and the Iahhel separate for good reason,' he said.

'Does it?' asked Thris, turning to him. 'Or is our separation simply one of the uncountable possibilities of the Rynth?'

'I …' began Ash, but then pale gold wings flashed into view as Ky dropped from above.

The three embraced, glad to be together again, but Ky remained unsmiling. 'I need to speak to you, Thris. I need to know about The Wheel.'

94

The meal Baraghan served was as sumptuous as Viv's room, although it was actually Baraghan's servants who served her along with the grey-haired woman who appeared to be the cook. Three younger women, who Baraghan introduced as Mishia, Derisi, and Verena, set the dishes on the table and refilled their goblets, while Baraghan kept up a patter of conversation about the pleasant jaunts within a day's ride.

He did not seem to expect her to contribute which left Viv free to concentrate on the lightly seasoned, tender cuts of meat; greens doused in a citrus sauce; and goblets of mead. The meal was delicious. The final plates were cleaned away, Verena set fresh goblets and a jug of urrut-sa on the table, and the hall fell quiet.

'I haven't had a chance to say how relieved I am to see you,' said Baraghan softly, as he filled her goblet. 'After Stelin Ridge, I feared the worse.'

'Thris collected me,' said Viv as she concentrated on her urrut-sa.

'Yes, I saw him. I also saw him in Ezam.'

'So, you *did* go there.'

Baraghan grinned. 'You chose the right rift.'

'Did Anetherey end up there too?'

'Anetherey?'

'An elddra. She rushed after you before I could stop her. The elddra have had me followed since I've been here. They want me to show them a rift.'

Baraghan's brows lowered. 'They've threatened you?'

Viv took a sip of her drink. 'Let's just say they won't be happy I've been gone for a while and will insist on knowing where I've been.'

'Where you've been is no concern of theirs!'

'I'll let you tell them that,' muttered Viv. 'If Anetherey *didn't* exit in Ezam, she must have ended up in some other fold. I just hope it's kind to her.'

'Unlike some of the folds you've ended up in, *according* to Ashdane,' said Baraghan.

'So you saw Thris in Ezam,' said Viv, ignoring his prompt to speak of the blue angel. 'What did he say?'

'Nothing. He was still drugged from his time here. I used hareesh to rouse him. The next time I saw him was at Stelin Ridge when he collected you.'

'Did he say anything then?'

'Not that I am aware of.' There was a long pause. 'Thrisdane knew you were in need. Is there some sort of link between you?'

'Not anymore.' She took a deep breath. 'Ash can see into other folds and would have probably sent him, but he shouldn't have. It's too dangerous for Thris here.'

'As it is for you on your own *or* at Ataghan en-Scintaril's compound.'

Viv shrugged. 'The Syld's never liked me.'

'Dislike is one thing, Violet Iris Vacia, violence is another. The traders didn't inflict the bruises on your face at Stelin Ridge, did they?'

Viv traced the table's engraving with her fingers. 'Why's he like that, Baraghan? You've known him a long time, haven't you?'

'I've known *of* him for ten zadicans when he first competed in the tournaments. He's always been violent, it's why he wins. He won this Fire Zadic too, in case you're wondering, but he didn't waste time celebrating. It's said he took men sunwise and breached the crests into Waradi Vale. Apparently bands of Genessi breached the crests too. What they did there is unknown, except word is the rill in Penrin-val ran red for days. He's been at the Scinta-ril for the last couple of zadics, rebuilding his sett, but he's back now.'

'I know. I went to his compound.'

Baraghan's eyebrows rose. 'And decided against *enjoying* his hospitality again?'

'He wasn't home and his guard wouldn't let me in. I want to see my lein, Baraghan. I have a *right* to see her! And I only have the clothes I'm wearing. Everything else I own is there.'

'Including your amè,' said Baraghan, his gaze on her neck.

'Yes,' said Viv and instinctively covered her bare skin with her hand.

'Well, at least I can solve your lack of clothing,' said Baraghan. 'My compound has a store of clothes, including some I hope you'll find suitable. Derisi will bring them to your room for your selection. Cadestone means you'll need warmer things than those you're wearing *and* ones that better show off your beauty.'

Viv said nothing and he lightened his tone. 'Cadestone celebrates the gifting of children and of lein-trysts, and there's music and dancing. It's a happy time and I hope you'll grant me the opportunity to show you that Esh-accom can offer more enjoyable things than those you've so far experienced.'

'Yes, thank you,' said Viv, hoping she had agreed to nothing more than clothes and sight-seeing.

Baraghan leaned back in his chair and surveyed her from under lowered lids. *Like the cat that's got the cream,* thought Viv uneasily. Judging by the compound, his healing skills were lucrative, unless he made his money in other ways. Women obviously found him attractive too, given Caibel, and his young servants' lingering glances, but what she really wanted to know was how he had managed to return from Ezam.

'Thris told me I couldn't go back to my home fold, because I was still there in *that* time, and returning would destroy me,' said Viv.

'The Host told me the same thing, but I didn't take their word for it,' he said with a smile.

'Maybe you were just lucky,' said Viv, irritated by his smugness.

'*Lucky*?'

'Fortunate.'

Baraghan smiled again, showing his teeth this time. 'I am indeed fortunate, Violet Iris Vacia. However, I'm inclined to believe that good fortune follows good planning.' Viv resumed her fascination with the table to hide what was probably a sour expression. As she had always had bad luck, she was obviously a crap planner!

Men appeared in the doorway and Baraghan rose. 'Kindly excuse me, Violet Iris Vacia. There are matters I must attend to. I'm reliably informed the wind will swing cloudwise this afternoon and become chill. It might even bring rain, so it would be wise to stay inside until you have selected some warmer clothes. I look forward to joining you again for the evening meal.'

He bowed and his steps echoed back down the passageway. Baraghan was used to getting what he wanted, concluded Viv as she surveyed the room's luxuries, including more than his fair share of luck, but what did he want with her? She still sensed it concerned the Syld, but she was in no position to walk away and she had yet to see Poss.

She went to her room and was at the window, watching the birds play in the fountain, when Derisi appeared with an armful of clothes. She even had a pair of beautifully stitched ankle boots. The soles were unscuffed and the clothes looked new too. 'Who owned these?' asked Viv, holding up an embroidered jacket with silver buttons.

'I don't know, *Violetirisvacia*. I've been in Baraghan's service only a short time.'

'Their previous owner appears to have been exactly the same size as me,' said Viv. 'How *fortunate*,' she added sarcastically.

'Is there anything else you require, *Violetirisvacia*?' asked Derisi. Like the other young servers, she had reddish brown hair and blue eyes.

'Are you elddra?' asked Viv curiously.

'Oh *no*, *Violetirisvacia*!' she exclaimed in mortification. 'I'm the seed-daughter of Daril en-Mena-ril.'

'I don't need anything else, thank you.' Derisi nodded and the door clicked shut behind her but Viv stayed where she was. It never got any easier being a member of a despised group, although it did not seem to worry Baraghan, who had *planned* for a fortunate life in Eshaccom and maybe something else too.

She took a turn around the room. According to Caibel, Baraghan had transformed his compound *after* Fire Zadic, brought Caibel to live with him, and employed Derisi and the other servants, probably including the men he met with now. He had made what had been an empty compound into a home, but had he done it for her?

Given the timing, Cadestone must just about be the last chance for men to secure children. Baraghan would have enjoyed many lovers, so maybe a luxurious compound was bait for a bit of *gifting* of the child variety. He might want a child or two he could call his own, and a si-tryst, or even a lein-tryst, although she doubted he had any interest in his *fortunate* life being curtailed.

Yeah, right Vivi. He's got someone else in mind which is why he's spent a fortune on a bed cover only the two of ya can understand. And on the clothes of course, which were obviously new, and probably on the room's furniture, and on the silver vases, and on their beautifully wrought silver leaves …

Bloody hell! They were glis! Baraghan had transited back from Ezam with his pockets full of glis leaves! She just hoped he had not topped up his flask with ambrosia or imported a pretty amethyst scarab or two. *And what does all this tell ya, Vivi?* It bloody well told her Baraghan had a fondness for *all* things *Angellus* including her.

Chapter 14

Baraghan's storm clouds rolled in as Viv hurried across Axian, head down and collar high, but she need not have worried about being seen. Those who had enjoyed the music and stalls had sought shelter and the stall-holders had secured their awnings. Viv's jacket was more decorative than weather-proof, and she broke into a jog as asht-voices filled the air. The wailing was unsettling, despite her knowing it was only the wind.

She hoped the worsening weather meant the Syld was snug in his compound, and his horse *was* in the stable, but she got no closer to the building than earlier that day. 'Your business?' demanded the guard.

'The same as this morning. Can you tell the Syld I'm here?'

'Wait,' the guard ordered, and strode off, but any thoughts of sneaking in after him were dashed by a second guard near the door. Poss's window shutters were closed and she hoped they were bolted as she jigged from foot to foot to keep warm. The majellus's branches creaked but there were no more blossoms to tumble to the cobbles, then the guard reappeared carrying her pack and a leather purse.

'The Syld returns your possessions and asks me to tell you that his daughter is happy and settled, and that if you love her, you'll allow her to stay that way.' He handed over her pack and the purse. 'The Syld gifts you coin to secure suitable accommodation during your stay in Esh-accom.'

The weight of the purse told Viv it held more money than she would need for a whole suite of rooms. 'Tell the Syld to keep his *bribe,* and that *unlike* him, I'm not motivated by coin. And tell him that I *always* keep my pledges, no matter how long it takes!'

Viv stormed off and was still angry when she reached the Anaten Quarter. She had pledged Syatha to turn aside from hate but it was bloody near impossible with people like the *Syld* around. The wind grew shriller and she did not hear the footsteps as she strode along until she was overtaken and the man swung back to block her path. One of Anfarena's men, she concluded, rather than some random attacker. 'What do you want?' she demanded, in no mood for bullying.

'Anfarena requests a meetin' at her compound.'

The street was empty of help and the weather meant it would stay that way, but Viv stood her ground. 'It's not convenient.'

'My orders are to be takin' you there.'

'I don't give a shit what your orders are. Anfarena can talk to me tomorrow. I'm going back to my compound.'

The man's hand fastened on her arm. 'You'll be comin' with me, elddra.'

'The elddra wishes to return to her compound,' a new voice grated behind her. 'You'll let her pass.'

The first man drew his knife and Viv swiveled. The second man was armed too and already crouched. 'It doesn't matter...' she began quickly, dreading a fight, but was knocked sideways as the first man lunged. 'Stop!' she begged, as the men struggled on the cobbles, but it was a strangled cry from the first man that ended the fight.

The second man rose and wiped his knife on the prone man's jacket. 'I'm Ershen en-Esh-accom,' he panted with a bow. 'Baraghan en-Esh-accom charged me with your care. I'll escort you back to his compound, elddra.'

102

The first man had not moved. 'You … you can't just leave him there,' said Viv.

'The wound is small. He'll make it back to his compound. Come, elddra, the rain is close. Baraghan Esh-accom won't want you getting wet.'

Viv grimly contemplating Anfarena's willingness to use force as she trudged along beside her rescuer. Her best bet would be to take herself off to Tahsin's sett, except she wanted to see Poss and, she conceded, spite the Syld in the process.

Memories of her time in the erathi were fading but not its truths and she grudgingly reminded herself of them. She had got into a car full of druggies because of hatred, and a child had died, and it made no difference her hatred had been for herself. It was hatred that fed the rats of memory too and robbed her of any chance of happiness. Hatred for Jimmy Wright, for the men who had abused her, for the systems that had failed her.

Since then, her only moments of happiness had been here in The Wheel: joining with Thris; finding Poss; living in Tahsin's sett; Sehereden's kindness and promise of a future. And even if Thris, Poss, and Sehereden were ultimately lost to her, Tahsin's welcome gave her hope of happiness *if* she could turn aside from hate.

Viv was hungry when she reached Baraghan's compound and had to use the latrines, something she had not done since her first days in Ezam. Erath was an angelic fold, but for some reason, she had returned more human than when she had left.

The compound was quiet, which suited her, and she went to her room, opened the shutters, and watched the rain pound the courtyard. The shrubs bent under its onslaught, and the fountain's water slopped from its basin, but the shining courtyard woke an intense longing, for what, she did not know.

She sighed, wandered back to the bed, and upended her pack. The Syld had tossed in her jewelry and she lay it to one side and sorted the clothes. Ithreya's cast offs showed signs of wear but they came without *expectations* and Viv preferred them to Baraghan's gifts.

She folded the clothes neatly back into her pack, then slipped the chain and owl tribute-charm over her head, holding the cool metal against her skin until it warmed. Sehereden had promised her a lein-tryst but she had always known the Syld would prevent it. The zadics she had spent in Erath Fold had changed her and if Sehereden had spent them in Ithreya's company, they would have changed him too.

She donned the amè casque next. She did not believe amès protected *anyone* in death, but the amè contained parts of Sehereden and Poss that were hers no matter what happened. That left the Waradi tryst-bracelet which, one way or another, had cost her dearly, including a slash to the arm for the Lefer. The Waradi rapist had used it to claim her and the Syld to reject her but the bracelet also reminded her she had survived both. It was also good to flash under the Syld's nose occasionally.

There was a knock but before she could move from the bed, Baraghan strode in. It was lucky she was not dressing, she concluded acidly. His eyes narrowed as he took in the bracelet, but his anger was for elddra. 'Ershen reports the man was willing to use force on you, at their behest,' he said, as he prowled round the room.

'Did you order Ershen to guard me?'

104

'My men ensure the safety of those of my compound.'

'I'm not of *your* compound,' said Viv tersely.

Baraghan's smile snapped back into place. 'Forgive my turn of phrase, Violet Iris Vacia. I meant *guests* of my compound.'

'I don't want your men to follow me around,' said Viv, nonplussed by Baraghan's flick from anger to charm.

'If you're asking me to abandon you to those who would harm you, then I must beg your pardon in advance for failing to do so, Violet Iris Vacia.'

'The elddra don't intend to harm me,' said Viv, but the claim sounded unconvincing, even to her own ears.

'*Yet*,' said Baraghan, and settled on the bed beside her. 'The elddra have only shown you the more pleasing parts of their natures, *so far*, but make no mistake, Violet Iris Vacia, they'll do whatever's necessary to achieve their masters' goals. Of course, you could show them a rift and rid The Wheel of them forever,' he said, and smiled again. 'It would solve a lot of problems, Violet Iris Vacia.'

'Only here. I don't have the right to inflict them on another fold, Baraghan. Apart from anything else, it would be a massive act of transference.'

'*Transference?*'

Viv went to the mantle, glad to put some distance between them, and brandished the vase of glis. '*This* shouldn't be here. Didn't the Host warn you against taking things from one fold to another?'

'They might have mentioned it,' he said, with a shrug, 'but I've always been attracted to beauty,' he added softly. Viv said nothing and he picked up the bracelet. 'As *you* are *unless* there's another reason you have a Waradi tryst-bracelet.'

'According to Ataghan en-Scinta-ril, it's a gift from my Waradi lover in payment for my spying services.'

'Is that what his lein believes too?'

'I no longer know what Sehereden believes,' said Viv and went to the window again. 'I haven't seen him since Fire Zadic.'

'You visited Ataghan en-Scinta-ril's compound again this afternoon?'

'Yes, for all the good it did me.' Viv smiled sourly. 'At least he returned my belongings. The only way I'm going to see my lein is to hang around Axian.'

'You won't see her that way,' said Baraghan brusquely. 'She'll be kept inside until you're gone or Ataghan en-Scinta-ril takes her back to his sett. If you want to see your lein, Violet Iris Vacia, you'll have to leave.'

'I don't see how …'

Baraghan raised his hand. 'What I *should* have said is, you're going to have to *appear* to leave.'

It was noon the next day when Viv strode out through Esh-accom's gates and was still in view of the wall when she struck sunwise towards the forests. But she did not enter them. She needed to remain visible to the men Anfarena would send after her, and to the men Baraghan had put in place last night to intercept them. At least the elddra's pursuit would reinforce the impression she had gone, she concluded glumly, sick of her life having turned into a game of cat and mouse.

Baraghan's compound believed she headed to the Kama-ril, as did the men assigned to prevent the elddra *troubling* her. Only Caibel and Ershen knew the truth. They would ride out later that day, Caibel on the back of

Ershen's horse, with his hood drawn close. The boy was similar to her in size, to the *casual* observer, or to others who had no reason to stare. And come dusk, Viv would ride back in, clad in Caibel's cloak, and take up residence in the compound that belonged to Caibel's mother.

Caibel would camp at Stelin Ridge, which was the last place Viv would have spent the night, but Caibel seemed untroubled by the prospect of bones, his glowing face telling of pride in being privy to information denied to nearly everyone else.

Viv would not be imposing on Caibel's mother long anyway. Once she assured herself Poss was well, she would head to Tahsin's sett on the Kama Rill. She was weary of being confronted by the Syld and Anfarena's crew, and doubted Baraghan's assurance she would blend in when he had presented her with a heavily embroidered head scarf. Apparently it was called an *Enda's Emblem* and worn by women during Cadestone to honour Enda, regardless of whether they carried.

Baraghan had gone to a lot of trouble on her behalf and she wondered when he would call in the debt. She suspected besting the Syld was insufficient compensation, but he was to be disappointed if he thought she would jump into bed with him. She had traded herself for safety or food in the past but those days were gone. She had a place with Tahsin now, paid for by working in the retsen stands. She looked forward to seeing his grizzled mop of hair again, and Doran's simple smile, and even Enesha's scowl.

Chapter 15

As far as Viv could tell, things had gone as Baraghan planned. No one accosted her, so either Anfarena had not bothered to pursue her, or had been thwarted and, as darkness fell, Ershen appeared from the direction of Stelin Ridge with Caibel's cloak, hauled her onto the back of his horse, and galloped her back to Esh-accom.

Music drifted from Axian as they made their way through the back streets to the shabbier area she had been in before. 'Which quarter is this?' she whispered as she peered at the dilapidated walls.

'Miraj.'

The same quarter as the Syld's compound, but that was all the compounds had in common. Melbourne had gracious mansions and rundown hovels, she reminded herself, as did most cities, and people had existed in separate worlds in her hometown too.

Ershen pushed the rickety gate open and rode in but the only person who seemed to be home was an ancient man so bent, he could only raise his eyes to Viv, and not his head. Ershen did not go beyond the yard, but Viv deduced the man's name was Morvin, and that the compound's occupants celebrated Enda's gifts at Axian.

She followed Morvin's shambling form down the passageway, hoping she was not the reason he missed the celebrations, to a room where everything from the bed to the clothing chest looked new. Baraghan's influence even extended to a single sprig of glis leaves on the mantel piece. 'Thank you, Morvin,' she said. 'You don't need to stay. I'll—'

'I will fetch your meal,' said Morvin and shuffled out.

Viv hoped he did intend to *fetch* it, not cook it, or she would be stuck there all night. She did not know exactly when Cadestone's celebrations ended, but the noise from Axian told her the square was crowded which meant Poss might be there.

Morvin's slow steps advanced up the passageway and she met him at the door to take the tray. 'Thank you, Morvin. I won't be needing anything else tonight,' she said, having to address the top of his head. 'As soon as I've eaten, I'm going out. I can let myself back in later. You don't need to be here,' she added, not knowing whether he needed to be there or not.

'I will be here for Baraghan en-Esh-accom's guest.'

'Oh … thank you,' said Viv. 'And thank you for the food,' she added awkwardly.

'It is as Baraghan en-Esh-accom ordered.'

Viv set the tray on the table. *Ordered*, not *requested*, or *asked*, or *gifted* by her hosts, the owners of the compound, unless Baraghan owned this compound too. He had provided the same luxury here, right down to the glis, but the glis, like the angel-adorned bed cover in his compound, were to remind her what only they two shared.

Baraghan had been to Ezam *and* seen Thris, although the Syld had seen Thris too, at the entertainments and at Stelin Ridge. She wondered what the Syld had told Sehereden about Stelin Ridge and was willing to bet it was nothing that showed her in a good light!

She ate quickly, which was not hard because the food was delicious and she was hungry. Having hunger return was inconvenient too given she had to journey to Astraal at some stage, and she wondered again why Erath had changed her. Maybe having to deal with the human

109

emotions of love and hate had made her more human, which was ironic, given the discovery she was almost all angel.

She set out through the darkened streets, the sound of revelry growing as she neared the square, the scarf tied firmly over her hair. The embroidered cloth matched her dark blue trousers and silver-buttoned jacket which she hoped matched the finery of others who celebrated *Enda's gifts*.

It was hard to imagine the pregnancies of so many unmarried women being celebrated at home. The press would have a field day at the *moral laxity* of today's young women although there would be no mention of the young men who had knocked them up.

Axian was so crowded she had trouble wedging into the throng. At least her chances of being seen by Anfarena's henchmen, or the Syld's, were small, unless she physically bumped into them, which was possible, given the crowd. She shuffled along in the same direction as those around her, then slid sideways towards the music, thinking it was as good a place as any to start her search.

The crowds were ten deep around the dance square but Viv edged closer as each medley ended, and dancers came and went, until she could see who danced. The musicians started a new tune, similar to that played on her journey with Amethen's sett when only the men had danced, and sure enough, the women cleared the dance square.

The music sounded Greek and the men danced in circles, hands linked, and heads thrown, back, the Syld amongst them. The physicality of the dance was intensely attractive; the men's finery adding to the spectacle, as it flashed in the lamplight.

Sehereden would not be far away and she slipped behind a tall woman with a red scarf and searched the crowd. The dance ended and most of the men moved off, but some remained, including the Syld. Then Baraghan joined them and as the music started again and the men linked hands, he looked directly at her and smiled.

Viv was sure she was hidden from the dance square, but Ershen probably kept tabs on her, and told his *boss* her whereabouts. The dance turned out to be a more complicated version of the previous one and some sort of test of strength, and dancers dwindled as the leaps became higher until only the Syld and Baraghan remained.

Viv watched enthralled as the dance reached its climax, then joined in the enthusiastic applause. Both men bowed to the crowd, but Baraghan bowed a second time in her direction. The red-scarfed woman dipped her head, so maybe he bowed to her, but Viv did not think so. She watched the Syld exit the dance square and as the crowd parted, she caught sight of Sehereden.

He embraced the Syld and smiled as he turned to the woman beside him; Ithreya, clad in a pale blue and silver Enda's Emblem, and heavily pregnant. Her arm was looped through his and she laughed up at him, then the Syld hoisted Poss into his arms, and she laughed too.

Viv stared at the tableau hungrily. Poss looked happy as she wriggled in her father's embrace, and Sehereden looked happy too and, as he glanced at Ithreya, in love. Viv jerked her gaze back to Poss, desperate to imprint her image on her memory knowing it might be a year before she saw her again.

The musicians started up, and the red-scarfed woman moved onto the dance floor. *Shift ya arse, Vivi. Ya seen the kid, and the state of things between the man ya fancy and the pretty blonde. Time to be on ya way.* But even as Viv turned, Ithreya glanced in her direction and froze.

Viv shook her head urgently and brought her finger to her lips, then slipped back into the crowd. Her heart thudded as she made her way towards Anaten but Ithreya had every reason to hold her silence. Despite carrying Sehereden's child, Viv's reappearance made Ithreya's lein-tryst less certain, and it *should* be certain, Viv told herself, as she hurried along.

She was tempted to grab her pack and take herself off to Tahsin's sett that night but Baraghan liked to win and the gangs had taught her the cost of thwarting men like him. He had done a lot for her too, including mending her arm, although that debt might be the Syld's, but whatever she owed, she was not paying it with her body.

Baraghan might not have his sights on her, anyway, except as an easy conquest. *Right Vivi, he's just a really, really, generous guy.* He would want children, which she could not give him, which might be her *get out of jail free* card, and he was promiscuous, so emphasising her desire for one true, *faithful* lover, might work too. She could also tell him her heart belonged to Sehereden, which would be easy, given it was not a lie, but none of it repaid the debt.

The compound was in darkness and she wondered whether Morvin had gone to the celebrations after all, but the lamps in her room were lit and Baraghan lounged at the table. 'Welcome back, Violet Iris Vacia,' he said, rising. 'I trust you enjoyed the evening?'

'Not really,' said Viv honestly.

'No,' agreed Baraghan. 'I imagine hiding from those who would harm you, like the elddra, and those you love, like the Syld's daughter and his lein, would be unpleasant.' Viv said nothing, and Baraghan produced a package wrapped in gold cloth. 'It's customary to give gifts during Cadestone's celebrations. Please accept mine,' he said, with a bow.

'You've already given me gifts,' said Viv, making no move to take it. 'You've gifted me beautiful rooms here *and* in your own compound, *and* clothes, *and* food. And you've gifted me a chance to see Poss again. I don't want to increase my debt.'

'Gifts do not elicit debts,' said Baraghan smiling.

Something she might need to remind him of later, thought Viv, as she accepted the package. 'Thank you,' she said, but her heart sank as she realised what it was. She had thought the Waradi tryst-bracelet beautiful, but this one was highly polished gold set with blue and white gems.

'To match your amè,' said Baraghan softly.

'I can't take it,' she said, and set it on the table. 'I don't love you.'

'Oh, I know that,' said Baraghan, picking up the bracelet and turning it over in his hands. 'You're in love with Sehereden en-Scinta-ril, who's in love with Ithreya en-Verra-ril, who carries his seed- or choose-child.' Baraghan settled on the chair again and clasped his hands behind his head. 'But Ithreya en-Verra-ril will only ever have a small part of Sehereden en-Scinta-ril's love, the small part Ataghan en-Scinta-ril allows his lein to give to others.'

Baraghan considered her from under half-closed lids.

'Ataghan en-Scinta-ril's a greedy man, Violet Iris Vacia, as well as a violent one. He takes his lein's love but gives little in return. Sehereden en-Scinta-ril seems unaware of this, but the Vale's women are more perceptive. Oh, they queue at the semna-firi tents to couple with the tournament's champion, but come Lirium, and Glimwing, and Cadestone, they gift their children to men who *are* capable of giving love.'

Baraghan straightened. 'I understand why you hanker after a man like Sehereden en-Scinta-ril but know this: only death breaks a leinship. Force Sehereden en-Scinta-ril to choose between you and his lein, and he won't choose you. And even if there were no leinship, consider how a tryst with him would end. You're Angellus, Violet Iris Vacia, and will live longer than any Valen. You will see your lover's hair go grey and the pleasure he gives you in bed fail. You will see him grow old and broken. You will see him die.

'And that won't be the worst of it,' he added softly, rising. 'The children Enda gifts you will be half his blood and you will see them wither and die too.' He smoothed the curls from her face. 'I am a quarter Angellus, but Angellus blood runs strong in my veins. I returned from Ezam, when the Angellus said it was impossible, and heal with my breath and hands, skills denied the elddra who view me with disdain.'

His fingers caressed her cheek and lifted her chin. 'I have many skills, apart from those of a surgeon, Violet Iris Vacia, that would bring you pleasure.' He lowered his head and his lips brushed hers. 'You would enjoy every luxury in my compound, including freedom from fear. Think on what I've said, and you'll find it's true.'

He stepped back and picked up the bracelet again.

114

'Cadestone's trysting ceremonies end tomorrow night, but I understand that might be too soon for you. We can lein-tryst any time and have Esh-accom's Sylds make it known.' He took her hand and slipped the bracelet on. 'Wear it to please me, but keep it hidden till then, if that's what you wish.'

Chapter 16

Viv took the bracelet off as soon as he had gone. The Waradi rapist had used a tryst-bracelet to seal his claim and Baraghan had done the same, not that she thought he would attack her. His weapons were different. He painted a bleak picture of her alternatives and he was right about Sehereden's love for his lein *and* for Ithreya, and that he would always choose the Syld over others. And he was right that Viv's angel blood meant she would out-live any man she chose, including Sehereden.

Don't fret, Vivi. Maybe ya'll meet Mr Right in Astraal. Plenty of Daimon and Du-Daimon there to choose from. But Baraghan was wrong about the Syld. The arsehole *was* violent and took more of Sehereden's love than he returned, but she had seen him with Poss and for all his faults, he *was* capable of love.

All very interesting, Vivi, but that kinda leaves ya high and dry, unless ya considering becoming Mrs Baraghan. Viv scowled. Jimmy Wright had cured her of the wish to be Mrs *anyone*, as had Rim in his own way. Love was transitory, and she would never trade her freedoms for the fool's hope it endured.

But being untrysted did not mean she was free. Baraghan would be on his guard tonight because of her reluctance to fall into line but leaving anytime would be difficult. She was pretty sure Baraghan did not know about her wings or he would have demanded to see them, so she could still fly away, but she wanted to leave on good terms. He would make a powerful enemy and she already had enough of those.

Sehereden downed his urrut-sa in a single gulp. Mereya had baked endesi, the spiced tocki special to Cadestone, and his jaw clenched as he stared at their ring-shapes. They symbolised tryst-bracelets but trysting this zadican ended tomorrow night. He had traded for a tryst-bracelet on his return from the Scinta-ril but was no closer to declaring his and Ithreya's new status to Esh-accom's Sylds. Even worse, Ithreya felt no such doubts and it shamed him he did not feel the same.

Most of At's band were still at the celebrations but Fariye and Ithreya's weariness had brought them back to the compound early. The sound of his lein's quick footsteps from the passageway told him Fariye had settled at last and he hoped she slept through the night. Bringing her back to Esh-accom had woken the terrors of her abduction and he knew Ataghan regretted not leaving her with Brithergen's kin. But Fariye had convinced herself Viv would return and look for them in Esh-accom, and had sobbed until Ataghan had relented.

She had enjoyed the celebrations' music and dance, and the shallit of course, but insisted they visit the wall multiple times a day to watch for Viv's arrival until Ataghan had been forced to explain why Viv would never return. But Fariye would have none of it. Her lein had pledged to come back for a final goodbye and come back she would.

Ataghan settled opposite and Sehereden watched him fill their mugs with urrut-sa. His face still wore the honed wariness of the fighting which Sehereden hoped would fade when they returned to the Scinta-rll. 'Here's to our second last night in Esh-accom, and to a lein-tryst for you,' said Ataghan, raising his mug.

'I can drink to the first half of that,' said Sehereden, as they clinked mugs.

'You've only got until tomorrow night, lein.'

'I know.'

Ataghan's eyes narrowed. 'I thought Ithreya was willing.'

'She's more than willing.'

'Then why the delay? She'll gift you a seed-child this zadican, and if Enda smiles on her, another next.' Sehereden half shrugged and Ataghan leaned across the table. 'What troubles you, lein?'

'The same thing that troubles, Fariye.'

Ataghan's mouth twisted. 'The elddra was dead when the Angellus retrieved her and according to Baraghan *if* he's to be trusted, her presence here was simply an accident anyway.'

Sehereden smiled. 'Maybe like Fariye, I need that final goodbye.'

'Don't make the same mistake as I did, lein,' said Ataghan, dropping his voice. 'You risk losing, Ithreya, *and* your child. Nothing is certain. There are many who would gladly take your place and *will* if you delay.'

'You're probably right,' said Sehereden, taking a gulp of his urrut-sa.

Ataghan emptied his mug and rose. 'I'm going out,' he said briefly. 'You'll see to Fariye if she wakes?'

'Of course.'

Ataghan strode away but Sehereden remained at the table. Even the mention of Viv angered his lein, and the only way he could expel his anger in Esh-accom's confines was through action. It was different when they were beyond the eyes of others but more damaging. Sehereden sighed. His lein needed time to heal, and the Scinta-ril's beauty would give him the place to do just that.

It was late when Fariye's screams woke Sehereden and he hurried to her room and lifted her from the bed. She clung to him, caught between sleep and wakefulness, and her sobs contained Viv's name, as they always did.

The door opened, and he turned, expecting Ataghan, but it was Ithreya. She had thrown a shawl over her sleeping gown and her loose blonde hair tumbled over it in a shining waterfall. She settled on a chair next to the fire and watched him pace. Sehereden watched her too, his gaze taking in the curve of her belly under her gown. Ataghan was right. He was a fool to risk losing it all.

When Fariye slept again, he slipped her back into bed and then kissed her forehead. Her hair was long and he remembered when his lein had first brought her to the Scinta-ril as a squalling baby with just a single tuft of hair. Ataghan had neither a lein- nor si-tryst with him but there had been other men's lein- and si-trysts in the sett and while Fariye had not lacked mothering, it had been he and Ataghan who had shared the joy of raising her.

'Come sit with me, Sehereden,' said Ithreya. 'We need to talk.'

'Yes, we do,' he said and settled beside her.

'I've wanted a lein-tryst with you since I first saw you here in Esh-accom nearly six zadicans ago,' she said quietly. 'When you came to Amethen's sett, I thanked Enda for a second gift, for Enda had gifted me early atunement. But Enda sent Viv too, or maybe Soaich did.' She half shrugged. 'It's hard for Valen women to compete with elddra, but Viv wasn't like other elddra. She was young, and the sett's men spoke of nothing else, and nor did the women, for that matter.

'When I asked her directly whether she sought you, she denied it, but I wondered if it were true then, and it's certainly not been true since and I know that you desire her. But she's been gone more than three zadics now and yet still you wait for her return.'

'I *do* wait for her return and it grieves me to cause you pain,' he said and sighed. 'Nothing was resolved between us and that last day she was here ...' He shook his head then took Ithreya's hands in his. 'I want my lein-tryst with you to be *because* Viv came back and I *chose* a future with *you*. I have to be certain for both our sakes' He rose and hefted another piece of wood on the fire, then stood staring down at it. 'Did Drasen tell you what happened at Stelin Ridge?'

'He said Viv had been stabbed and went into the sidari stands, that the Syld followed her, and that he came back alone. He said the Syld told him another of her kind had taken her.'

'And about Baraghan en-Esh-accom?'

'He said Baraghan hadn't been part of the Syld's band and had ruined their attack. He said if Viv hadn't reached Fariye first, the traders would have killed her. It was how Viv was stabbed.'

'Drasen might not know there are places apart from The Wheel,' said Sehereden turning to her. 'It's where the Angellus came from and probably where they returned to.'

'That's what my father believed.'

'Viv came from one of those places.'

Ithreya stared at him. 'Are you saying she's Angellus?'

'Not according to Baraghan en-Esh-accom,' said Sehereden, and briefly described what Baraghan had told his lein.

There was a long silence. 'But … *if* Viv came here by accident, why didn't she just leave?' asked Ithreya. 'If Baraghan en-Esh-accom could, surely she could as well?'

'I think she stayed because of Fariye.'

'And you think she'll come back because of Fariye?'

'*If* she survived Stelin Ridge, I am certain of it, but Ataghan said she was dead when Thrisdane retrieved her.'

'She wasn't dead,' said Ithreya.

Sehereden's eyes narrowed. 'How can you be so sure?'

'Because I've seen her.'

'What?! Where?'

'Here, in Esh-accom, at the dances tonight. And you're right, Sehereden. She came back for Fariye.'

Dawn was close when Sehereden set off on Fara. Taris was still in the stable, which meant his lein was on foot, wherever he was, but Sehereden could wait no longer. He needed to speak with Viv and depending on their conversation, he needed to leave enough time to visit Esh-accom's Sylds. He knew his delay hurt Ithreya, but entering a leinship with doubt in his heart could hurt her even more.

He had no idea why Viv had not come to the Ataghan's compound but *if* she had returned for Fariye's sake, she would need to *speak* with the little girl to fulfil her pledge. He did not know where Viv was staying either. She had nothing to trade, given her belongings remained at the compound, and she had no friends in Esh-accom to call on, and that meant she might have left for Tahsin en-Kama-ril's set straight after seeing Fariye.

He urged Fara to a gallop, glad the streets were deserted. Esh-accom's Sylds prohibited riding at speed in the settlement but last night's revelers still slept. He would check the Old Quarter first where Viv had visited the elddra and who might offer one of their own a bed.

He clattered across Axian, and swerved down the narrow street, slowing as Fara stumbled on the cobbles. The shabby building looked even more dilapidated than he recalled and he beat on the door. It was discourteous to visit so early, but his need was urgent. He waited, beat again, and the door was opened by a man with his arm in a sling.

Sehereden gave a brief bow. 'I beg your pardon for disturbing you. I am Sehereden en-Scinta-ril, and I'm searching for an elddra called Viv. Is she within?'

'No.'

The man's surliness went beyond displeasure at being pulled from his bed and Sehereden eyed him shrewdly. 'Has she been here?'

'Not *here*. If you're wantin' to speak to her, you're too late. She's gone. If you're wantin' to know where, her *lover* Baraghan en-Esh-accom might help *if* he chooses.'

'I thank you for your help,' said Sehereden and with another brief bow, leapt back onto Fara. The servant's dislike of Baraghan was obvious but his claim that Baraghan was Viv's lover told him where she was. And if she *had* left, she most likely headed to Tahsin en-Kama-ril's sett but having seen Fariye, she might also use the *door* at Stelin Ridge to quit The Wheel for good.

He needed to know if he were to catch her. He galloped back along the narrow street, reached Axian, and sped into Anaten quarter. Baraghan's compound was quiet but as he considered the need to be discourteous *again*, a servant emerged from the stables with water buckets and Sehereden hurriedly introduced himself. 'I seek the elddra Viv, who I believe was here.'

The man nodded. 'She was,' the man confirmed, 'but has gone to Tahsin en-Kama-ril's sett. Shall I tell Baraghan en-Esh-accom of your arrival?'

'There's no need to disturb him,' said Sehereden as he urged Fara towards the gate. 'And I thank you for your aid,' he called over his shoulder.

Chapter 17

Sehereden left Esh-accom at a full gallop but did not follow the track long before he struck sunwise towards the Ristaval Forests. Viv would have sought safety in the trees as she had before and his jaw clenched he imagined her trudging through the darkness alone. He just hoped she had not gone far before resting, then recalled she rarely slept. She would be keen to reach Tahsin's sett, and the fact that she went there rather than left The Wheel explained why she had been content just to see Fariye last night, rather than speak to her.

He rode hard and when sunlight pierced the trees, slowed to call her name. Even if she had walked all night, he should have caught her by now, *unless* she was deeper in the trees. She might even have cut towards Stelin Ridge to seek shelter in its tunnels *or* be running. He had seen her push herself past the point of exhaustion before.

Sehereden urged Fara into the trees but had to slow. Stelin Ridge was a long way off but pockets of icestone popped up here and there, as if the ridge sprawled underground. He skirted an overgrown crevice, too small for a man to fall into, but enough to break a horse's leg, and concentrated on helping Fara find a way through.

Juts of icestone broke the surface and he cursed as he realised he had chanced upon a secondary ridge. The shadows told him the sun was clear of the horizon and he briefly considered heading back to the forest's margin but pushed on, and was rewarded with a smooth sweep of ground. He sped up again and urged Fara up a small rise. There was a drop on the other side, steep but less demanding than the ridge jumps Ataghan led, and he let Fara choose the route down.

Fara leapt and landed, and leapt again, but the second landing was less sure and Fara's haunches went from under him sending a slurry of stone down the slope, then more followed as he struggled to find purchase.

Sehereden considered jumping off to aid his mount's recovery, and then the slope gave way completely and Fara rolled. Sehereden was aware of being airborne, and of shock as his head slammed into a tree, and then nothing.

Ataghan watched the sun rise from Esh-accom's wall. He had spent the night prowling the streets but his body allowed him to rest now, at least for a little while. The celebrations ended tonight but knowing he would not be gifted a child lacked its usual bitterness. Ithreya would gift Sehereden and the leinship meant the child would be his as well.

He would take his band and their kin back to the Scinta-ril tomorrow, but Ithreya would stay in Esh-accom to birth. There were birth-women here to aid her, and Baraghan was here, whose surgeon's skills extended to labouring women. Then Sehereden would return at Horse Zadic to bring his lein-tryst and son or daughter to the Scinta-ril.

Ataghan smiled as he imagined Fariye's excitement and came down the wall steps two at a time but for some reason his good mood dissipated in the Miraj quarter's shadowed streets and he quickened his pace and scanned as he entered the yard. Fara was missing and he waved over Shornon who guarded. 'Where's my lein?' he demanded,

'I don't know, Syld. He left before sunrise and was in a hurry.'

Taris moved restlessly but the stallion's fragmented images told Ataghan nothing and he strode into the building. The flow of conversation from the hall suggested his band enjoyed a late breakfast, and then Fariye sped from her room and leapt into his arms. 'Da! You're back! Come and eat. Mereya's made more endesi. They're *so* nice!'

'In a moment, Fariye. Is Ithreya there?'

Fariye shook her head. 'I think she's still sleeping. Hurry, won't you, da? Or there'll be none left!' She wriggled from his arms and darted back towards the hall and Ataghan continued up the passageway, knocked on Ithreya's door, and was invited to enter.

She sat by the fire, a shawl over her sleeping gown, but her pallor was obvious even in the dim light. 'Are you unwell?' he asked, wondering if Sehereden's dash had been for Baraghan.

'I'm well, thank you, Syld.'

'Do you know where my lein is?'

'Not exactly. He's gone in search of Viv.'

'The elddra? Why would he search for her *now*?'

'Because she's here and he wants to be sure—'

'Sure of what?' he broke in angrily. 'He has *everything* a man could want!' His hands came to his hips. His watchers had reported the elddra leaving so Sehereden must have seen her *before* she had gone but if he had, he would have told Ataghan. 'How did he know she was here?'

'I told him.' Ataghan stared at her in disbelief. 'I saw her at the dancing last night. It was obvious she wanted to see Fariye, and when I noticed her, she gestured me to keep quiet.'

'Then why in Soaich's name, didn't you! You know what you're risking, don't you?'

Ithreya clutched her shawl as she wedged herself upright. 'I've always known what I'm *risking*, Syld! That Sehereden would lein-tryst with me when his heart belonged to Viv. And I was willing to risk it when I thought her dead, but not when I knew she lived. Sehereden's choice has to be made freely.'

'Do you know *where* he searches?'

'No. Viv didn't come here so I've no idea where ...' She stopped and her eyes narrowed. 'But she *did* come here, didn't she, Syld?'

'I won't have the elddra distressing Fariye again, not now she's started to settle.'

'*Started to settle*? She cries for Viv every night! And you forget, Syld; Viv's her lein!'

'I forget nothing!' he said and strode to the door. 'And *you* would do well not to forget you carry and that upset can injure you both!' he said, and slammed the door behind him.

He went back to the yard, too angry to join his men in the hall. Taris *was* agitated now and while the images of storm clouds might be triggered by his own upset, every bone in his body screamed something was amiss.

The elddra was probably with Baraghan, but Sehereden knew nothing of Baraghan's claim on her, and would not have gone there. It was also possible the elddra was in the Old Quarter with her own kind, but if she were, Sehereden would have returned by now and that suggested he searched beyond the walls.

Ataghan's thoughts raced. If Sehereden believed she headed back to Tahsin's sett of misfits, he would be in a hurry to catch her; he was short on time whether he wanted to lein-tryst with her or with Ithreya. And even if he simply wanted to salve his conscience by giving the elddra a proper farewell, he still had to get back in time to visit the Sylds.

Ataghan's anger surged anew but was matched by dread. If the elddra were at the dancing last night, she would not have got far unless ... He strode back inside and his men fell silent at his appearance. 'Taris needs a gallop and I'd like some company,' he said brusquely. There was a chorus of volunteers but he chose only the men from his original band *and* Drasen, because he was from Ithreya's sett. 'We meet at the gate,' he said, and the men hurried out.

'But da, you'll miss out on the endesi,' said Fariye plaintively.

He bent so his face was level with hers. 'Ithreya's not feeling well, Fari. Will you take her some and ask Mereya for some semna?' Fariye nodded solemnly, and he kissed her on the cheek. 'And ask Mereya to bake some more so I can have mine when I get back.'

Ataghan said nothing as they left the settlement but his men knew him well enough to know that this was no pleasure jaunt. He passed word back that his lein had ridden out that morning and not returned and to fan out. Some stayed parallel with the track and some rode several lengths inside the trees, but he took Brithergen and Drasen with him sunwise.

Neither spoke as they rode but Ataghan barely noticed, his attention on what Taris sent. Escadi horses communicated more powerfully than other Valen horses, both between themselves and with their riders, and the link was especially strong between Taris and Fara. He and his lein had chosen their stallions together and ridden together since, and what Taris relayed sent sweat oozing from Ataghan's body.

'Syld!'

It was Drasen and he brought Taris to a stop but it was Brithergen who pointed away to the trees to their left. Taris whinnied, but Fara remained mute, flanks dark with sweat, head hanging.

'His leg,' hissed Brithergen.

Even from a distance they saw the bone was through the hide. Brithergen and Drasen looked at him uncertainly but Ataghan reeled under the onslaught of images Fara sent. 'Wait here,' he ordered, and slid from Taris's back. He kept his steps even, despite the horror that battered him, and went on past Fara into the trees. There was a small ridge above him and a fresh slide of stone and he followed it down to Sehereden.

He was on his back, unmarked by even the smallest scratch, his neck broken. Ataghan fell to his knees. 'Lein,' he whispered. 'Lein.' He smoothed the hair from Sehereden's forehead. 'We swore we would never leave each other. Remember that, lein? Remember? You swore never to leave me, Sehereden,' he said hoarsely. 'You swore!' he cried, and collapsed forward onto his body.

Fire ravaged Ataghan and he slashed his arms, crouched there panting, and slashed again. When he was able, he cut a lock of Sehereden's hair then kissed him, once on each cheek, and once on the mouth. Then he pulled down his sleeves to cover his bloodied arms, stumbled back to Fara, and used his knife again, this time to open the big veins on the stallion's neck.

All he could offer Fara was a quick death but he let the blood-flow disguise his own, and when Fara lay as still as Sehereden, he went back to Drasen and Brithergen. 'Bring the men back, Drasen,' he said hoarsely, and when Drasen had gone, he turned to Brithergen. 'I need your help with a pyre.'

Brithergen thumped to the ground and pulled Ataghan into his arms. He did not say anything, just held him, and then they made their way back to Sehereden and worked together to collect the wood. The men returned in twos and threes and did not speak either, even when they gently laid Sehereden atop the branches, and Brithergen set them alight. But they sang as the band sang at the end of a long foray, a song that told of the beauty of friendships, of the Vales, and of the constellations Enda sent, but they sang it without joy, like a dirge, and Ataghan stood with his eyes on the flames, and felt himself burn.

When the fire sank low, he leapt onto Taris and led the men back through the trees, and when they reached the track, broke into a gallop. He rode at their head, as silent as his band, but after a while Brithergen brought his horse level with Taris and Drasen did too, so that they rode either side of him. Esh-accom's gate swung open and they continued in formation across Axian and into the Miraj quarter.

People stared as they passed, disturbed by their silent grimness, and when Ataghan reached his compound, he left Taris in the yard and entered the building. Mereya's greeting died on her lips, as she took in his face and blood-stained shirt, but he said nothing, just continued to his room, went in, and locked the door.

Chapter 18

By late that morning, Viv had decided there was probably no way to quit Baraghan's company without making an enemy of him and that meant waiting until dark, climbing out the window, and flying straight upwards, all the while hoping no one noticed. Baraghan might come after her but once she reached Tahsin's sett, she would be under his protection; even *Ataghan en-Scinta-ril* had discovered that!

Others moved around the compound, but she stayed in her room, uncomfortable at being the *guest* Baraghan had foisted on them. The sun was well up before Morvin brought an immense platter of food, which seemed to be breakfast and lunch combined, and once she had eaten, she folded the ornate clothes Baraghan had gifted her neatly on the bed and packed Ithreya's plainer ones.

She stowed the pack behind the bed and pushed Baraghan's tryst-bracelet up inside her sleeve, ready to display if he visited. Now all she had to do was wait for dark *again*. She occupied herself by pacing around the room and was tallying up her fifty-second lap when Baraghan burst in.

'Sehereden's dead!'

Viv stared at him uncomprehendingly. 'But …'

Baraghan seized her and wrenched her close. 'The Syld's already known as Mad At but his lein's death will tip him into insanity. Do *not* go *anywhere* near his compound for *any* reason. Is that understood?'

Viv nodded dumbly and Baraghan strode to the door. 'Sehereden en-Scinta-ril broke his neck between here and Stelin Ridge searching for *you* and that means Mad At will hold you responsible. He's damaged himself before *and* others, but my concern is Sehereden's would-be lein-tryst and I go to her now. If her child comes early, it won't survive. Stay here!'

The door slammed and Viv's legs gave way. There was immense pain in her chest, as if a fist had smashed its way into her ribcage, clamped itself around her heart, and squeezed. She curled into a ball, scarcely able to breathe, battered by the horror of what Ithreya endured and by a gut-wrenching guilt she had not felt since the child's death. 'You offered me roses, Syatha,' she choked, 'but it was a trick. There's nothing in the world but thorns, just endless, endless thorns!'

She struggled to her feet, numbly set the bracelet on the table, and hauled on her pack. Ershen would have orders to keep her here but she must go for everyone's sake. She climbed out the window and surveyed the scene. A ramshackle wall separated the compound from its neighbour, and she took a running jump at it and used her momentum to flip herself over, sprinted on through the next compound's yard, and repeated the manoeuvre until she was in the street.

Her thieving days had given her a knack for choosing cover and she had always been fast, and she reached the wall unchallenged. The gate was open, probably to admit the horsemen who were near the stables, and Viv hurried through. The muddy track was empty *and* the flat land to either side but she had not gone far before she heard hoofs behind.

Every nerve tensed as the horse slowed then came alongside. She expected it to be Anfarena's henchmen or Baraghan's but it was Drasen and Viv kept walking. 'Viv, you have to come back to the compound.'

'That's the last place I'm wanted,' she muttered, keeping her head down. 'I killed Sehereden.'

'What? Who told you that?' demanded Drasen. 'Sehereden died in an accident.'

'While searching for me!'

'Viv! Will you stop? We need to talk.' Viv shook her head and trudged on, but Drasen jumped from his mount and caught her arm. She did not struggle, but she would not look at him either. 'Viv, Ithreya sent me.'

'I might have killed her too,' she said.

Drasen gave her a shake. 'Listen to me,' he said urgently. 'The Syld's locked himself in his room and no one has authority to enter. Even Baraghan en-Esh-accom won't risk it.' Drasen paused. 'He's harming himself, Viv. He might die.'

Viv's head came up. 'But then Fariye will have no one!'

'Which is what Ithreya said, which is why she sent me. She said to tell you that if you have *any* love for Fariye, you'll come back.'

'And do what?' demanded Viv. 'The Syld hates me!'

'That was her message. Will you come? We don't have much time.'

Viv swore, which Drasen obviously took to mean *yes* because he leapt onto his horse and dragged her up behind him. The Wall Guard must have seen them coming for the gate swung open and Drasen swept across the yard and up the streets into the Miraj quarter, taking the turns so fast Viv feared she would be killed. At least, it would save the Syld the trouble, she concluded grimly.

They reached the compound intact and Drasen hauled her up the passageway. The hall was full of men, but their mutters fell silent at her appearance, and then Ithreya struggled from the throng and caught Viv's hands. 'Thank Enda you've come.'

Her face was whiter than the walls and Viv searched the room for Baraghan. 'You need to rest,' said Viv. 'Didn't Baraghan …'

'Forget him! He's gone off to patch up his men after some brawl in Axian. Come, Viv, we don't have much time.' Ithreya tugged her back along the passageway, Tormis in tow, his craggy face grey with worry. They stopped at the Syld's door and Ithreya beat on it. 'Syld?'

There was no answer and Viv glanced down. 'Shit!' Blood seeped from under it, and Tormis caught Ithreya's arm as she swayed. 'Where's Fariye?' asked Viv, watching the seep in horrified fascination.

'I told Brithergen to take her to his compound.'

Ithreya seemed the only person capable of doing anything. Everyone else was under the Syld's command and that meant letting him die. Viv's mind raced. 'Are the shutters locked, Tormis?' she asked urgently. Tormis nodded. 'Can they be opened from the outside?' Again, the nod. 'Do you have a bloody key?'

'I'm not permitted to use it, elddra.'

'Well, do you have a piece of wire? Or a hammer?'

'I have a hammer, elddra.'

'Then bring it,' said Viv and hurried off down the passageway. Ithreya followed and she stopped. 'Go sit down before you fall down,' she told her, and gave her a gentle push towards the hall, then went out into the yard. The Syld's window was the only one shuttered and Viv ran her fingers over the lock. She could have picked it in a flash had she been in Moonsun, but The Wheel never had anything useful lying around like hair clips or ring-pulls.

She wrenched off the owl charm. It was filigreed metal and might just work.

Tormis appeared and she snatched the hammer and smashed the charm until a thread of metal unraveled. Tormis's disapproval was palpable but she concentrated on the lock, and when the metal bent, twisted it to double strength and tried again. Picking locks was about sensitivity not speed, but Viv struggled not to shake. The Syld's room was quiet which meant he might already be dead.

The lock turned, and she twisted the bolt and eased the shutters open a crack. The Syld was still on his feet near the door but it was too dim to see which way he faced. She gestured to Tormis to move away, but then Ithreya appeared. 'I told you to sit down,' hissed Viv.

'I drank the bitter concoction Baraghan left,' whispered Ithreya. 'I'm all right, Viv, but I'm worried about you. What if he kills you?'

'Then I'll be dead.'

'Viv …'

'We agreed he needs to live for Fariye's sake. Stay well clear.'

Viv eased the shutters open and climbed in with all the stealth of a thief, but the light flooded the room, and he spun. He had knives in both hands and as he dropped into a crouch, Viv feared he would throw them. 'Go,' he ground out, 'before I kill you.'

Viv remained rooted to the spot. His arms and torso were drenched in blood, his trousers saturated. 'You don't have a right to do this,' she said unsteadily. 'Fariye needs you.'

'Go,' he repeated, then slashed himself again, opening another gaping wound. He was suiciding, cut by cut, but even as she watched in horror, the wounds began to seal.

God in Heaven! How could she have been so effing, bloody blind? It had stared her in the face since day one. The explosions of aggression, the bursts of heat, the recklessness that earned him the title *Mad At*. Even Sehereden had alluded to it, but she had been too full of hatred to see.

Help me, Syatha, she entreated as she dropped her pack to the floor. Her jacket and shirt followed, leaving her naked to the waist, then she unbedded her wings. He swayed, but his gaze was unrelenting as she stepped towards him. He could throw his knives or stab her, but she forced herself on. He swayed again, slipped in his own blood, and fell to his knees. He was too weak to get up and Viv knelt too, and cradled his head against her breasts.

'Let it go, Ataghan,' she whispered. A shudder ran through him, but he was rigid, the knives in his hands cold, as they pressed against her skin. 'Let it go,' she whispered again, and brought her wings about them both.

'Sehereden!' The cry was so full of pain that Viv sloughed citrus, then he collapsed against her and she lowered him gently to the floor. She was covered in his blood and she bedded her wings, poured water into a bowl, and washed herself down. Then she dressed, unlocked the door, and went back to the window.

'Viv,' cried Ithreya. 'Thank Enda! Are you hurt?' Tormis hovered, grinning in relief.

'No, the Syld's unconscious. Tormis, can you bring water and cloths? The door's unlocked. The Syld needs his wounds seen to and the room cleaned.' Tormis hurried off and Viv and Ithreya considered each other in silence. 'You should hate me,' said Viv finally.

'Because Sehereden loved you? That was his choice.'

'If I hadn't come back …'

'Sehereden had all of Cadestone to lein-tryst with me but he *hoped* for you. It was his choice,' she repeated.

Viv glanced down at bulge under Ithreya's gown. 'You've still got a part of him. He's not truly dead.'

'Yes,' said Ithreya thickly. 'Enda gifted me early atunement and certainty.' She drew a ragged breath. 'But I loved the man.'

'He was an easy man to love,' rasped Viv. 'What will you do?'

'I haven't decided. And you?'

'I'm going to Tahsin's sett. I'm welcome there.'

Ithreya caught her hand. 'You're welcome here, Viv, and Fariye needs you.'

'Fariye needs her father, and her father needs Fariye,' said Viv, with an unsuccessful attempt at a smile. 'They need time together to heal. The fighting, her abduction, and now this …' Viv swallowed several times. 'Fariye needs to be a little girl again, to laugh and play, to feel safe, to have her father's love.'

'She's always had that.'

'Yes, the Syld loves his daughter.' Viv forced another smile. 'Fariye's a fortunate little girl to have a father who loves her.'

'Viv—' began Ithreya, but the door opened behind Viv, and Tormis came in with buckets and cloths. Drasen and Mereya were with him, and Mereya locked the door while Drasen and Tormis lifted the Syld onto the bed. Viv was glad they kept the Syld's suffering private, but it was time for her to go and she clambered out the window and slipped on her pack. 'Take care, Ithreya,' she said, and briefly touched her belly. 'You carry something precious.'

'You might carry one day too, Viv.'

137

'No possible. I'm barren.' She shrugged. 'A story for another time,' she said, and went to move off, but Ithreya embraced her.

'Take care, Viv.'

Viv nodded, but knew she would probably need a giant dose of luck to make it out the gates a second time in one day without Baraghan or the elddra's henchmen catching her.

Viv made her way back to the gate, jumping at every shadow, and expecting a hand to descend on her shoulder at any moment, but she arrived there without incident and when the Wall Guards opened the gate, she walked through. Maybe Anfarena thought Viv had already gone or maybe the brawl Baraghan's men were involved in concerned Anfarena's men and none of them were in any state to report anything.

She just wanted to get to Tahsin's sett, curl up in bed, and shut out the world. She had told Ithreya that Fariye and the Syld needed time to heal, but she needed time too. The sky faded to a delicate blue as she walked, then blushed an intense pink, and she recalled Mt Silvercrest and the colour-change game she played with her mother. Viv hoped her mother *was* in Astraal, but if she was not, Viv might have to accept she had gone beyond her reach.

The idea of wandering the Rynth alone for the rest of her very long life was terrifying and there was much in The Wheel she loved, including Fariye. Tahsin's sett gave her a home where she was safe and which allowed her to still see Fariye occasionally. It was a simple life and harvesting retsen monotonous, but she had done plenty of worse things to earn her keep.

She took to the air as soon as it was dark, and flew high to avoid stray Lefer and hunters' barbs. It was hard to see much beyond the vals' dark crags and the shine of rills, but she had no fear of getting lost. Erath Fold might have woken her need to eat, sleep, and pee, but it had also honed her sensing skills, and she came to earth near Tahsin's bounds just as Cadestone burst into the sky.

Its light made the bob of Doran's lamp visible long before he saw her, and she waited for the signs of recognition to appear on his broad face. 'Viv en-elddra. You've come back.'

He grinned but forgot to lower the lamp, and Viv squinted up at him. 'Can you tell Tahsin?' He would want to put her on a work roster, and she needed to be assigned a room. Tomorrow would be a normal harvesting day, and she would be expected to work.

'Doran will tell Gothral.'

'No, you need to tell Tahsin.'

Doran scratched his chin and thankfully, lowered the lamp. 'Doran must tell Gothral who comes to the sett and who leaves the sett,' he said carefully.

'Alright,' said Viv giving up. 'Tell Gothral.' She followed Doran into the building, wondering if Tahsin were away and all but collided with Enesha coming from the washroom.

'Viv! I didn't expect to see you again.'

Viv grinned, knowing it was as warm a welcome she was likely to get from Enesha. 'It's good to see you, Enesha. Maybe we can eat together after I've seen Tahsin.'

Enesha's eyes flicked to Doran. 'Didn't you tell her, you big lump?'

'Doran will tell Gothral who comes to the sett,' said Doran stolidly, and Enesha shook her head in disgust.

'Tell me what?' asked Viv.

'Tahsin died at Fire Zadic. It's Gothral's sett now.'

Chapter 19

Thris and Ash followed Ky through the Bokos, holding their silence to avoid distracting him from his counting. Thris was too astonished to speak anyway. He had known the Bokos was immense, but the vast rows of shelves jammed with yellowing scrolls pressed in on him like a living creature. Surely the answers to *his* questions and to the questions of *every* angel in Ezam, whether Dane or Archae, were already here? And if they were, why did angels labour over their own sheets of blank parchment?

But the immensity of the angelic knowledge posed its own problems. The scrolls were stored without apparent order, so that the writings on Wheel Fold discovered by Prime-archae Serith, were not elaborated on by the scrolls to either side or on the surrounding shelves. The relevant scrolls could be anywhere in the Bokos *or* nowhere at all.

'There will be empty shelves soon,' said Ky.

'How do you know?' asked Thris, staring at the shelves groaning under scrolls.

'Because I have taken four thousand steps, and at four thousand five hundred steps, the shelves empty.'

'We might be approaching from a different direction,' pointed out Thris.

'It makes no difference,' said Ky. 'It is a nine thousand step round journey to where the *scrolls* end, and another three thousand steps after to where the *shelves* end. Prime-archae Serith calls it a trinity of trinities. He says it is important in other folds too.'

Thris stared at him in confusion. 'A trinity of trinities?'

'Multiples of three,' explained Ash. 'Like Paendane, Anasdane, and Senquar-archae, and we three, of course.'

'Did Prime-archae Serith say what a trinity of trinities means?' asked Thris.

Ky grinned. 'Of course not.'

'It would be nice to have answers instead of more questions,' said Thris.

'Which is why we are here,' said Ky sobering. 'It is where you returned from Wheel Fold.' The scrolls gave way to empty shelves, as Ky had predicted, and Thris found himself counting as they went on, and sure enough, the shelves ceased after three thousand steps, as did the muted light. The gloom closed in and Ky brought them to a stop. 'I do not know how large this central area is,' he admitted. 'It has been too dark to search except for when we found you, Thris. Then it was filled with a golden light.'

'You were wet,' said Ash. 'Even your plumage was saturated, which means you passed through water with your wings unbedded. Have you any memory of it?'

'I was caught and caged,' said Thris slowly, 'and they burned me.' A shudder passed through his body. 'And then, the cage was gone … and I woke in Haven,' he finished raggedly.

Ash and Ky's arms came around him and held him enclosed and it was Ky who eventually spoke. 'This is the centre of the Bokos and according to Prime-archae Serith, the Bokos is the centre of Ezam,' he said softly. 'You came back into the very heart of Ezam, Thris, and I am guessing you came through a water rift.'

'I heard your heart stop,' said Ash tremblingly, 'and knew I must come here.' There was a long pause. 'Is there water in Wheel Fold?'

'Yes,' said Thris. 'It flows down valleys set as evenly as the petals of a glis bloom and there is a peak at their centre. It makes the fold the same shape as the wheels some human caste folds use to aid travel, hence its name,' he added.

'Which proves angelic scholars have been there,' said Ky. Thris and Ash stared at him. 'The Tome lists the *correct* names of all known folds but most angels simply call them after their main features. The Tome lists the fold as Wheel Fold, the same name those who live there call it, whereas the shekinah does not call her fold Moonsun as we do.'

'What does the Tome call Moonsun?' asked Thris curiously.

'Space Fold.'

'The male daimon caste who visited said that *Angellus* engendered those such as him but had not stayed,' said Ash. 'The daimon caste the Angellus left behind wish to join them, wherever they were. The male daimon caste thought we might be the Angellus.'

'What exactly did Prime-archae Serith's scroll say about Wheel Fold?' asked Thris.

'*The Wheel the way, the Wheel a knife; the way of water, the way ...*' recited Ky. 'The rest of the scroll had been torn off.'

'*Light is the lure and light the trap, light the maze and light the map. The red, the blue and the white don't show, what mantise, scarab and sumi know,*' quoted Ash. 'I think Senquar-archae wrote those words about Wheel Fold too.'

'Probably, considering how obscure they are,' grumbled Ky.

'They might have been clearer in their entirety,' said Ash. 'The way of water, the way of ... *life*?'

'Or *strife*,' suggested Thris darkly. 'Whoever damaged the writing, might have removed the angel lore stored here as well. But why?'

143

'*The way of water,*' murmured Ash.

'Water rifts are unstable,' said Thris uneasily as he peered up. 'I would prefer not to linger.'

'No,' said Ash. 'There is nothing more to be learned *for the present.*'

Viv stared at Enesha in shock and for a moment had trouble breathing. It seemed Lady Unlucky was running true to form again, she concluded bitterly, and her first impulse was to leave. If Tahsin were dead, she had no place in the sett, but Enesha's hand fastened on Viv's arm and she marched her to the hall to meet Gothral. He was a lot younger than Tahsin, with black hair and an unsmiling face, and simply nodded when Enesha identified Viv as a returning sett member, and then Enesha marched her out again.

'You can have your old room back, next to mine,' said Enesha, as she hauled her along, her grip still fastened on Viv's arm. 'Gothral won't care. He's too busy working out how to run a sett.' Enesha pushed open the door and deposited her on the bed. 'Wait there,' she ordered, and disappeared to return a moment later with a lamp and a flask. She set the lamp down and unstopped the flask. 'Take a swig of that,' she said, and guided it to Viv's mouth. The liquid burned all the way down and Viv coughed, but the world came back into focus and Enesha grinned. 'Hareesh; does the trick every time.'

'How did he die?' asked Viv hollowly.

'He had water in his lungs but he knew his days were running down before that. He summoned Gothral and gave him a list of the sett's members and what they did, and a list of the traders, the regular ones and the ones who come occasionally. Gothral's Tahsin's choose-brother,' she added. 'He's from Bracken-ril.'

'I never thanked Tahsin properly,' said Viv, staring at the floor. 'I thought he would be here when I came back. I …'

She choked to a stop, and the bed dipped as Enesha plonked down beside her. 'You didn't have to tell Tahsin much. He knew. Which reminds me.' She disappeared again and returned with a small box. 'He told me to give you this *if* you ever came back.' Viv stared at it uncomprehendingly. 'It's a puzzle box called Enda's Aim. Tahsin used to carry it about with him but I never saw him play it. He seemed happy enough without knowing whether Enda or Soaich had control of his fortunes. It's good you're back. I thought I would be stuck minding it forever.'

'Why?'

Enesha shrugged. 'I kind of thought you would get a better offer than the Kama-ril.'

'This is the first place that ever welcomed me.'

'Oh, elddra are never welcomed,' said Enesha, matter-of-factly, 'but they get plenty of offers.' Viv said nothing and Enesha picked up the flask. 'Come back to the hall and eat, Viv. Gothral will have you working tomorrow. That's one thing he's got sorted,' she added dryly.

'I want to see him,' said Viv, staring down at the box. 'I want to see Tahsin.'

'He went to the pyre at Fire Zadic, Viv. That's over three zadics ago. There won't be much left of him to see.'

'I want to see him!' cried Viv, scrambling up and pacing the small room. 'People die or disappear, and everything's left unsaid, or said badly, or misunderstood, or passed on as damning, damning lies! Then it's all too

145

late, and *everything's* lost. For once in my life, Enesha, I want to say what needs to be said!'

Enesha simply stared. 'I didn't realise his death would be such a shock to you,' she said slowly. 'Or maybe the sett saw it coming and you weren't here. Eat first, Viv, then I'll take you.'

They sat with Merhen and Fahan, but Viv did not recognise the rest of the table. Two men, who she guessed were in their thirties, a third probably in his sixties, and three grey-haired women. Their names ended in en-Bracken-ril, so Viv assumed they were Gothral's friends he had brought with him. Merhen and Fahan were excited to see her and Merhen even kissed her cheek.

'Cazir and Jered are still at Esh-shallin's celebrations,' Fahan told her. 'They'll be back soon to join our team.'

'Gothral decides the teams,' the older man said.

Viv was too relieved they were not at Esh-accom and privy to what had happened there to care whether they rejoined the team or not. 'Help me collect the gorash,' said Enesha, heaving herself up. Viv followed her to the kitchen door and waited while Doran and Prenya loaded the trays. 'Don't say anything in front of the Bracken-ril people you don't want Gothral to hear,' she muttered. 'There's at least one in every team.'

'Doesn't he trust us?' asked Viv, keeping her voice low. Tahsin's sett had seemed like a sanctuary but maybe it was just another snake-pit now.

'He doesn't know us,' said Enesha, muscles bunching as she picked up a tray. 'Bring the retsen and milk jugs,' she instructed and headed back. Enesha's appetite had not diminished, and nor had the twins' but Fahan managed to keep up a constant stream of talk between mouthfuls. Gothral's people sat at the far end of the table and spoke amongst themselves, but one of the younger men, *Orthagh*, watched her and Viv became increasingly uncomfortable. She could tell Enesha was irritated too.

'So, you've been in Esh-accom, elddra,' he said, when Fahan drew breath.

'Her name's Viv,' said Enesha tartly.

'I was there for Fire Zadic,' said Viv quickly as the man rankled.

'For what purpose?'

'To visit my lein,' said Viv. It was none of his bloody business but she did not want a fight. 'She's the daughter of Ataghan en-Scinta-ril,' she added politely.

'Ataghan en-Scinta-ril's known to us,' the man said. 'And we've heard of you as well.' Viv sipped her milk but found it hard to swallow. There was *nothing* friendly about Orthagh.

Enesha swigged down her milk and rose. 'Time to sort out that room of yours, Viv. Gothral likes an early start.' She nodded to those at the table and strode away, and Viv hurried after her. 'Never did like that man,' said Enesha, as they stepped into the cool air outside.

'What did he mean about knowing *of* Ataghan en-Scinta-ril?' asked Viv, as she followed Enesha into the darkness.

'Mad At's known to many people,' she said. 'Orthagh's probably had a run in with him. Lots have and lots have come off second best. Take note of where we're going, Viv. You'll have to find your own way back. I've got better things to do than hang around a pyre.'

Enesha led her on through a stand of trees and down to the Kama Rill. The water glinted in the dull wash of stars

147

and Viv watched it as they walked along its bank. Insects chittered in the rushes but it was too early for owls.

They came to a crossing made of boulders, and Enesha slipped and put her foot in the water. 'Stinking Soaich,' she muttered, but continued across and up the bank to another stand of trees.

Their scent was familiar, and Viv's stomach tightened. 'What are they?'

'Sidari. Tahsin liked them. It's why he asked his pyre be set here.' Enesha shrugged. 'The advantage of knowing you're dying, I supposed. Don't stay late, Viv. We breakfast at first light and leave at dawn.'

She thumped away and Viv picked her way forward. The darkness was thicker under the trees and she was wary of treading on bones. She came to a small clearing which she guessed was the pyre site and Cadestone's arrival confirmed it. Bones glimmered in the constellation's light and Viv settled on a mossy log and pulled the puzzle box from her pocket.

The night was still and the trees' spice heavy in the air. It had been the last thing she had smelled at Stelin Ridge and the idea she had died there returned. Maybe life was a series of deaths, barely noticed because of the swift start of another life. One life had ended with her mother's disappearance, another when she had fled Jimmy Wright. A third when she had got into that car, *intending* to die, a fourth when Kald had taken her down the rift. A fifth when she had imagined a life with Thris, and then with Sehereden, but death had intervened again. Then she had come here, expecting things to be the same, but death had stolen that life too. And now she sat in a place of death with no hope of another life to come.

She gripped the puzzle box, knowing Tahsin's fingers had gripped it too. He had said little but his kindness had clothed the sett. She wondered whether it had dissipated along with his funeral smoke. She did not know what Gothral was like, but she already disliked Orthagh.

The night chilled but Viv stayed where she was, holding the puzzle box. Enesha believed Tahsin's spirit had gone, but gone where? To Thris's Great Beyond? Only angels went there, or so the Host believed. Jimmy Wright believed the dead rotted like garbage, and in his case, she hoped he was right. She grimaced as she imagined Syatha's disapproval. 'Okay, okay,' she muttered. 'Roses, not thorns.'

Chapter 20

Enesha was right about the early starts and Viv found them wearisome now her need to sleep had returned. The days fell into a rhythm of early rises, harvesting, and eating with the work team in the hall each night. Jered and Cazir returned, and Viv was glad of their familiar faces, but they were assigned to another team.

Sometimes there was dancing at night, which even Enesha joined in, but Viv sat in the sidari trees with the puzzle box in her hands and her eyes on the stars. She still searched for the right words to say, not just to Tahsin but to Sehereden, but nothing would come.

The days grew chill and they harvested closer to the sett, which shortened the trek. Enesha's team included Pitren and Norsen from the Bracken-ril, but Orthagh had disappeared. The Bracken-ril men kept to themselves and only harvested the lower branches, which suited Viv. She liked being high with Methren, who had overcome his fear of heights and now climbed higher than Fahan.

He did not speak much and nor did she, but he liked birds and named them for her. Redwings, greywings, shrills, reets, rakes, and when they harvested late, arling and sengling owls. 'The senglings have a longer call,' he explained as they made their way back one blustery evening. They walked at the tail of the group and Viv hugged herself in an attempt to keep warm. 'You won't see them as often as arlings, especially tonight,' said Methren. 'They don't like the wind.'

'Neither do I,' said Enesha, dropping back. 'Vorash is early. We won't harvest for the next few days, which is a relief,' she added, lowering her voice, 'given the company.'

It was raining by the time they reached the sett and Viv was keen to change her wet clothes, but she needed the latrines. 'I'm going to the washrooms,' she called after Enesha, who now walked with Fahan in front. Enesha grunted, which was her usual response, and Viv peeled off down the passageway. The shutters banged in the wind and some of the lamps had blown out. She hurried along and was almost to the washrooms when Orthagh stepped from the shadows.

She jerked to a stop as a knife flashed, but he sliced his own palm, and held the wound up to her face. Viv stared at it in confusion then gasped as the edges started to seal. 'Anfarena sends greetings, Violet Iris Vacia,' he said with an icy smile and stalked off.

The rain beat against the shutters but Ataghan pushed them wide, needing the chill wetness against his skin. There would be frost at the Scinta-ril, and new snow on Astraal's peak. It would reach far into the vals and ice the Scinta Pool. It did not matter; his expanded band and their kin were already snug in his sett.

Only Jethren, Sandagh, and Inaghan kept him and Fariye company at the compound *and* Drasen en-Verra-ril but he was not here now, he was with Ithreya, and Ithreya was in childbirth.

Drasen hoped to be named choose-father, as did other men of Amethen's sett, and he was a worthy candidate. He had fought to reclaim Fariye *and* to rid the Vales of the Waradi filth, but he did not stay with Ithreya only to strengthen his claim; he stayed as a friend.

It was more than Ataghan could claim, given their last exchange. There was no chance she would name him choose-father, despite the leinship, but if she chose Drasen, and Drasen joined his sett, the child would grow under Ataghan's care. It was the most he could hope for, and in the meantime, he waited. Ithreya was young but there was always risk, and he had traded for Esh-accom's best birthing-women to attend her. He just hoped they would not be needed.

The compound was quiet, and he knocked on Fariye's door and went in. She no longer slept in the room and it had an air of desertion. Since Sehereden's death she had slept in Ataghan's bed, curled against him for comfort and having her safely in his arms had gifted him sleep too.

She sat cross-legged on her bed, her feather collection laid out around her, and he perched on its edge. Fariye's first collection had been destroyed along with his sett, but she had amassed another one thanks to Sehereden. His lein had interrupted their travel whenever he saw a feather she lacked, and Ataghan had made his irritation clear.

He subtly flexed his hands and took a deep breath. 'Which is your favourite?' he managed to ask.

'The one Viv gave me,' said Fariye, carefully picking out a glossy bronze feather. 'It smells of Viv too. Smell it, da.'

Ataghan brought the feather to his nose, careful to exhale. 'Yes, it does,' he said, and handed it back.

'She found it at the Kama-ril, but Sehereden didn't know which bird it belonged to, and he knew *all* the birds. Do you know, da?'

'There are lots of birds hidden away in the cloudwise vals,' he said, wandering to the window. The rain continued to pound and he glanced back. Fariye still held the feather, but her face was so sad, his guts knotted. 'As soon as Vorash eases, we'll go back to the Scinta-ril, Fari. And if the snow allows, we'll hunt for parien feathers. I know places where they might still be found. Would you like that?'

Fariye's dark eyes came to his. 'But I won't be here when Viv comes back, and she won't know where to find for me.'

'I've explained to you why I don't think she's coming back,' he said gently.

'She will! She always comes back! She promised!' Tears rolled down her cheeks and Ataghan lifted her into his arms. 'Ser ... Ser's dead ...' she said, between gulps of air, 'but my lein ... might still come back. I ... want her, da. I want ... my lein back. I want Viv.'

Ataghan paced until she had calmed, then carried her down the passageway to the hall. Tormis drank urrut-sa at the table and Mereya portioned retsen flour on the bench. 'Want to make some tocki with me, Fari?' she asked cheerfully. Fariye sniffed and nodded and Ataghan set her down. 'Go wash your hands then,' ordered Mereya, and Fariye trotted out.

'Some urrut-sa, Syld?' said Tormis, filling a mug. Ataghan took it and settled opposite. 'An early Vorash means a chill Horse Zadic,' said Tormis sagely.

'And wet traders,' said Mereya. 'There's always a few who delay for those last trades, even when their wiser friends have departed. Axian's a miserable place with no shelter and no custom.' Fariye came back and Mereya tied a cloth around her waist, pulled a chair to the bench so she could reach, and portioned her some flour.

Ataghan drained his mug and rose. 'I'm going out,' he said.

Fariye swiveled, scattering the flour on the floor. 'When will you be back, da?' she asked anxiously.

153

'Before dark, Fari. I promise.'

He kissed her on cheek and Tormis hastened after him as he headed for the store. 'I'll help you with a cape, Syld,' he said. Ataghan needed no help to toss a cape over his jacket, but it was Tormis's way to show he cared, and he nodded his thanks.

Ataghan had the streets to himself, not surprising given the rain beat without pause. It dashed the last of the blossoms of late flowering bushes to the cobbles and he stared at their broken petals as he walked. Movement was more bearable than stillness, but nothing was bearable anymore, even drawing breath. There was no Fara in the stables, and no lein by his side. There was no quiet presence who, in Ataghan's darkest moments, had held him close.

He should have sent his men back and followed Sehereden into death, and now he was trapped. Fariye needed him, but he needed something Fariye could not provide. He jammed his hands into his pockets and felt the feather he had found on the feed-store floor. It came from the same stinking place as Fariye's and he closed his fist over it and felt it break. Then he pulled it out, and held it cupped in his palm, until the rain washed it to the cobbles. And then, without knowing why, he brought his fingers to his nose.

There was a jag, and an exquisite sense of peace, then he was back in the rain, the ruined feather at his feet. It glinted gold against the rain-slicked cobbles, and he picked it up and thrust it back into his pocket, and somehow managed to keep walking.

It was close to dark when he returned and Drasen taking his meal with Tormis in the hall. The warm smell of fresh-baked retsen filled the air, and Ataghan tossed his sodden cape in the corner and took a seat. 'Good news, Syld,' said Drasen with a smile. 'Ithreya's birthed a girl-child.'

Ataghan filled his mug with semna and emptied in a single gulp. 'A Vorash child is blessed by Enda,' said Tormis as he refilled Ataghan's mug.

'Why?' asked Drasen curiously.

'Vorash is a time between,' said Ataghan, his gaze on the cooking-fire. 'Neither one zadic nor the next. A time full of possibility.'

Tormis nodded as he ladled gorash into a bowl. 'A child born then can be anything it wants,' he added.

'I hadn't heard of that before,' said Drasen, using retsen to mop up his gorash.

'Different sayings in different setts,' said Ataghan briefly, as Tormis set the bowl of gorash in front of him. 'Thank you, Tormis. You won't be needed again tonight.'

Tormis bade them a good night, and Ataghan ate in silence even after the sound of a door closing told him Tormis had reached his rooms. 'It was a difficult birth,' said Drasen quietly. 'Ithreya needed aid in the end but she's well enough now, as is the child.'

'She's named the choose-father?'

'Not yet.' Ataghan looked at him sharply. 'She wants to see you, Syld, but not for a few days. She asks for time to recover and settle with the baby.'

'Do you know what she intends?' asked Ataghan tightly.

'She's kept to her rooms since your lein's death and the birth-women feared her grief would imperil the birth. Perhaps it did. She loved your lein but ...'

'Has no love for me,' finished Ataghan, and pushed his gorash aside. 'We didn't part on the best of terms but whatever her intentions, Drasen, I offer you a place in my sett.'

'A place I gladly accept, Syld, and I thank you for it. If Ithreya returns to Amethen's sett, I'll see her settled there first, so it could be as late as Cascade before I join you.'

'You're welcome any time, as is any si- or lein-tryst you might bring.'

Drasen smiled grimly. 'I'll have to wait until *next* Fire Zadic to have a chance of that, Syld.'

Ataghan spent the following days readying the compound for his departure but his nerves were so taut he had to reassure Taris more than once that all was well. Ithreya had asked for time but Ataghan would have delayed his journey back to the Scinta-ril in any case, having no intention of exposing Fariye to the bitter weather.

Ataghan had no idea why Ithreya had summoned him but whatever her reasons, it was not to make him choose-father. Some women named the choose-fathers of their babies before the birth and all were gifted within a day or two so the child would have been gifted by now. He just hoped it was to Drasen.

The uncertainty did not help his mood as he set out for her compound, nor did being greeted by older women in no hurry to do anything. Most of the compound's inhabitants had departed to Amethen's sett before Vorash, but a dozen or so lived in Esh-accom permanently, and they kept him waiting in the hall until *Tonera*, who was even more ancient and hampered by a heavy limp, escorted him with excruciating slowness to Ithreya's room.

She sat by the window, her face as pale as her hair, but Ataghan remained poised in the doorway, his gaze on the cradle. 'I congratulate you on Enda's gift,' he said finally with a stiff bow.

Ithreya inclined her head. 'Enda is worthy of thanking,' she said, giving the ritual response of a new mother, and Ataghan's gaze returned to the cradle. 'I didn't ask you here to open old wounds, Syld,' she continued, 'but to see your lein's daughter.'

Ataghan bowed again and forced himself across the room. The baby slept, hiding her eye colour, but her dark hair, brows, and the set of her lips, were all his lein's. Pain burned through him and it was hard even to breathe.

'I know your suffering,' she said softly. 'Sometimes the pain is so great, I think Soaich had a hand in Enda's gift too. I watch her face as she suckles and feel a mother's love, but I would trade her in an instant to have Sehereden back.' She bit her lip and it was a moment before she could speak again.

'There are two things I want you to know, Syld. The first is that I've named her Vivreya.' Ataghan looked at her astonishment. 'The second, is that I will make you choose-father *if* you meet my conditions.'

Ataghan's blood roared and he fought to control his body's burn. 'What are the conditions?' he demanded harshly.

'Listen carefully, Syld, for I will not tell you a second time or grant you longer than Pool Zadic to meet them. Vivreya will be weaned by then and ready to gift. Whether I gift her to you, or to another, is up to you.'

Chapter 21

Viv decided that Horse Zadic was the most spectacular of all the zadics she had seen, although she suspected its brilliant undulations were helped by the icy air. No one spoke of zadics being hot or cold, but The Wheel certainly headed towards the equivalent of winter. The sidari took the edge off the air, but Viv shivered as she sat on her usual log beneath their branches. Wearing her shirt halter neck did not help but after Orthagh's little knife demonstration, she had traded warmth for safety.

She came to the clearing most nights. She liked the trees' solitude and she felt close to the man who had shown her kindness. She felt close to Sehereden too, but it was harder to think of him, his death was too raw.

The silver dapples on the leaf-fall dimmed as the zadic ebbed, and she headed back to the sett, chaffing her icy hands. The stable yards were full of horses, which was nothing unusual, the flow of traders constant in recent days. Apparently most vals had *some* retsen stands, but not of the quality or quantity of Gothral's sett, and Enesha said trade picked up in Horse Zadic because people were loath to risk the weather later.

The horses turned at her approach then went back to their grazing, except for one, which watched her all the way past. Viv still found Valen horses unnerving and this one was particularly intent. It was big enough to be the Syld's, in fact, she was bloody well sure it *was* the Syld's!

The hall's rumble of conversation told her people lingered over their final mugs of milk, keen for news from other parts of the Vale, but Viv hurried past to her room and wedged the chair under the handle. *If* the Syld were here, he would simply be tracing for retsen like everyone else. *Sure, Vivi. He'll just bid ya a good day and go about his business like he has every other time ya crossed paths.*

Someone knocked at the door, making her jump, then tried to enter. 'Viv? What in Soaich's name have you done to this door?' It was Enesha and Viv pulled the chair aside. 'Why are you blocking the door?' she asked, eyeing the chair. 'Gothral's sett is safe, or is someone troubling you?'

'It's a habit I've got into.'

Enesha plonked down on the bed. 'Ataghan en-Scinta-ril's here.'

'I know. I saw his horse.'

'There's a whole party from the Scinta-ril, come for our retsen,' said Enesha dryly and paused. 'You know Sehereden en-Scinta-ril's dead?'

'Yes.'

'How did he die?'

'In a riding accident.'

Enesha's breath whistled. 'That man followed his lein into more fights than I care to count, and he dies in a stinking riding accident!' She glanced at Viv sideways. 'He's the reason I didn't think you would come back. His intentions were pretty clear when he collected you at Pool Zadic.'

'Pool Zadic precedes Fire Zadic.' said Viv with a shrug. 'Every man's intentions are clear then.'

'Sehereden en-Scinta-ril wasn't *every* man.' Viv said nothing and Enesha eyed her. 'It's why you go to the sidari every night, isn't it? Not just for Tahsin, but for Sehereden.'

'I never got to say goodbye to either of them.'

Enesha snorted. 'There's lots of folk I've never said goodbye to, which was probably for the best,' she said, then sobered. 'The dead are gone, Viv. You need to stay with the living.'

It was so unlike anything Enesha ever said, that Viv stared. 'It would be good if you came to the dancing too,' continued Enesha. 'Otherwise some in the sett will think you're a typical elddra who thinks the Valen are below them, when I know you're not.' She got to her feet. 'It'll be interesting to see how much madder Mad At gets now his lein's gone,' she said cheerfully.

Viv knew when the Syld entered the hall the next morning, not just because she faced the door as she breakfasted, but because she saw the animosity on Orthagh's face. The Syld was with others of his sett who had been at Esh-accom with her, but no one acknowledged her including him.

Enesha sat opposite, but Viv concentrated on her retsen and honey, despite Enesha's puzzled gaze flicking between her and Gothral's table behind, where Viv assumed the Syld and his party sat. The Syld would trade for retsen and go home, she told herself, as she followed Enesha out. He might even be gone by the time she finished the day's harvest.

'We're picking the nightwise stands,' said Enesha, as they set out, but instead of leading as usual, she ordered Merhen and Fahan to walk with the men ahead and fell into step beside Viv. 'What is it between you and Mad At?' she asked, dropping her voice. 'He ignored you when he came in then spent the entire breakfast staring at the back of your head.'

'He's my lein's choose-father.'

Enesha gaped. 'Your *lein*? But the way he dragged you into the sett when you first came here, you would have thought you were his worst enemy.'

'I found his daughter after the Esh-embrin massacre and travelled with her,' said Viv briefly. 'We became lein but were separated by the Waradi. They were killed by the Syld's party and he decided I was a Waradi lein-tryst. When his men found his daughter and he discovered I had cared for her, he brought me here.'

'You've missed a few bits of the story,' said Enesha as she stomped along. 'Like the urrut leash, the Grey Fire, and your burns.'

Viv glanced at her. 'I love my lein, Enesha, and she loves her father.'

'So you say nothing about what he did to you? And what of Sehereden?' Enesha laughed sourly. 'Oh, I can imagine how *happy* Mad At must have been at his lein's interest. And exactly how far did that *interest* go, Viv?'

Viv stopped. 'You told me to stay with the living, Enesha. My lein's safety depends on her father's standing, and that little girl is all I care about. If you care about me, *at all*, you'll keep silent too.'

The day's fine start did not last long. Clouds scudded in, followed by slithers of icy rain, but the team continued to pick. Viv bore the brunt of it, as she harvested highest, but being half-frozen was preferable to a warm sett shared with the Syld, because given the foul weather, he would still be there.

Viv rarely suffered retsen splinters but she had collected two deep ones by the time she climbed down. Doran extracted them with his usual lack of sentimentality,

161

shouldered the retsen bags, and lumbered off. Viv sucked her stinging hand as she walked. Sehereden had used saliva to soothe her scorch-berry burns and she recalled his other acts of kindness, right back to when he had stilled the Syld's knife as it plunged towards her heart.

If she had trusted him earlier, *if* she had told him the truth …Viv shook her head. Enesha was right; she had to stay with the living, it was just that the Syld's arrival had opened wounds old and new. *Unfinished business has a habit of comin' back to bite ya, eh Vivi?*

Viv trudged on, oblivious to the rain. She had planned to live in Tahsin's sett but it was Gothral's now and she had planned to check Astraal for her mother and yet she loitered here, in a place she no longer believed she could be happy. She needed to farewell her dead and go to Astraal. If her mother were there, she would live with her, and if not? Viv had no answer but the prospect of wandering from fold to fold was so awful, she could not bear to even think about it.

Viv went straight to the sidari grove despite her wet clothes. She was not given to prescience, but she had a feeling her time at the sett was running out. Her usual log was sodden, but she was too restless to sit anyway. The scattered bones were evidence enough Tahsin had gone but she had no evidence Sehereden had gone except the Syld's agony.

She wandered around the derelict pyre, weaving between the bones. She had read somewhere a labyrinth was different to a maze because a maze was a puzzle that had to be solved, and a labyrinth conjured useful thoughts. Given her head was empty of anything remotely useful, she decided the route between the bones must be a bloody maze.

She stopped and pulled the puzzle box out from her pocket but the usual sense of connection to Tahsin was missing. What she did sense though, was a rift. Unsurprising given the clearing was a place of death and useful if Orthagh decided to visited. 'Speak of devil,' she muttered, as she heard someone approach, but it was the Syld.

He stopped on the edge of the clearing and they eyed each other across the bones. 'Gothral said I would find you here. I would like to speak with you *if* you're willing.'

The Syld had never given a toss whether she was *willing* or not before 'About what?' she asked, not moving.

'Living in my sett.'

Viv actually laughed. 'Living in your sett?'

'It was rebuilt in your absence. My new band lives there with their kin. There will be plenty of company for you.'

'You don't want me anywhere near your sett.'

'Fariye wants you.'

'Fariye's happy and settled, and if I love her, I'll allow her to stay that way,' she quoted back at him. The Syld stepped into the clearing and Viv edged towards the rift. 'If you're making some sort of gesture for Sehereden's sake, don't bother.'

'It's for *your* lein!'

'No, it isn't. You've wanted me out of Fariye's life since the moment we met. I saw her in Esh-accom and she *did* look happy, so maybe it's for the best I stay away. One day she'll reach an age when she'll sense your hatred of me and I never want her to have to choose between us. I'll stay away, Syld, if you let me see her once a zadican when you come to Esh-accom. Is it a deal?'

His face twisted in contempt. 'You're content to spend your life *here*, harvesting retsen?'

'Tahsin welcomed me.'

'Tahsin's dead and Gothral's a very different man, as you'll discover. You would be better off accepting my offer.'

'I've *never* been better off accepting *anything* you've offered,' she spat. 'Harvesting retsen is an honest way to earn my keep, and there are enough misfits here for a stinking elddra like me to blend in!'

'Whatever you are, you're not elddra, *unless* Baraghan and Thrisdane lied.'

Viv was tempted to toss back that he was not Valen either, but she was too concerned about what Baraghan and Thris had actually said. Maybe the Syld intended to expose her as some sort of witch. She shoved the puzzle box in her pocket and turned towards the rift.

'Don't, Viv! Stay!'

She stopped. It was the first time he had used her name, but she was more shocked by his apparent ability to sense the rift. Or maybe it was a lucky guess. As a street fighter, he would be super sensitive to his enemy's intentions. 'There's no reason to stay,' she said, watching him cautiously.

'Fariye's here and your mother might be too. I know the best route to Astraal and can aid your search.'

Why was he suddenly so bloody keen she stayed? She wondered whether he and Baraghan had a bet going who could bed her first, then dismissed the idea. Baraghan might strut his stuff like a farmyard rooster, but it did not ring true of the Syld. And if he *did* know Astraal *and* who

164

was in charge, it could shorten her search. On the other hand, having to walk there, rather than fly, would lengthen the whole undertaking. 'I'm leaving at first light,' she said.

'First light it is,' he clipped out, and disappeared back into the trees.

Chapter 22

Are you as mad as Mad At?' exclaimed Enesha when Viv shared her plans. Enesha was sprawled at the table in her room and Viv sat opposite. 'No one goes to Astraal unless they're Called, and *then* they think twice.'

'The Stonash do.'

'Trade makes it worth *their* while,' Enesha tossed off. 'It's a hard journey, whichever way you go, and don't expect a welcome at the other end. The Astraali barely tolerate our visits to *their* sacred lake.'

'I need to see if my mother's there.'

'Why in Soaich's name would your mother be there?'

'She looks like me.'

Enesha grunted. 'And why go with Mad At given your history together?'

'He's been there before, and he's good with knives,' added Viv, dredging up a smile.

'And what does he want in return for being your little guide?'

'Nothing.'

Enesha laughed mirthlessly. 'Believe that if it makes you happy, Viv.'

'Just delay telling Gothral I've gone for as long as possible, will you? I want to be clear of the sett before he knows.'

'Gothral's no Tahsin, Viv, but you don't need to fear him.'

'He's from the same sett as Orthagh, and I don't want Orthagh knowing.'

Enesha's brows lowered. 'He *has* been troubling you, hasn't he? You should have told Gothral.'

'They're from the same sett,' she said with a shrug. 'And it's not what you think. I *was* troubled by the elddra in Esh-accom, and they weren't happy I left. Orthagh is part of the same group. He's let me know I'm being watched.'

'Why would Orthagh be mixed up with elddra?'

'Because he's elddric.' Enesha looked at her blankly. 'The male of elddra,' explained Viv, and rose. 'If my mother's not in Astraal, I'll come back. If she *is* there, I don't know what I'll do. And if the journey's as bad as you say, I mightn't make it back anyway, so I'll say goodbye now.' She took a deep breath. 'Thank you for being kind, Enesha.'

'I haven't been kind.'

'It's all relative,' said Viv, with another attempt at a smile. 'You haven't tried to kill me.'

'Not since the first day,' said Enesha and enclosed her in rib-cracking hug. 'Take care, Viv.'

Viv nodded. 'You too.'

The predawn air was icy and despite her jacket, Viv shivered as they walked. They headed cloudwise up the val, keeping to the Kama Rill's bank, but when a breeze sprang up, the Syld pulled a jacket from his pack and tossed it to her. 'Wear that,' he said. Mittens followed. 'You'll need those later.'

'Thank you,' said Viv, putting on the jacket and stowing the mittens. The jacket was fleece-lined and her size, so he had probably got it from the sett's store. The exchange was the first words they had spoken but Viv was happy to walk in silence. She had put off searching Astraal for so long it was a relief to actually start the journey. The jacket was warm, and she felt almost cheerful as she watched the redwings in the trees and the occasional shrill.

'Are the birds the same as where you're from?' the Syld asked. 'Or doesn't *Moonsun* have birds?'

She had been walking behind him but he stopped so she came level. There was no friendliness in his face and she wondered if he tested her honesty. Baraghan had obviously told him about Moonsun but what else had he passed on? 'There were lots of birds where I grew up,' she said briefly.

'Why didn't you stay in Moonsun with your choose-father?' he pursued, matching his pace to hers.

'He was an arsehole who beat my mother, and when she disappeared, he beat me. Then my seed-father turned up and told me my mother was still alive in another fold, and made Thris my guide, as Baraghan's probably told you.'

'Why not stay with your seed-father in Ezam?'

'Because Kald's an arsehole too. Not violent like my choose-father, but self-serving and vindictive. Moonsun isn't like here. Mothers are more important than fathers who often abandon their seed-children and have no interest in choose-children. It's why I'm glad I can't have children.'

There was a surge of heat and Viv braced herself. 'Sehereden wanted to lein-tryst,' he rasped. 'He traded *everything* for it, including his life.'

'I told Sehereden I could not have children but he believed I would have a child with him because it would be seeded with love, and then it would grow up safe and happy in your sett.' The heat from the Syld was like a furnace now, but Viv pressed on. 'I knew Ithreya loved him and could give him a child, then I saw at the celebrations

168

she carried. I would have said goodbye to Sehereden as well as Poss had you let me into your compound.'

'You blame *me* for my lein's death!?'

The Syld looked positively murderous but Viv held her ground. 'What Ithreya said was true. Sehereden *chose* not to lein-tryst with her and he *chose* to search for me. He had a choice in everything he did.'

'Not once he'd seen you!'

'If you believe your lein was a maragh boar, so be it,' snapped Viv. 'I know you loved him, and that Ithreya loved him, and that I loved him.' Viv's voice cracked. 'He was an easy man to love, your lein. He was the *only* man I've loved. I'm truly sorry for your loss, Syld, and thank you for the offer to aid my journey to Astraal, but it was *never* going to work.'

She dropped her pack to the ground, removed the fleece jacket, and unbuttoned the lighter jacket underneath. At least her shirt was halter neck, which saved time. 'What in Soaich's name are you doing?' he demanded.

'Parting company,' she said, pushing the jackets into her pack.

His hand fastened on her arm. 'You'll stay with me!'

'No, I effing won't!' she retorted and wrenched herself free. 'Tell me why you're *not* trading retsen at Gothral's sett, or *not* back with Fariye at the Scinta-ril. Tell me why you're *really* here or I'm gone!' His eyes blazed but her anger matched his. 'Tell me!' There was a long silence and she saw how he sifted possible responses.

'I came to an understanding with Ithreya.'

'Ithreya?'

'She's birthed a girl-child.'

Viv cursed herself. Between dealing with Tahsin's death and the likes of Orthagh, she had lost track of when the baby was due. 'And they're both well?' she asked anxiously.

'Yes.'

'Thank God,' she muttered. The Syld's face was expressionless but his neck muscles roped. 'The baby's Sehereden's, isn't she?'

'Yes.'

'And Ithreya will give her to you, if …?'

'Ithreya's yet to choose the father, but she wants you safe. It's what Sehereden wanted too and the safest place is in my sett.'

'*Then* she'll make you choose-father?' pursued Viv. 'Is that the deal?'

'Ithreya's yet to choose the father,' he repeated.

Ithreya had dangled a bait in front of the Syld he could not refuse. Not only had she offered him the chance of another child, but the child of his *dead* lein. But why? Ithreya had been kind to Viv but this was something else. Maybe she wanted to see the Syld squirm, but Viv had never seen them argue. There had been none of the animosity she had *enjoyed*.

'You should have told me the truth earlier *if* this is the truth. I would have understood, but we both know it's impossible for me to live in your sett. I'll visit though and argue your case with Ithreya. You're a loving and protective father to Fariye, the sort of father I wish I'd had. You would be doubly loving and protective *if* that's possible, to your lein's child.'

Viv took a breath. Syatha would be proud of her little speech, though not how grudgingly she had delivered it. 'What did Ithreya name Sehereden's daughter,' she asked curiously, 'or is naming the choose-father's privilege?'

'Vivreya.' Viv's mouth fell open. 'The name's not uncommon around the Verra-ril,' he added tersely. Perhaps not but Viv shivered. 'You need to stay with me,' he repeated. 'Astraal isn't a kind city. Put your jacket back on before you freeze.'

He waited while Viv dressed and heaved on her pack, and they went on in silence. He would have known why she had undressed but had not alluded to her wings, and she knew why. She had seen him at his most vulnerable, and that was the last thing he wanted to be reminded of.

It was completely dark by the time they stopped. The land had grown steep with gnarled trees that clung to the slopes to either side, and the Kama Rill reduced to a narrow bed, full of foam and fury. 'We'll need wood,' the Syld said, as he cleared a space for a fire.

Viv dropped her pack and peered about. The slopes were bare, the only windfall probably in the trees further up. *Can you collect some firewood, please*, would have been nice, she thought sourly, as she clawed her way up. They had walked in silence since their little *chat* about Ithreya though she could have made more effort to be sociable too, she conceded, particularly as she needed to learn more about The Wheel.

The windfall was thick under the trees, as were the spiders, and there were crumbling bones that looked human. She avoided them, and the spiders, loaded her arms with wood, and picked her down. She supposed burning people where they fell made sense given the sparse population and a legal system that seemed to consist of payback.

The Syld had set a fire and she headed for the orange glow. He had pitched a maark too, and sat on boulder in front of it, toasting retsen rounds on a sharpened stick. The fire burned well and she tossed down her load of windfall in disgust. 'You didn't need wood,' she said. 'You had oilstone.'

'Oilstone won't last the night and if mercats turn up, neither will we.'

He had positioned other stones around the fire and she sat on one. 'Caibel said mercats weren't around anymore.'

'Caibel?'

'Baraghan's son.'

'Baraghan doesn't have a son.'

'He does whether he acknowledges him or not. A relationship doesn't cease to exist because one side ignores it.'

His jaw tightened but there was no sign of anger when he spoke. 'Mercats roam the higher vals and don't like fire,' he said, as he handed her a round of retsen. 'Honey and cheese there,' he said, gesturing to one of the stones. 'Have both. We have a long walk tomorrow. Refill your flask before we leave too. There's no water for two days.'

'How far is Astraal?'

'That depends on the route you choose and whether Enda smiles on you.'

'So what route will you choose?' asked Viv in exasperation.

'That depends on you.' He turned, and the fire lit the planes of his face. Rim or Sehereden; he could have been either. 'How tolerant are you of darkness? Of stone close all about you? Of trusting those who've done you harm?'

It seemed to be an acknowledgement of his arseholery unless other enemies lurked ahead. 'I've survived all three,' she said slowly, wondering whether it *was* some sort apology.

'That route is four days, *if* Enda smiles on us. Or we can take a route through land like this, which takes double that, *if* Enda smiles on us.'

'What if Soaich sticks the boots in?' asked Viv, thinking of the way her luck *always* ran.

'Then no one ever sees us again. You can decide in the morning,' he added when she said nothing.

'If the mercats don't get us,' she muttered.

'We'll be safe enough in the maark *if* we keep the fire high.'

'I'm sleeping here.'

'You're sleeping *in* the maark. Mercats have taken sleepers in the open before, despite the nearness of flames. You might think *me* dangerous, elddra, but you've not seen a mercat.'

He was angry again and Viv shrugged. She guessed his deal with Ithreya meant he would be the perfect gentleman, even if he still could not bear to utter her name. And then the zadic burst into the sky with its usual splendour, and Viv forgot everything but it.

'You have no zadics in Moonsun?' he asked.

'No, nor elsewhere I've visited,' she breathed, staring up at it. 'I've seen Pool, Cascade, Fire, Cadestone and now Horse Zadic. How many others are there?'

'Eight. Ice, Lirium, and Glimwing passed while you were absent. They last between forty and forty-five days, depending on Vorash.'

'What about the zadic that only lasts a few moments?'

He stiffened but again his voice betrayed nothing. 'That's a Call Zadic. It appears to those who Enda summons to Ourassin, the sacred lake the Astraali renamed Astraal after themselves.'

'Why did I see it?'

'Because you've been Called.'

'But why?'

'The Called don't speak of what they discover in Astraal,' he said and packed the food away. He built the fire until it roared, then rose. 'Time to sleep,' he said, and Viv reluctantly followed him into the maark.

Chapter 23

Despite the elddra's repugnance at sharing his maark, she was soon asleep, unlike him. The maark's oiled cloth muted the zadic's silver but she had shimmered like an otherworldly creature, which she was, and one here by an accident that had twice saved his daughter's life and cost him his lein's.

Heat beat through him, exacerbated by her scent, and he ducked back out the maark into the chill night air. There was no guttural snarls that signaled mercats but senglings sounded beyond the ridge, their calls faint as if they headed cloudwise too. He would keep his time in Astraal short, then take the elddra back to the Scinta-ril by the quickest route.

He reviewed his plans as he paced around the fire. He had thought delivering her to his sett the simplest of Ithreya's demands but the elddra had only tolerated him for Fariye's sake and the message Shornon had passed on, that Fariye was happy and settled, later confirmed by the elddra's own sighting, now gave her no reason to tolerate him at all.

Even worse, her belief Fariye no longer needed her weakened her links to The Wheel, as did Sehereden and Tahsin's deaths. Baraghan suggested rifts were easy to use, once you found them, and if the elddra's mother was not in Astraal she had no reason to stay. And then there was Thrisdane. The sight of him was etched into Ataghan's memory, as was his tenderness as he cradled her. If they *were* lovers, it all but guaranteed she would leave.

His body's burn grew and he wrenched off his jacket, and slashed his arms, and when the sear had dulled enough to breathe, staggered down to the Kama Rill and washed away the blood. The water rushed into the darkness and he was tempted to let it take him too but forced himself back to the fire and slumped onto a stone.

His life had been one long fight and this was just another one, but for the most precious prize of all. Some fights needed trickery, others strength, but all required him to understand his adversary. To win Sehereden's daughter he must meet Ithreya's demands, but Ithreya was not the enemy, the elddra was. To defeat her, he must counter her strengths and exploit her weaknesses, and he had until the end of Pool Zadic do it.

Viv was greeted by spits of sleet in the face when she crawled out of the maark next morning. 'Just another day in paradise,' she muttered as she pulled her jacket close. There was no sign of the Syld, so she guessed he attended to matters quarash, which she did too, keeping an eye out for whatever mercats looked like.

Then she scrambled down to the Kama Rill to wash her hands and fill her flask. The sleet was like needles, not the prick of being watched and as she felt the latter, she turned, expecting a mercat to be crouched above but it was the Syld. Not much different, she thought, as she came back up the bank.

He packed away the maark and quenched the fire, all in silence, and only spoke when he tossed her a cape. 'You'll need this,' he said.

'Thank you,' said Viv, *you surly bastard*. The cape was a good fit, and looked new, in fact, as new as the fleece jacket and mittens. She suspected they were not from Gothral's store after all but traded in Esh-accom. It seemed the Syld was a planner like his elddric mate Baraghan.

He strode off and she followed, pleased not to have him behind her, despite the risk of mercats slinking in their wake. The cloud hid the ridge-tops and she strained for sound. Mercats, pig-bears, Orthagh and his ilk, and even Baraghan, who would not take her desertion philosophically, might all lurk. Her skin continued to prick which told her *something* watched and she hoped it was just the shrills.

'You'll need to make a decision soon,' the Syld tossed over his shoulder.

'What?'

'Whether we take the four-day route or the eight-day one.'

'You choose.'

'Shorter is better when Horse Zadic deepens.'

'Shorter it is,' said Viv, and wondered if she had just signed her death warrant. She had been trapped underground with Thris in Hearth Fold and almost drowned in Melbourne's sewers so maybe this would be third time lucky for the Grim Reaper. At least any pursuers would be less likely to follow *unless* they decided an ambush in a pitch-black tunnel was a grand idea.

The Syld turned upslope and followed a path more stone than earth, and slippery stone at that. It wound its way up into the clouds and the world became a soft place adrift with grey.

She followed the Syld's shadowy back until a sheer rockface emerged from the fog. 'How are your climbing skills?' he asked sardonically.

'Every thief can climb.'

'You go first, elddra, in case you miss your footing.'

'I've learned not to have people behind me,' she said.

177

'I'll try not to ruin your deal with Ithreya by falling but if I do, don't burn my body. You can bury it, or if that's too much trouble, leave it for the mercats.'

He scowled as if he were going to argue, but started to climb, and she followed, using the same hand- and toe-holds as him. It was not easy, and she had not gone far before she wished she had shed the cape.

She toiled on through the cloud, in a mesmerizing rhythm, and then his feet disappeared. 'Almost there, elddra,' he called down. His hand appeared through the fog and as he yanked her over the ledge, his jacket sleeve rode up to reveal fresh wounds. 'We'll eat before we start,' he said and dropped his pack near a crevice in the stone. He handed her retsen and cheese, then took his own food to the far end of the ledge and ate there, staring into space.

The cloud was too thick to see above or below which gave the strange sensation of being suspended in the middle of nowhere. Viv perched on her pack and considered him as she ate. She guessed Sehereden's death had triggered his self-mutilation but the whole crap-show was a hell of a lot more complicated than that. For a long time she had thought him tanked on something but the fold appeared to have no drugs. Nor was his Angellus blood the sole cause of his self-destructiveness or Baraghan would be the same. Orthagh was violent, she reminded herself, but he was more of your run-of-the-mill thug, whereas the Syld seemed on the verge of breaking apart.

Having her angel part emerge in Ezam had been harrowing, but the effects of her human-angel mismatch went back much further than that. She had been powerless to stop Jimmy Wright's violence but she had *chosen* Rim and reacted to his violence by directing her own inwards until finally, she had got into that car, that night, in search of death.

The Syld channeled most of his violence outwards. It made him a merciless killer and the champion of tournaments but rarely a father. He had gained only a single child from all his tournament wins and now he had the chance of a second child, more desired even than Fariye, because it was all he had left of Sehereden. But to have that child, Ithreya had stipulated Viv must live in his sett.

It still made no sense and the crevice that loomed nearby added to her unease. The Syld suggested they were in for four days of total darkness *if* things went well. She only hoped the tunnel did not rearrange itself like those in the Blue Helixai and that it held a rift as a nice little insurance policy.

'Ready, elddra?'

Viv grimaced. If she could manage *Syld* instead of *arsehole*, he could bloody well make an effort too. 'If it's four days in darkness, *Syld*, it'll give you plenty of time to practise my name,' she said, as she heaved on her pack. 'I've got more than one, so feel free to choose the least repulsive. Most people call me Viv, which is short for Violet Iris Vacia, the names of my mother, grandmother, and great grandmother. Violet Iris Vacia is a mouthful but Baraghan used it. Rim called me Vivi, so I prefer you don't use that.'

'Because he was your lover?' he sneered.

'Because he was a violent arsehole that I don't want reminding of.'

'Elddra is sufficient,' he said impatiently.

'We agreed I wasn't elddra, remember. Sehereden called me Viv if that helps. You can think about it as we walk.'

It was pitch black within twenty paces and Viv knew because she counted. Four whole bloody days of this, she thought, as she walked, her hand on the wall as a guide, and with a man who was hardly the life of the party. At least he kept the pace even and spoke now and then, if only to ensure he had not lost her.

She refused to respond when he called her elddra and he finally called her *Iris*, although it sounded more like *Ilris*, the way he said it. No one had called her *Iris* before, but she had given him the choice, and could hardly complain.

'Tell me about Rim,' he said, after a while.

'I've told you about him. He was an arsehole.'

'How long were you with him?'

'Why do you want to know?'

'I'm interested in your life before you came to The Wheel.'

She doubted it; the Syld was only ever interested in weapons to use against her. 'When Sehereden was bringing me to Esh-accom, he wanted to know about my previous life too, and I wanted to know about The Wheel for obvious reasons, so we agreed to trade. He would ask a question, and I would ask a question. Do you want to trade?'

His irritation was palpable. '*If* you insist,' he grated. 'Your question?'

'Why didn't you lein-tryst with Fariye's mother?' There was a pulse of heat and Viv wished she had started with something less sensitive. She wanted to know what made him tick, for Poss's sake, but if he sank back into an angry silence, at least he would stop badgering her.

'A lein-tryst locks out the chance of choose-children and I was young. How long were you with Rim?'

'The equivalent of three zadicans here, on and off. He took other lovers.'

'If he were an *arsehole*, why did you stay with him?'

'That's two questions and it was my turn. 'Where were you born?' Again, the pulse of heat. 'Astraal. And the answer to my question?'

'I was fifteen when I met Rim. I had been on the streets almost a year, which is a zadican

here. I had been hungry a lot of the time, and frightened, and cold. I had been raped once and escaped another time. I had traded sex to save my skin and put food in my belly. I felt safe with Rim, *at first*, so I stayed.' She struggled on as her throat tightened. 'He made me feel worthwhile, as if I were lovable after all. And he had food, and a bed, and a way of getting coin. He taught me how to thieve and how not to get caught. He gave me a group to be part of, like a family almost.' She sleeved her eyes, glad of the darkness.

'Why do you call him an arsehole?'

'That's two questions,' she said thickly. 'How old were you when you left Astraal?'

'Fourteen. My question?'

'He took drugs. I used to think you did too. They're things you sniff, or eat, or smoke, or poke in your veins. People do it because it makes them feel good, but it makes them violent and unpredictable. They need more and more to get the same effect, and in the end, they can't live without them. Rim could be loving but once he cut me up with a knife and burned me several times.' She cleared her throat. 'Why did you leave Astraal?'

'I was expelled. Why in Soaich's name did you stay with the man?'

'He said he loved me and I kept hoping it was true.' She stumbled to a stop and his footsteps ceased too.

'*Ilris*? Are you all right?'

'That's two questions,' she choked.

'We need to keep moving.'

'Yes,' she said, and forced herself on.

Chapter 24

They walked in silence for a time, Viv as weary as if she had journeyed many days. 'Tell me about Thrisdane,' the Syld said.

'That's not a question and it was my turn. Why were you expelled from Astraal?'

'The rulers of Astraal expel elddric regularly. I was one of them. Is Thrisdane your lover?'

'Yes,' said Viv, copying the brevity of his answers. 'The Astraali are elddra or elddric. Why expel some and let others stay?' He had only been fourteen, for God's sake, the same age as when she had lost *her* home.

'Some elddric are more worthy than others,' he said bitterly. 'If you and Thrisdane are lovers, why is he content to be so far from you?'

'You had lots of lovers during Fire Zadic that you don't seem to want around.'

'Thrisdane doesn't want you?'

'That's another question. Really Syld, you're not very good at this, are you?'

'As you failed to answer the original question it doesn't count.'

His tone was not light-hearted exactly, but at least it was not angry. 'No, you're probably right.' She paused. 'I don't know what Baraghan told you about Thris's fold of Ezam.'

'He said they were all males and there was no food.'

Viv laughed. 'I can see why he came back, but Ezam's more complex than that. Its angels exist in a hierarchy and must complete various tasks to work their way to the top so they can transcend. Thris's task was to guide me to my

183

mother, a task allocated by my father, Kald, who's near the top in the hierarchy. But there are things that pull angels in the opposite direction. Sex is one of them, or coupling, as you call it here.'

'But you said you were lovers.'

'Thris seduced me on Kald's orders. I had decided to search for my mother on my own, but Kald wanted me back with Thris, and decided sex was a good way to achieve it. I didn't take much persuading,' she admitted. 'Thris is beautiful, not just what you see, but in his heart too. Kald ordered him to couple with me, knowing it would damage Thris's chances of transcendence. He betrayed us both. The last time I saw Thris he was bound and burned. I don't want him here. It's too dangerous.'

'You intend to go to him in Ezam?'

'No. He has to forget about me to transcend.'

'You're willing to give him up?'

'Isn't that what love's all about, Syld?' she asked ironically. 'It's why coming to your sett is such a bad idea. I love Poss but I'm part of the horrors of Esh-embrin and Stelin Ridge. I want her to forget these things.'

They walked on in silence, but Viv's head was full of Thris. Their second encounter had been love not Kald's coercion and while her renouncing of Thris sounded noble, it was messy, and desperate, and ultimately fragile and if she ever saw him again, it would probably fall apart.

'It was a lie.'

'What?' asked Viv, struggling to collect her thoughts. 'What was a lie?'

'That Fariye was happy and settled and had forgotten you. She sobbed for you every night in Esh-accom, she *still* sobs for you every night *and* during the day now

Sehereden's gone. She wants her lein. She hasn't forgotten you and nor will she ever. Only death breaks a leinship.'

Viv stopped. 'How dare you!' she choked, incoherent with rage. 'I thought you loved your daughter and you've done this to her! For what? To get one over me? Because you hate what I am? Because you hate what *you* are? God in Heaven! I didn't think you could lie! You've got angel blood, but you've dodged the honesty bullet! How much else that you've said are lies? All of it?' Viv dragged in a harsh breath. She could have seen Poss in Esh-accom, but she had walked away. She could have comforted the little girl after Sehereden's death, but she had believed this arsehole instead! Rim was right. She *was* a bloody moron!

'I can't lie.'

'Tell that to some other gullible idiot!' she screamed into the darkness. 'Your *whole* life is a lie!' She felt the burst of heat, heard him step towards her, turned and ran. She pelted through the darkness, hand skimming the wall, horribly aware of feet running behind her.

He shouted for her to stop and she quickened her pace and then cannoned into something and was thrown backwards. She had a split second to realise someone else lurked in the darkness, then her head hit stone.

Ky swept into land on Ash's favorite ledge on the Blue Helixai and dashed into the cavern, relieved he did not have to go far. Ash played his lyre near one of the opaque pools and Thris was with him but they scrambled up as he appeared. 'It was strife,' cried Ky, and Thris and Ash looked at each other blankly. 'The Wheel the way, the Wheel a knife; the way of water, the way of strife. The rift can give, the rift can take; do not disturb the sacred lake,' he recited excitedly. 'We have found the rest of Senquar-archae's writing,' he panted. 'Prime-archae Serith wants you to come.'

They did not speak as they powered over Ezam's glittering landscape, sliced through the glis close to the Bokos's door, and hastened through the shelves. Prime-archae Serith sat at his usual place and the three angels bowed and palmed. 'Ashdane, Kydane, and Thrisdane,' he said, 'or is it Senquar-archae, Anasdane, and Paendane?'

'A most interesting development,' said Prime-archae Mirek as he bustled from between the shelves laden with ambrosia and goblets. He set the goblets down and filled them. Prime-archae Serith's attention was now on the lacewings beyond the window and the Dane looked at Mirek questioningly.

'Behold the scroll, or what's left of it,' said Prime-archae Mirek, carefully setting a ragged piece of parchment on the table 'It has been wet,' he said, as the Dane stared at it.

'Where was it?' asked Ash.

'On the shelf behind the rest of the writing but stuck to a larger scroll,' said Ky. 'It has taken me most of the cycle to separate it.'

'It is a warning,' said Thris, staring down at the words.

'And refers to the fold you visited,' said Mirek.

Thris raised his head. 'You think I should go back?'

'No!' exclaimed Ky. 'You barely escaped with your life last time.'

'Senquar-archae, Paendane, and Anasdane,' murmured Serith, his gaze roving over them again.

'If this concerns us all, we must all go,' said Ash.

'It is too dangerous,' said Thris sharply. 'I am familiar with Wheel Fold's dangers. I will go alone.'

186

'Most likely Ashdane is right,' said Mirek thoughtfully. 'But aid can be rendered in many ways. Kydane aids the discovery of important writings and Ashdane's *dreams* take him to many folds. That might be sufficient.'

'For a little while,' said Serith.

Ataghan heard the thud and wrenched oilstone from his pack, swiftly calculated the distance to the sound, and smashed his heel into the stone. Flame illuminated the outline of a man and Ataghan crouched and drew his knives. The man did the same and they confronted each other over the motionless body of the elddra and then Baraghan sheathed his knives and rose. 'More oilstone, Syld,' he ordered and hurried forward. Ataghan smashed another lump in time to see Baraghan pull his surgeon's kit from his pack.

'Why are you here?' demanded Ataghan.

'Men prefer to be near their future lein-trysts,' said Baraghan as he held a pad to the elddra's head. It filled with blood and Ataghan's guts clenched. 'There's also the little matter of Anfarena's men.'

'Whose?'

'Hold this, while I check whether she's cracked her skull. Keep the pressure firm.'

Ataghan did as he was bid while Baraghan's hands moved over her. Her curls spilled onto the stone where blood pooled and he jerked his gaze back to Baraghan. His face held the far-off expression it took on whenever he healed, and Ataghan held his breath.

'No permanent damage but she's going to be sick and sorry when she wakes.' He took a bandage from the kit, and Ataghan supported her head while Baraghan bound the pad in place. 'You have an unfortunate habit of inflicting damage on Violet Iris Vacia, Syld.'

'She collided with *you*.'

'While fleeing from *you*,' retorted Baraghan.

The oilstone's light dwindled and Baraghan stowed his surgeon's kit. 'We need to keep moving,' said Ataghan.

Baraghan nodded. 'We take turns carrying. She'll not be well enough to walk today, even if she rouses.' Ataghan took her pack and Baraghan swung her into his arms and the last thing Ataghan saw before the dark closed in was Baraghan lower his head, inhale, and smile.

'Tell me about Anfarena's men,' ordered Ataghan as they walked.

'Violet Iris Vacia hasn't mentioned Anfarena?'

'No.'

'She's one of Esh-accom's elddra. Your lein sought information from them about Violet Iris Vacia before he brought her to Esh-accom. They knew nothing of her but their interest picked up when they realised the key to the door out had just dropped into their laps. They had her watched *and* accosted, until *my* men suggested threatening her wasn't a good idea. One of the elddra followed me into the rift when I went to Ezam, but she never arrived, which confirms the dangers Violet Iris Vacia warned of.'

'You think they follow us now?'

'I doubt they will enter the Ourian Way, even if they know of it. Anfarena's orders come from her masters at the Bracken-ril, and theirs from our friends in Astraal. The distance to the Bracken-ril doubtless delayed her men being more forceful in Esh-accom but her spies would likely know where we head.'

'The new sett leader at the Kama-ril is Gothral en-Bracken-ril,' said Ataghan. 'He brought his people with him.'

'Then they certainly know. My poor Violet Iris Vacia,' he muttered. 'Beset on all sides.'

'The Astraali will want her to show them a rift.'

'Yes and she won't agree. You see, Syld, there's a thing called *transference*. Everyone who transits affects the new fold. Violet Iris Vacia was agitated by me going to Ezam and angry I brought a few keepsakes back. The beautiful Violet Iris Vacia has affected us too, but in a *good* way, don't you think Syld, given your daughter survives. Her impact here has been very different to that of the Angellus and she won't agree to their descendants repeating the catastrophe in another fold.'

'The Astraali won't take no for an answer,' said Ataghan tersely.

'Indeed, they won't. Violet Iris Vacia will be in danger the moment she sets foot in Astraal, and so will anyone who interferes with the Astraali's grand plans. This jaunt might well prove the death of us, Ataghan en-Scinta-ril.'

Viv knew she was being carried, but the understanding was dim, unlike the sickening throb of her head. The pain ricocheted with every heartbeat and bile burned its way up her throat. 'I'm going to be sick,' she gasped. She was set down and hands steadied her as she vomited, then the pound escalated, and she groaned.

'Some light, Syld.' It was Baraghan's voice, there was a sharp crack to her right, and yellow light pierced the darkness. 'Hold her a moment.' Other hands replaced

Baraghan's and she heard the glug of liquid. 'Drink this, Violet Iris Vacia.'

It smelled like grass-clippings and Viv feared Baraghan would shortly have it back, but she managed to keep it down, and it quelled the nausea. 'Why are you here?' she rasped.

'Because you're here, Violet Iris Vacia. How are you feeling now?'

'Shit.'

'*Shit*?'

'Matters quarash,' said the Syld briefly. 'I'll carry. It will shorten tomorrow's journey.' He sounded like he discussed a package, and he picked her up like one, but she was too ill to protest. She rested her head against his chest, desperate for sleep to escape the pain. The strong beat of his heart reminded her of Thris and Sehereden, of being in *their* arms, but they were lost to her and tears slid down her face. 'Sleep, *Ilris*,' the Syld said softly, and she did.

Chapter 25

Ky hurried through the glis, staring at everything he passed, as if to imprint it on his memory. The red and yellow blossoms high in the tree-tops; the lacewings feeding on spent blooms on the forest floor; the vines that linked the two, alive with mantises and scarabs. He thought of the greys of the Hollow Hills and Thorny Mountains; the four shining aqua lakes; the Red, Blue, White, and Green Helixai as they twisted up towards a sky that was sometimes umber and sometimes peach. Ezam had seemed eternal to him but now he feared for its very existence.

Resonance heralded a stele but he did not deviate and when a font appeared, drank deeply then glanced up as Dane streaked overhead. Once winning trials was the most important thing to him, transcendence clear-cut, his mentor's words wise. He had thought the Bokos the refuge of angels too weak to prove themselves in more demanding ways but he had endured more terror among its scrolls than he had in any desperate dash against Thris. And now he journeyed to *aid* Thris not defeat him, and to save the fold they called home.

The Halls' gleaming portico sheltered its usual gathering of Archae engaged in oratory and he bowed and palmed courteously as he detoured around them, then quickened his pace along the Halls' vast passageways to Archae Dejon's rooms.

He dreaded the visit but the Archae had reached the very brink of transcendence and might possess the wisdom that had eluded Ky in the Bokos. He knocked and was given permission to enter, bowed and palmed, but the

Archae barely glanced at him. 'Your business, Dane?'

'I seek your advice, Archae Dejon.'

'In what matter?'

'On a disturbing writing Prime-archae Serith discovered in the Bokos.' Dejon's lip curled but Ky pressed on. *The Wheel the way, the Wheel a knife; the way of water, the way of strife. The rift can give, the rift can take; do not disturb the sacred lake.* Prime-archae Serith believes it refers to Wheel Fold, and that a water rift connects Wheel Fold to Ezam. He fears—'

'Serith is a *Prime*-archae, Dane. He has a long journey ahead to achieve the wisdom of an Archae *if* he ever does. What he believes is of no consequence.'

'Which is why I seek your advice, Archae Dejon,' said Ky, bowing and palming again.

'My advice, Dane, is to seek company other than that of an addled Prime-archae.' He looked at Ky for the first time, and for some odd reason, Ky was reminded of the oldest scrolls in the Bokos, ancient and decayed. 'It is a pity you were incapable of accepting the wisdom I offered as a mentor. I guide other Dane now whose journeys to ascension will be shorter than yours.'

Ky bowed and palmed again. 'I thank you for your time, Archae Dejon.'

He closed the door gently behind him and hurried on to Archae Kald's rooms and while the Archae was similarly dismissive of Serith's discovery, he *was* interested in Dejon's response. 'Archae Dejon is ill-informed if he believes the Bokos holds nothing of worth though he may come to understand its importance in the coming eons. Whatever the case, I shall no longer be here to witness to it.'

Ky took to the air as soon as he cleared the Halls and sped to Haven, desperate to see Thris before he left but was only halfway there when he sensed This's resonance below and landed. Thris was already clad in human caste clothes but Ky was relieved to see he had left his shirt and jacket unbuttoned. 'I sought advice from Archaes Kald and Dejon,' he panted.

'And did you receive it?'

'I received advice about *my* inadequacies from Archae Dejon and about *Archae Dejon's* inadequacies from Archae Kald.' He took a steadying breath. 'I do not want you to go, Thris.'

'And I do not want to go,' admitted Thris, 'but I sense Ezam's peril, as you and Ash do, and do not believe the threat to us lies here.'

'It might do. The Bokos is vast. If I had time—'

'Time is one thing none of us have but it is not the only reason I go. I pledged to take Viv to her mother and my pledge still binds me.'

'Given what has happened, I do not think—'

Thris's head swiveled. 'A stele.'

Ky nodded. 'I sensed it earlier.'

Thris strode off in its direction and Ky hurried after him. It was the Larimar, which Ky had seen many times, but its familiarity never dimmed its glorious blue and aqua pulses. Thris laid his hands against its faceted crystal surface, and Ky followed suit and then the air moved as Ash came into land. 'The Larimar nourishes the spirit,' he murmured.

'We are going to need its aid,' said Ky darkly. 'This parting is bitter.'

'There is no parting,' said Ash, laying one of his hands over Ky's, and the other over Thris's. 'We are one.'

Viv woke, snug in her cover, her headache reduced to a dull throb. It was no longer dark, and she carefully turned her head, wondering if she had been carried senseless through three entire days. She was in a cavern. The Syld and Baraghan's sleeping-covers lay to either side, but they stood some distance away, backs turned, in conversation too soft to hear. They faced a small lake, as still as a mirror that, like a mirror, reflected the cavern's arching roof in all its exquisite detail.

Viv eased herself up. Stalactites hung from the ceiling, as translucent as icicles, and light shafted in through breaks in the roof to create a glittering aqua haze. The whole cavern was tinged aqua and she wondered whether the pool's deep turquoise reflected onto the cavern's walls. She winced as memories of the Principae flooded back, but memories were not the only things that resonated; there was a pervasive buzz in the air.

Baraghan turned, and then hastened back. 'Still feeling *shit*?' he asked dryly, as he crouched beside her.

'No. Thank you for your aid,' she said.

He inspected her head. 'I think we can dispense with this,' he said, and carefully removed the bandage. 'The remarkable healing capacity of the Angellus,' he murmured, as his fingers probed the wound.

'I'm not Angellus,' she said automatically, 'but I'm not what you call elddra either.' The Syld had come back too, and given she had accused of *him* lying, she felt obliged to clear the air.

'Kydane told me your mother was human caste and your father the Angellus or *angel* Archae Kald,' said Baraghan. 'Was that untrue?'

'It's what Ky believed. Angels can't lie *knowingly*. My father *is* Kald, but my mother was daimon caste, *and* her

mother, and probably her mother too.' She glanced at the
Syld but his face was unreadable. 'I learned that in Erath
Fold,' she added, 'where Thris took me after Stelin Ridge.'

'Erath Fold?'

'Home of the Iahhel, female-aspected angels,' said Viv
softly. 'They taught me what I was, or what I could be, if
I chose.'

'And that is?' pursued Baraghan.

'Before the Iahhel, I didn't need to eat or sleep much,
but now I do. But I can track rifts now, not just stumble on
them, *and* sense where they lead. The Iahhel heightened
my angel *and* human sensibilities.'

'Your heritage makes you all but Angellus,' insisted
Baraghan.

'My blood doesn't define *what* I am,' she said tersely,
and glanced at the Syld again but his face still revealed
nothing and she gave up. 'What is this place?'

'Ourassin Hall,' said Baraghan, 'home to the sublime
Ourassini Lake, so named after its parent, the sacred lake
of Ourassin, or Astraal, as our friends the Astraali would
have it.'

Viv struggled from her cover and Baraghan helped her
up. 'Allow me to show you,' he said, and shifted his grip
to her hand. He staked his claim, but she was too unsteady
to shrug him off.

She wanted to see the pool up close, and sure enough,
the buzz grew as she neared it. 'It's a rift,' she said.

'*In* the water?' said Baraghan. 'Surely you would
drown?'

'It's how I ended up at Esh-embrin,' she said and felt
the Syld tense. 'But Esh-embrin wasn't my first visit to
The Wheel. I became separated from Thris and Ky in
another fold and a rift tipped me out into the Leferen,

although I didn't know it was the Leferen then. I made my way out and ended up in a mist-filled valley, where Thris and Ky found me. Then we were besieged by long-armed creatures who drove us over a cliff.'

'The Rimming belongs to the Long-arms, kin of the Stonash,' said the Syld, speaking for the first time. 'The cliff was likely the Argine. I'm surprised you survived.'

'Ky was injured and the creatures pursued us even on the cliff-face. We found a rift and Thris managed to get Ky into it, but I was attacked before I could follow. I fell into water and woke near Esh-embrin, soaking wet.'

'And that's where you found Fariye,' said the Syld tightly.

'No, I found her in the slopes behind,' she said, and took a deep breath. 'When I saw Esh-embrin, I wanted to get the hell out of the fold. Rifts are commoner in caves, so I climbed the hills behind and found a cave. It held a rift too but I was curious about whether the cave had a false back like others I had seen.'

'They were used as storage holds for those who visited the sacred lake,' said Baraghan. 'Food was left there for the return journey. They have no use anymore,' he added sourly.

'The cave *did* have a false back and Fariye was crouched deep inside. I thought she was a little animal at first,' said Viv. 'I guessed she had come from the massacre and knew how frightened she must be. I wanted to get away incase the murderers came back, but I didn't want to drag her out either.'

'So, what did you do?' asked Baraghan curiously.

'I sat down on the stone near her and sang.' Baraghan's eyebrows rose. 'My mother used to sing to me, when we hid in the dark, when my choose-father raged and smashed things and threatened to kill us both.'

Baraghan looked shocked and Viv stared at the water. 'After a while, Fariye crept out onto my lap, and I held her through the night, and when it was light, we set out to find her family.'

Baraghan still gripped her hand but it was as if she spoke to the Syld alone. 'She went with you willingly?' the Syld asked.

Viv smiled at the memory. 'She clung to me like a little possum, which is an animal from where I grew up, hence the nickname Poss.' Viv glanced at the Syld. 'I was a better bet than being alone, but it took her a long time to trust me. You taught her well, Syld. Her caution kept her alive and now she's safe, which is all I ever wanted.'

'But *you're* not,' said Baraghan bluntly. 'Have you considered the risks of going to Astraal, Violet Iris Vacia? It's full of those wanting a rift out, and they'll know you can provide it.'

'I don't have the right to send them to someone's else's fold,' said Viv.

'The Astraali won't ask you nicely.'

She glanced at the Syld but his face was a mask again. Her search for her mother was not about him anyway or about Baraghan. If anything, it was about Thris who had pledged to guide her. But Thris was in Ezam and that meant she was alone again. 'I only left home because I was told my mother was still alive and I could be with her, but even if she's here, the Astraali's demands mean I won't be able to stay. I'll visit the Syld's sett to say goodbye to Fariye and take a rift out.'

'You can't go off alone into the unknown!' exclaimed Baraghan.

'I've done it before,' she said, and extricated her hand from his grip. 'I'm well enough to walk now, thank you, Baraghan. Maybe we should make a start.'

Chapter 26

The dark closed in all too quickly, its oppressiveness worsened by Baraghan's insistence on walking behind her. He should have walked with the Syld, she concluded irritably, given they kept up a conversation that did not include her. They had not mixed in Esh-accom but clearly shared some sort of history. 'Were you expelled too, Baraghan?' she asked after a while.

'*Expelled* is too strong a word, Violet Iris Vacia. Let's just say I was invited to leave.'

'Why?'

'Astraal has always been a closed city, Violet Iris Vacia, but the lake wasn't always shut off and in the early days of the Angellus, there was a stream of visitors, both men and women from all the Vales. Ourassin even had its own festivities, where the champions from each Vale competed. Hard to imagine now, isn't it, Syld? The Morvadi, Sonori, Terissi, Beshadi, Genessi, Waradi, Ascadi and Eshadi all dancing together like one big happy family.

'It gave the Angellus the choice of the women who visited, and they favoured those with red-hair and blue eyes. The women were happy to stay too. The Angellus had the finest of everything including music. The Scharii of Ourassin were legendary.

'The children the Angellus seeded were far less welcoming, especially after the Angellus suddenly departed. The Daimon and Du-Daimon wanted the coin the Valen brought but not the Valen themselves, especially not Valen men. It became harder to visit Ourassin, or Astraal as the Astraali re-named it, and soon only a Call Zadic guaranteed admittance to those without trade. The Astraali enjoyed their newfound power but some of them finally grew tired of counting coin and turned their attention to following their forebears out.'

Baraghan's description more or less fitted with what Ithreya and Anfarena had told her, but still did not answer her original question. 'So, why were you *invited* to leave?'

'A simple matter of numbers, Violet Iris Vacia. Astraal's rulers don't wish to compete for the Valen women they attract *or* the elddra they seed.'

It was actually a simple matter of *sex*, realised Viv in shock. The Astraali threw out the next generation of young men in order to keep the next generation of young women for themselves.

'But it means they expel their own sons!' she exclaimed. She felt the Syld's burst of heat but her own blood ran cold. A father was *everything* in The Wheel and the Syld's father had rejected him. Baraghan's had too, but he seemed less affected. 'How old were you, when you were *invited* to leave, Baraghan?'

'Seventeen. *Astraal is a city of peace*,' his resonant voice mimicked. '*There is no place for those whose blood is heavy with the baser taint of the Valen's violence.*' He laughed sourly. 'The Astraali saw me as less of a threat than Ataghan en-Scinta-ril and let me stay longer. I'm hoping they'll learn the error of their ways, eh Syld?'

The Syld said nothing but Viv fumed. 'What a pack of arseholes! It would be good to send them all off to Sand Fold!'

'What's in Sand Fold?' asked Baraghan eagerly.

'Nothing but sand, which is all very peaceful until the wind blows, then it suffocates you.' Viv paused. 'But if you were both *invited* to leave, they're not going to let you back in, are they?'

'There are other ways in apart from the gate,' said the Syld briefly.

'Always good to know a hole to duck down and a tunnel to run, when you're young and elddric in Astraal,' said Baraghan cheerfully.

'How close to Astraal do these tunnels exit?' she asked.

'A half day's walk,' said Baraghan.

'Is the way in easy to find?'

'You're not going in alone,' said Baraghan firmly.'

'Astraal's pretty obviously dangerous for both of you. I'm guessing they won't simply ask you to leave if you're discovered.'

'It's more dangerous for you, Violet Iris Vacia.'

'I'm a thief, Baraghan. I can slip through windows, pick locks, run fast, and climb. I can find rifts. I can concoct stories. Ask the Syld here. He knows I can lie without actually lying. It's kept me free in the past. Besides, I've seen a Call Zadic. You said they let in those who've been Called.'

'They'll let *you* in regardless, Violet Iris Vacia, but they won't let you out. We're coming with you.'

'I've been alone a long time, Baraghan. No one's going to miss me but you've got Caibel, and the Syld's got Fariye. And if they put a knife to your throat, or to the Syld's, I'll do as they say. It's best we part company.'

'You underestimate the affection you generate, Violet Iris Vacia,' said Baraghan softly.

Viv took a deep breath. 'I'm never going to be your lein, Baraghan, although I'm flattered by the offer and thank you for it.'

'*Never* is a long time, Violet Iris Vacia.'

'We stay together,' said the Syld.

'Shit,' muttered Viv.

'You need to stop for matters quarash?' asked Baraghan.

'I was commenting on the Syld.'

Baraghan laughed. 'I really do enjoy your company, Violet Iris Vacia.'

Ky stopped at the end of the empty shelves and peered out. According to Prime-archae Serith, the circle of darkness was the exact centre of Ezam, and given Ezam's symmetry, Ky knew it must be significant. A circle of empty shelves enclosing a disk of empty space, like the Hollow Hills enclosed the Dendrinai, except the Dendrinai teemed with life. He moved restlessly. Maybe the dark space in front teemed with life that he lacked the wisdom to see.

He unbedded his wings, intending to fly the perimeter, but feared if he strayed into the darkness, he might never come out. Instead he plucked a feather, wedged it into an empty shelf, and set off on foot, arriving back at his feather, six thousand steps later. A double trinity was not as auspicious as a trinity of trinities but must still be important.

The Halls, Haven, and Bokos made up a trinity too, he noted, but the lakes and Helixai existed in multiples of four. His brows kinked in thought and he set off again, stopped after fifteen hundred steps, turned into a passageway between the shelves and when he reached the first of the scrolls, selected the foremost scrolls from the top, middle, and bottom shelves. Then he returned to the circle of darkness, continued for another fifteen hundred steps, turned down a passageway and collected three more scrolls. He repeated the procedure twice more, and by the time he reached his feather, carried twelve scrolls.

The scrolls could be full of obscure musings on glis blooms for all he knew, but he was desperate for a quicker strategy than plucking random scrolls from the shelves. Ash lay dreaming in the Blue Helixai but Thris had gone back into terrible danger, and Ky wanted their threesome together again safe in Ezam.

Prime-archaes Serith and Mirek were where Ky had left them, but they had set a second table beside the first to accommodate an immense book Ky recognised as the Tome. Its brittle pages were notorious for their contradictions and he had preferred to explore the scrolls instead.

He leaned his collection against the wall and came to Mirek's side. 'We are investigating what the Tome says of Wheel Fold,' the Prime-archae said.

Ky's interest quickened. 'Does it add to our understanding?'

'Indeed it does. See for yourself, Kydane.'

Ky leaned over Mirek's shoulder and gasped. The name of the fold was listed with the others, but its brief description had been inked out. 'I do not understand, Prime-archae,' he said.

'Senquar-archae warns against Wheel Fold, and the fold's description has been erased,' said Mirek. 'Given his warning, Senquar-archae is unlikely to have erased information about it but other angels obviously wished to negate Senquar-archae's warning *or* to strengthen it.'

'I fear for Thris,' whispered Ky.

'And I fear for Ezam,' said Serith. Ky stared at him, shocked by his directness, but the Prime-archae's vague expression returned.

'You have more scrolls, I see, Kydane,' said Mirek as if Serith had not spoken.

'I returned to the heart of Ezam,' said Ky and described his strategy to select the scrolls.

'*If* the central scrolls were removed because they related to The Wheel, then any residual writings *might* be amongst those you collected,' said Mirek thoughtfully. 'Or if the rift *does* connect to The Wheel's lake, and there *was* a breach, these might be the first row of scrolls to have survived the deluge. Or they might be as random as the others we have found,' he added dryly.'

'A double trinity, Kydane,' said Serith, making Ky jump. 'I had not thought of that.'

Mirek carefully closed the Tome and placed it on the floor. 'Let us see what you have discovered.'

Serith had sunk back into contemplation and Mirek gave half the scrolls to Ky and they settled at the tables. Lacewings came and went outside the window and Serith wandered off but Mirek left only to replenish the ambrosia. The hue of the glis leaves softened as the umber sky cycled to peach but still Ky worked.

Commentary on obscure folds; a treatise on the configuration of the Halls; poetry dedicated to Crystal Lake; a theory that glimmers travelled Ezam via vast networks of underground tunnels. The last gave Ky pause for thought but he dismissed it. Even if it were true, it was useless in protecting Thris.

A hand rested on his shoulder and he looked up into Mirek's weary face. 'Rest, Kydane. You are exhausted.'

'I need to finish these scrolls, Prime-archae,' said Ky. 'How many remain?'

'Four,' said Mirek. 'Perhaps that itself is significant,' he added ironically.

'I no longer know *what* is significant,' admitted Ky.

'You study two, and I will study two, then we will rest,' said Mirek.

Ky unrolled the next scroll and struggled to focus. The words were clearly Senquar-archae's but his tired brain could make no sense of them. 'I have found something, Prime-archae,' he said hoarsely. Mirek was suddenly beside him and Ky read slowly. '*Red mountains rise, red mountains fall, a home for bears and angel Halls. The Great Beyond, a gift is given, the sacred lake must not be riven. The journey in, will still suffice, be thankful for the fold of ice.*'

'The sacred lake again,' muttered Mirek, 'and another clear warning.'

'Might it be another lake entirely?'

Mirek shook his head. 'We know Thrisdane transited from The Wheel and arrived wet in the centre of the Bokos. Given the importance accorded to symmetry, we must assume he transited the lake rift. But this writing contains more than a warning which, were you not exhausted, you would have noticed.'

Ky rubbed his eyes. '*Red mountains rise, red mountains fall, a home for bears and angel Halls* ...' he read hoarsely. 'It sounds like Redice Fold.'

'Indeed it does.'

'Why would Senquar-archae speak of Redice, with its blood-red ice and foul-smelling bears?'

'Because it is also a home to angel Halls. *Be thankful for the fold of ice,*' read Mirek thoughtfully.

'It is a gift from the Great Beyond,' said Ky suddenly. 'To use Redice Fold instead of the lake. But *use* for what?'

'Or to live there rather than Wheel Fold? We have parts of a puzzle that some sought to hide but that Senquar-archae fought to reveal.'

'Thris might know more given his time in The Wheel.'

'If only he were still here,' said Mirek regretfully.

'Ash can tell him. He passed messages from Archaes Kald and Dejon to us before. It's as if he speaks into your head.'

'I see,' said Mirek softly. 'Then I believe he should communicate Senquar-archae's words to Thrisdane as soon as possible. I fear that time is short.'

Thris stepped gingerly from the rift, glad it was the fold's dark cycle. He was in a valley like the one where he and Ky had searched for Viv. He knew he needed to be higher in the fold to see the lake but feared taking to the air. It was how human caste had captured him last time.

He set out on foot and had not gone far when he felt a second rift and was surprised to sense it also exited into the fold. He had not come across such rifts before but it was helpful and he stepped into it. The fold had cycled to light when he exited into trees. Their shelter made him feel safer until he noticed their branches were full of birds.

He grimaced as he stowed his shirt and jacket in his pack and set off upslope. Its steepness told him he was nearer the peak and he toiled on, sensing for rifts as he went. The light ebbed and the birds quieted, which was a relief, but the trees dwindled too and he was considering waiting for the fold's dark cycle, when Ash's voice sounded in his head.

His message of Senquar-archae's words was astonishing. It could mean … Birds thrashed from the nearby branches and then something cannoned into him, he was hurled to the ground, and the cold metal of a blade pressed against his throat.

Chapter 27

Baraghan and the Syld stopped as birds broke from the trees ahead and the Syld gestured urgently for quiet. Viv's heart raced. Then he flicked his fingers in what was obviously a signal and slipped away through the trees. Baraghan gestured her into the lee of a broad trunk, crouched in front and drew his knives, and Viv silently slid off her pack and unbuttoned her jacket.

Nothing happened and she licked her lips, and then she heard people coming their way. Baraghan's muscles bunched but it was the Syld and he dragged a prisoner with him. The man's head was down and he was bound. God in Heaven! It was Thris! She leapt from her hiding place and was to him in an instant.

'I needed him to know friend from foe,' said the Syld, as he cut Thris's bonds.

His face was bruised and there were cuts on his neck and chest. 'You shouldn't have come back,' she said hoarsely.

'I am bound by my pledge to guide you to your mother but that is not the only reason I have returned. Ezam is in danger.'

'What—'

'We need to keep moving,' interrupted the Syld. 'Speak later.'

They went on, the Syld leading and Baraghan bringing up the rear. Horse Zadic came and went, and Viv grew weary, but she did not care. She leaned into Thris as they walked so that his body brushed hers and she breathed in his scent. He might disappear again at any moment and the next time, she had a horrible feeling, it would be forever.

The darkness thickened as Ataghan led them down into a narrow ravine but he needed no light to find his way. He had been fourteen when he had last been here and the tunnels under the detritus bigger. He smiled sourly at the notion and at the desperate bravado of his fourteen-year-old self.

It was icy in the ravine and he cleared a fire site and set a fire, knowing the thick roof of twig- and leaf-fall masked smoke. The elddra sat with the Angellus on the far side of the fire and her gaze on him was like Ithreya's had been on Sehereden.

'The Astraali had him?' asked Baraghan softly as he returned with a load of windfall.

Ataghan nodded. 'And now the mercats have *them*.' Baraghan's eye-brows rose. 'There was an active den nearby,' added Ataghan, as he heated urrut-sa.

Baraghan glanced across the fire. 'They could be seed-brother and sister,' he murmured. Baraghan was right. They shared the same face shape and curly hair, although the Angellus's hair was dark and the elddra's shone like molten metal in the firelight. She had human blood, Ataghan reminded himself, but the Angellus's reappearance was a complication he did not need.

'Why's he here?' asked Baraghan.

Ataghan thought the reason was obvious but he simply filled their mugs. 'We'll let him explain himself after we've eaten,' he said.

Given the mercats, Ataghan kept the fire high as he listened to the Angellus outline the likely water rift between The Wheel and Ezam, their dangerous instability, and the writings that warned of a threat to Ezam should the sacred

209

lake be disturbed. The elddra's pallor told him she had just realised the consequences of what the Astraali would force her to do.

'Do you think the Angellus *were* from Ezam and used the lake rift to return there?' she asked when he had fallen silent.

'We do not know,' said the Angellus. 'Ky found no scrolls that speak of their home fold but Senquar-archae knew of them, so it is possible. Whatever their origins, his writings suggest they went to Redice Fold after they left here.'

'Senquar-archae?'

'A blue angel who appeared in Ezam with Anasdane and Paendane. They disappeared but the scrolls do not speak of them transcending.'

'A threesome, like you, Ash, and Ky,' muttered the elddra and Ataghan saw her dread deepen. 'What do Senquar-archae's writings actually say?'

'*The Wheel the way, The Wheel a knife; the way of water, the way of strife. The rift can give, the rift can take; do not disturb the sacred lake.* That was the first writing discovered. Ky discovered a second one while I was here. *Red mountains rise, red mountains fall, a home for bears and angel Halls. The Great Beyond, a gift is given, the sacred lake must not be riven. The journey in, will still suffice, be thankful for the fold of ice.*'

'Is Redice Fold like Ezam?' asked Baraghan curiously.

The Angellus shook his head. 'It is icy and has a dangerous animal caste of bears. Their fumes are corrosive to angel caste.'

'Not the sort of place the Astraali will clamour to visit,' observed Baraghan dourly.

'Is there a rift to Redice Fold in Astraal?' asked Ataghan.

'I do not know,' said the Angellus. 'Rifts come and go. They can be open for eons, then shut for eons, or open and shut in an instant. But *if* the Host of *this* fold went to Redice Fold, there must have been a rift.'

'*If*,' murmured the elddra.

She looked ready to drop and Baraghan noticed too. 'You need to sleep, Violet Iris Vacia, unless you want your headache back. She suffered an injury on our journey here,' he explained to the Angellus.

The Angellus's concern was immediate and obvious. He gently cradled the elddra's face between his hands and breathed over her. Ataghan knew Angellus breath was healing; Baraghan used it as a surgeon and Ataghan had used it too after the elddra's injury at Esh-telin, but pure Angellus scent was far more potent. Her face regained its colour but also a longing painful in its intensity and she struggled to her feet, took the Angellus's hand, and led him away into the darkness.

The fire cracked as Baraghan added more wood and poked it into position. 'Easy to see the *real* reason Thrisdane en-Ezam returned,' he said, 'but I'm unclear why you're here, Syld. You've shown Violet Iris Vacia nothing but antagonism or was that just a feint to throw me off?'

'Ithreya en-Verra-ril's offered me Sehereden's seed-child but there are conditions.'

Baraghan's breath hissed. 'Which are?'

'Bring the elddra to live in my sett.'

'Stinking Soaich.' Baraghan laughed mirthlessly. 'I rarely feel sorry for you, Ataghan, but this is one such occasion.' He topped up his mug of urrut-sa and took a gulp. 'It's a pity you didn't pretend kindness for her earlier,' he added, and laughed again. 'Although you do have one thing I've never been able to trump, and that's a little girl called Fariye. Violet Iris Vacia will even put up with your company to be near her.' He drained his urrut-sa and eyed Ataghan as he wiped his mouth. 'And what would you have done had Violet Iris Vacia chosen me?'

'Whatever was necessary.' There was a strained silence and Ataghan shrugged. 'As it is, the elddra wants to see if her mother is in Astraal and I offered to guide her.'

'She knew of Ithreya's offer?'

'She does now.'

'And now the magnificent Thrisdane en-Ezam's turned up. Hardly a welcome development for you, eh Syld?'

'The danger extends beyond our personal wants, Baraghan,' said Ataghan, booting an errant coal back into the fire. 'The elddra was always going to be a rich prize for the Astraali but the Angellus exceeds even her worth. He's fresh from the fold they claim by right of inheritance and he knows how to take them there. The elddra is far more valuable to them now too. The Angellus would do anything to save her, and she to save him.'

'It's best they keep clear of the Astraali's stinking walls then.'

'But they won't. You heard what he said. He's bound by a pledge to find her mother and now *his* fold is threatened, I imagine those higher in the Angellus hierarchy direct him too.'

'He won't need much directing if he fears for those in Ezam,' said Baraghan. 'I spoke with his friends Ashdane and Kydane. The three are akin to lein.'

Ataghan surveyed him through narrowed eyes. 'What's your plan, Baraghan? You always have one.'

'That we all turn around and go home now. And a very sensible plan it is too except I never expect sense from *Mad At*, especially when he has a rather pressing reason to stay.' Baraghan's teeth flashed in a smile. 'We'll need to speak to the Council, so subterfuge is pointless. I suggest we roll up at the gate and demand to see them. We'll tell them about Redice, *if* we get the chance, and hopefully either Violet Iris Vacia or Thrisdane en-Ezam will find them a rift and they'll all troop off there. Then we'll explore the empty city at our leisure and enjoy our old haunts.'

'And if they insist on being shown the rift to Ezam?'

'Then I hope our beautiful visitors will talk them out of it. But we won't be there anyway, At.'

'No. They'll separate us as soon as possible. And have you planned for that?'

'I've planned to continue to enjoy my usual good fortune, and your ability to dodge Soaich is legendary, Syld. Together we make a good team.'

Ataghan's mouth twisted. 'Or a dead one.'

Astraal looked like an extremely fancy wedding cake, thought Viv, except the happily-ever-after plastic man and woman on top had been replaced by guards who escorted their little party up a walkway carved into the cake's side. It ascended in a series of steps and terraces that gave a spectacular view of the city.

Soaring arches, domes as delicate as eggshells, and fretwork-rimmed windows; all picked out in white stone. It was not marble, but the duller stuff of the walkway underfoot. Viv stared at the snow-capped peak at the city's back and at the immense aqua lake below. She could see why angels had been drawn here but she sensed no rifts. She just hoped there *was* one, it went to Redice, and it was nearby.

There were lots of people along the walkway, as if festivities were in progress, but given their stares, Viv had a horrible feeling she and Thris were the main attractions. There were few youngsters among the crowd and most of the women were faded versions of Anfarena while the men looked hard and hungry. If her mother *had* stayed here, Viv could not imagine her being happy.

Smaller streets were visible to either side but not nearly as ordered as the grand sweep of the walkway they followed. Given their tangle, she suspected it would be hard to find a way out if she had to make a run for it unless she stayed on the walkway which she guessed would be guarded. She could fly, she supposed, presuming they had no darts.

'Lots of elddra and elddric here to welcome us,' the Syld said softly to her, as they walked. 'You should keep a look out for your mother.'

'My mother was loving. She would not have stayed *here*,' said Viv angrily. She had no idea why the Syld had positioned himself next to her at the gate, and Baraghan next to Thris but they would have their reasons. 'Your movements have been known for some time,' he continued. 'Those with Angellus blood have poured in from the Vales in happy anticipation of joining the glorious Angellus in Ezam.'

'Redice Fold,' corrected Viv, but he was right. The crowd held an air of expectation although the men were clearly antagonistic towards Baraghan and Ataghan.

'They'll lack any interest in going to Redice and it would be wise if you feigned a similar lack of interest

214

in Thrisdane. They'll use your love for him to force your cooperation or his love for you to force his.' Viv swallowed dryly, her gaze on the grand building ahead. Its pillars reminded her of Ezam's Halls. 'Behold, Astraal Hall,' he said, and Viv's tension escalated as she thought of Kald and Dejon's callous ambition.

'The rift to Ezam could kill *every* angel there and a lot of people here,' she muttered as she glanced down at the lake. 'If the water rises, it will flood the lower terraces and some of the higher ones as well.

'I know the Astraali,' he whispered urgently. 'They'll see your refusal to cooperate as a willful denial of the splendours their ancestors now enjoy.' His voice sunk lower. '*Whatever* happens, Ilris, know this: I will *never* abandon you.'

Viv blinked. 'But you'll be with us.'

He subtly shook his head. 'Baraghan and I will be escorted back to the gate *if* we're fortunate. We've prepared as best we can.'

Viv's stomach twisted into a sickening knot and she had wild thoughts of fleeing but they were already at the Hall's steps and then sure enough, as they reached the portico, muscular guards smoothly separated her and Thris. They were marched through the massive doors and she screwed her head back for one last glimpse of the Syld and Baraghan, and then the doors slammed shut behind them.

Ataghan descended the Hall's steps steadily, Baraghan by his side, the guards hard on their heels and then as he reached the street, flicked his fingers, and ran. Their explosive speed took the guards by surprise, but they did not take long to recover or other men to join the chase.

Ataghan let Baraghan lead and they passed three streets to their right before Baraghan threw himself into the fourth. They raced down its narrow way, took a second turning at breakneck speed, and pelted on. The streets became alleyways, and the alleyways rat runs, their pale stone stained with refuse.

Their narrowness reeked of a trap but Baraghan sped on and Ataghan followed until they were confronted by a sheer wall of stone and Baraghan slewed to stop. The pound of feet grew closer, but the wall had a drain at the base. 'Stinking Soaich,' gasped Baraghan. Its heavy metal grate had been bolted shut but they seized it anyway in a vain attempt to wrench it free. 'Who would have thought they would repair the Daen sector?' he panted.

'Still feeling fortunate?' demanded Ataghan, as the first of their pursuers appeared. They were armed with cudgels to keep them out of knife-range, and as they moved in, Ataghan and Baraghan took up position back to back.

'It's all relative, Ataghan,' said Baraghan with a grim smile. 'I'm fortunate to be with you, here at the end.'

Chapter 28

Astraal Hall was even grander inside, its white stone polished to a high gloss, its ceilings cavernous. Built to impress, thought Viv acidly, as they were marched past its soaring columns. Doors were set to either side, their guards' uniforms decorated with silver braid. They would have to be elddric, given their age, but deemed worthy of staying, unlike the Syld and Baraghan. Her heart gave an uncomfortable thud. The punishment for returning would not be a slap on the wrist.

Heavy double doors loomed ahead and she kept her eyes on them, despite yearning to grab Thris's hand and run. The Syld was right; coming to Astraal was a terrible risk, that risked those in Ezam too and she glanced sideways at Thris. He had already been brutalised in The Wheel and she wanted him *anywhere* but here.

Denying her need for him last night had left her with a longing as punishing as pain but she *had* to remove reasons for him to stay. She clutched her amè as they were marched past still more stony-faced guards. It now held one of Thris's feathers along with locks of Fariye and Sehereden's hair and she gritted her teeth as she considered how much more vulnerable Thris was than her.

His angel blood meant he would answer the Astraali honestly but she had learned to dodge and weave, skip key information and paint misleading pictures. She was experienced in dealing with arseholes too and, as the heavy double doors swung open to reveal a room full of Kald and Dejon clones at a gleaming table, she knew exactly what to do.

'I had heard Astraal was a place of courtesy, but two of our party have been dragged away by your guards. Where are they?' she demanded.

A Kald-clone rose from the table's head and bowed. 'I am Archae Thero, Syld of the Council. Welcome to Astraal, Violet Iris Vacia, and welcome also Thrisdane of the Angellus. Please join us.'

He gestured to the table, but Viv refused to budge. 'I'm more interested in our friends' welfare than your welcome.'

'The elddric you refer to were expelled from Astraal some zadicans ago and were not permitted to return.

'You've had them murdered?' Viv managed to keep the anger in her voice despite the sickening drop of her stomach.

Thero's lip curled in disdain. 'We are not the Valen.'

So they were still alive *if* Thero were to be believed but she wondered how dilute the Astraali's *inability* to lie had become. The dozen or so daimon around the table looked pure angel but their looks had probably helped them rise through the ranks, given their contempt for all things Valen.

'Kindly take your seats,' said Thero again. 'We have many things to discuss and there is much anticipation in Astraal as to their outcome.'

Viv sat next to Thris, which gave her the opportunity to kick him under the table, but knowing Thris, he would probably simply politely move his leg. Thero remained standing as he introduced those seated, all of whom were Archae something-or-other, and all of whom had variations of silver or silver-streaked red hair, waves or curls, and dark or light blue eyes. Thero was the only Syld, a title obviously borrowed from the *lowly* Valen.

218

A servant filled silver goblets with a pale liquid, which Viv declined, needing to keep her wits about her, but she accepted several of the delicate biscuits, not knowing where her next meal was coming from. The Syld had carried all the food.

'I will begin by—' began Thero.

'I'm here because I've been Called but I'm also looking for my mother,' interrupted Viv. 'The two things might be related. Her name's Violet Wright, but she might also be known as Lettie. She looks like me. Do you know whether she's in Astraal?'

Viv knew she was rude and hoped that, despite her looks, the Archae would conclude her crassness stemmed from a high dose of Valen blood. 'She is not in Astraal,' said Thero, parading the room with the same arrogant strut as Kald. He just needed to steeple his fingers, thought Viv, and the transformation would be complete.

'How do you know?' she demanded.

'No female in Astraal looks like you. Your appearance is the result of exceptionally high levels of Angellus blood. Tell me of this *Lettie Wright*, Violet Iris Vacia.'

So much for Plan A. 'My mother gave birth to me in a human caste fold called Moonsun,' said Viv, careful to maintain her insolent tone. 'She disappeared when I was ten zadicans. I didn't know I had angel blood until my father, Archae Kald, turned up in Moonsun and told me. I left Moonsun to find her.'

'And your father was an Angellus from Ezam Fold?' he asked, pausing behind her.

'My father *is* an angel from Ezam Fold,' said Viv, keen to divert Thero from her mother. Lettie was just a run of the mill human caste woman who could not have produced an almost angelic daughter, especially one with *wings*.

'You went to Ezam to search for your mother?'

He was still behind her and Viv willed him to move. 'To *start* the search for my mother. My father appointed Thrisdane as my guide.'

'Why?'

He had strutted on, thankfully. 'Seeding daimon is frowned upon in Ezam. By reuniting me with my mother, my father would cancel out his bad deed.'

'Why did you come to The Wheel? Did you know of us and believe your mother was here?' Thero's glance included Thris in the question, but Viv jumped in before Thris could answer.

'I arrived here by accident. Transiting rifts is *extremely* dangerous and I got separated from my guide. Before that, we travelled with another angel who was *badly* hurt by *savage* creatures and Thris had to take him back to Ezam.'

'So you know how to find and transit rifts, Violet Iris Vacia?'

Viv's heart migrated to her throat. 'After a fashion. It's very hard to know where they lead. I arrived here after nearly suffocating in a fold full of sand.'

Thero's pale eyes swung to Thris. 'And you, Thrisdane? The purity of your Angellus blood surely makes you a skilled rift traveller?'

'I am an *angel,* Archae, but I am more experienced than Viv. Even so, many of our transits have gone amiss.'

'And why are *you* in The Wheel?'

'I am bound by my pledge to guide Viv to her mother but I must also ensure that Ezam and The Wheel remain safe.'

'*The Wheel* remains safe?'

'There are more senior angels in Ezam who believe a rift connects The Wheel to Ezam and that the rift passes through the sacred lake. Water rifts are rare, often unstable, and dangerous to use.'

There was a burst of conversation from the rest of the gathering that the *Syld* had trouble stilling. 'What evidence is there for your claim?' he asked when he was able.

'I was held by the Valen for a time, and while I have no memory of my escape, I was found in the centre of Ezam soaking wet.'

'Hardly evidence,' a curly-haired Archae scoffed.

Thero gestured for quiet. 'Patience, Meresh. Is there *further* evidence of this rift, Thrisdane?'

'There is a vast store of scrolls in Ezam which contain the writings of angels who have transcended. Two of the scrolls warn of the danger. The first reads thus: *The Wheel the way, the Wheel a knife; the way of water, the way of strife. The rift can give, the rift can take; do not disturb the sacred lake.* And the second: *Red mountains rise, red mountains fall, a home for bears and angel halls. The Great Beyond, a gift is given, the sacred lake must not be riven. The journey in, will still suffice, be thankful for the fold of ice.*'

Again the silence gave way to a torrent of speech and Viv glanced at Thris. He looked calm but angels were not skilled at reading human or *half-human* emotions. The Archae were actually excited rather than fearful, and Viv's hands clenched under the table.

Again Thero had to wait for the noise to ebb before he spoke. 'Do you know the author of these writings, Thrisdane?'

'We believe it to the angel Senquar-archae.'

'By *we*, you mean the more senior angels of Ezam?' Thris nodded. 'And are all Senquar-archae's writings so obscure?'

'We believe he wrote so to ensure his warnings endured. Ezam houses its angel lore in a circular hall called the Bokos. It contains uncounted scrolls, but the central part is empty. We believe the scrolls that referred to the rift were removed to prevent the rift being used.'

Another murmur rippled through the assembly but Thero spoke over it. 'Our store of Angellus lore is also empty. The Angellus took the scrolls with them when they departed.'

'Probably for the same reason,' broke in Viv. 'I've seen the lake here. If it were to empty into Ezam, it would destroy it.'

Thero paused in his stroll and his shrewd gaze swung to her. 'A rift is not a purely *physical* pathway, Violet Iris Vacia, as I am sure you know.'

'There is a fear it might become so,' said Thris. 'The writings tell us Senquar-archae was blue, and one of three angels who appeared in Ezam simultaneously eons ago. I appeared with two other angels also, one of whom is blue. There are no writings that tell of Senquar-archae or the other angels' transcendence, which is unusual. But we do have the warnings I have shared with you.'

'A *blue* angel? That would be a strange sight indeed,' said Thero and those at the table tittered. 'You obviously believe we repeat the circumstances of the first three angels' demise, but the Angellus were not given to belief in the fanciful, and neither are we. The writings you quote might contain warnings, but we know nothing of their veracity. Senquar-archae's writings might have been removed because he suffered from a mental affliction.

'However, what they do suggest is a rift between The Wheel and Ezam, and despite the subtle change in name from Angellus to *angel*, I believe the Angellus came from

Ezam and returned there. The rift in Lake Astraal will allow us to follow them, under your guidance of course.'

'It's too dangerous!' cried Viv in panic. Thero had stopped behind her again and she had to screw her head around.

'The Council will depart first and are few in number as you see,' said Thero, gesturing to those at the table. '*If* there is a danger of disturbance, the effect of our passing should be small. Those of lesser Angellus blood will follow.' And so suffer any *fatal* consequences, thought Viv grimly.

'The risk is too great,' said Thris slowly.

'Risk is comparative, Thrisdane,' said Thero and with a lightning speed, seized Viv by the hair, jerked her head back, and brought a knife to her throat.

'Let him kill me,' gasped Viv, horribly aware of the blade against her skin. 'You can't risk all of Ezam *or* those here!'

Thris's face was agonised. 'I am pledged to protect you,' he cried.

Thero released her and strolled on, as if nothing had happened, and Viv felt her throat, surprised she was uninjured. 'We are not the Valen,' said Thero contemptuously. 'It was simply a little demonstration of our *determination* to leave.

'Violet Iris Vacia will remain in Astraal and be released once we have safely transited. She can follow or not, as she chooses. There will be few left in Astraal to keep her company, but some elddric will remain whose baser blood she might find appealing, although I suspect not as appealing as yours, Thrisdane.'

He nodded to the door guards and they strode to where Viv and Thris were seated. 'You will be accommodated separately, so I regret you will not have time to say your goodbyes. I trust the separation will be brief. We will depart at dawn to give those of lesser blood time to prepare, but it is also when the sacred lake is at its most glorious.' He smiled coldly. 'It will be a fitting time to farewell it.'

Chapter 29

Ataghan? Ataghan? Stinking Soaich. You've slept long enough. Come back to me, Syld.' The gravelly voice came from afar and Ataghan opened his eyes, or at least one eye, the other was glued shut. His head thudded in a sickening rhythm and there was not a part of him that did not hurt. He groaned and spat blood from his mouth. 'Not a pleasant wakening, is it?' said Baraghan hoarsely. 'Drink this. You'll have to hold it till I get my arm working again.'

Ataghan fumbled the flask to his mouth and gulped down the hareesh. It brought the feeling back to his body in bursts of jagged pain, and he panted as he squinted around.

'We're in trees, about ten lengths from the wall, which is as far as I could drag you. Didn't want to stay where any passing Astraali might be tempted to finish us off. Our cudgel-wielding friends dumped us like refuse outside the gate *and* our packs. Generous of them, really.' Ataghan groped for his missing knives. 'They weren't *that* generous, Syld.' Baraghan coughed. 'All in all, we've been fortunate.'

Ataghan heaved himself into a sitting position. The bracelet he had traded in Esh-accom had gone, but that was the least of his problems. Baraghan was half-propped against a tree, his eyes blackened, his lips split. There was an egg-shaped swelling on his brow, and one arm was limp.

'Not a pretty sight,' he croaked, 'and you're no better. Although, I tell a lie, unusual for an elddric.' He laughed harshly and coughed again. 'You escaped broken bones, at least. I need help to sort my arm.'

225

'I'm no surgeon,' said Ataghan. The trees spun as he fought waves of nausea.

'No need to be,' croaked Baraghan. 'I need your elddric breath, lots of lovely pain-dulling, strength-building, elddric breath. I'll do the rest. I need it *now*, Syld. I've used mine to help you wake.'

Ataghan half-crawled to him. 'Tell me what to do.'

'Help me off with my jacket and shirt.' Ataghan did as he was bid, then rolled up the shirt to serve as a sling for Baraghan's arm. 'You missed your calling,' muttered Baraghan, with a ghastly smile.

'What next?'

'Deep breathe directly into my mouth. Keep it up till I tell you to stop. I need your strength to build mine. I don't need to see a break to mend it, but I need to keep the pain at bay.'

Ataghan knelt beside him, placed his mouth over Baraghan's and emptied his breath into Baraghan's lungs, careful to keep rhythm with Baraghan's breathing. He closed his eyes to avoid seeing what Baraghan did; the crunch of bones was bad enough.

Baraghan's breath bathed Ataghan too and his pain ebbed enough to think. It was dim under the trees which meant he had been unconscious most of the day. He had not suffered a beating like that since he had left, but revenge was not uppermost in his mind.

The Astraali would have come to a decision by now and given how long they had waited to follow their *majestic* fathers, he knew what it would be. He also had a pretty good idea what threats they had used to ensure their decision was implemented.

'Enough,' gasped Baraghan, and Ataghan sank back on his haunches. 'Always good to have your bones where they should be.'

'Shall I splint it?'

Baraghan nodded. 'We'll make a surgeon of you yet.' Ataghan used a bandage from Baraghan's kit and the straight pieces of windfall he could reach without crawling, and carefully splinted the arm. 'Now we rest until after Horse Zadic, then go back in.'

'There's no reason for you to come.'

'There's plenty of reasons,' said Baraghan. 'I know where the knife stash is.' Ataghan looked at him. 'I was older than you when they threw me out, remember. I had longer to prepare for my return.'

'Like using the drain in Daen sector,' said Ataghan sourly.

'Let's not dwell on the past, Syld.'

'You're in no state to run and fight, Baraghan. I'll retrieve the elddra and get out fast. The Angellus will have to look after himself.'

'Retrieve the *elddra*? Why do you have such trouble saying her name?' Ataghan shrugged then regretted it as pain speared through his shoulders. 'If you want her at your sett, I suggest you get accustomed to her name. Perhaps admitting she isn't the same as the stinking Astraali would help.'

'I don't need your advice.'

'I think you do, but I'll desist. Rest while you can, Ataghan.'

Viv stared down as Horse Zadic turned the sacred lake to liquid silver, but the cold light also made the city's stone look more like a graveyard than a wedding cake. She had expected to be hurled into a dungeon, complete with wall-chains, but the guard had marched her up countless steps at the back of the Hall to a plushly appointed eyrie which gave her an excellent view over the water.

It was still a prison cell, with bars on the window to prove it, and no window-lock she could find. She clambered onto a chair for a more thorough inspection and swore. The bars were set into the stone. They might be there to stop people falling out, but it seemed more likely the Astraali had imprisoned their *guests* before.

'Pack of arseholes,' she muttered but was too full of dread to conjure hatred. They would force Thris into the rift with them, and if it tore, he would drown with them too. And their deaths might be just the start. As well as the risk to Ezam, the lake could send great waves of water surging down the Vales.

She faltered as she thought of Poss at the Scinta-ril but the sett would likely be safe, as would Gothral's on the Kama-ril, and Amethen's on the Verra-ril because rills were high in the smaller vals. It were the settlements like Esh-accom on the Eshacade and those on the main rivers in the other Vales that would be destroyed.

Thero had insisted rifts were not physical things, and they were not *normally*, but water rifts were a different beast altogether. And *if* water rifts were safe, Senquar-archae would not have gone to such lengths to leave his warnings behind.

Viv pressed her face against the bars and peered down. There was a lot of activity around the lake, the small shapes of men, women, and children milling about as they prepared to go to their wonderful new home of Ezam *or* to their deaths.

Get ya arse into gear, Vivi. Ya not a thief for nuthin'.
The window was not an option and there was no man-hole
or fireplace in the room, which left the door. The problem
was the guard who patrolled outside. She pressed her ear
against the wood and listened to his steps recede then
grow nearer. She had about a ten-pace interval to pick the
lock and she had it picked in seven, using the broken owl
charm.

It was the easiest lock she had ever picked but not
the easiest room to get out of, given the guard. He would
be elddric and want to catch the rift out too, but his
replacement might be less interested in leaving, given he
was to be stuck here with her. It meant he would probably
be older and slower, or so she hoped. If not, it would be
time to fly.

To do what, Vivi? 'I have no effing idea, Rim,' she
muttered, 'but I'm sure as hell not sitting here on my
backside while Thris drowns.'

Ataghan flexed his favoured throwing hand, then the
other hand, squatted several times and sprang upright.
Everything hurt and it had been agony crawling through
the tunnels, but they had finally reached a disused storage
turret and he could stand. Baraghan's elddric breath, his
own elddric blood and snatched sleep, had healed the
worst of it, but having knives again was the best balm.
They were in perfect condition, despite having spent
thirteen zadicans wrapped in oiled leather, and wedged in
a rat run under the city.

Baraghan's foresight had been admirable, but he
had always planned to return, whereas Ataghan had
sworn never to set foot in the stinking place again. 'This

would be a fine city without its present inhabitants,' muttered Baraghan, as he peered out through a chink in the stone. 'Hard to see much now Horse Zadic's done, but lots of Astraali hurrying about carrying their *precious* possessions.'

'Preparing to leave,' said Ataghan shortly. 'I need to see where the Council will leave from to check whether they have the elddra with them or the Angellus, or both.'

'They'll take Thrisdane,' said Baraghan, glancing back. 'They'll have more trust in his rift skills and they'll hold Violet Iris Vacia somewhere as a nice little guarantee of his cooperation. I'm guessing they'll use the pleasure barges popular in the warmer zadics, given the numbers leaving. The barges dock at wharves just sunwise of the Hall.'

'Can we get there from here?'

'I hadn't *planned* to but we can probably get closer than this if the runs haven't fallen in, or been blocked, or have shiny new grates.' Baraghan smiled humourlessly. 'There are hatches we can use though and I suspect most of Astraal's citizens will be more interested in joining their venerable forebears than beating us up again.'

'We hope,' muttered Ataghan.

Thris's fear escalated as he watched the shore recede. Daimon caste rowers propelled the craft towards the lake's centre, carrying the Archae he had met last night, and other craft followed, crowded with daimon caste of all ages. He stared up at the Halls and sensed for Viv but felt nothing, unlike the faint resonance that rose from the water around him.

The snow-capped peak soared behind the city, gilded by the new sun, its glorious image reflected on the lake's still surface. Archae Thero had said the lake's crystal depths fed eight mighty rivers and Thris peered down. The water was clear but so deep, he could see no bed.

His thoughts went to Ky labouring in the Bokos, to Ash in the Blue Helixai's heart, and to the uncounted angels, Dane and Archae, who lived their lives under Ezam's gentle skies. And he thought of Viv, a prisoner like he was, of those who cared only of themselves.

'Do you feel anything, Thrisdane?' demanded Archae Thero, coming to his side.

Thris chiefly felt dread but it was not what the Archae wanted to know. 'There is a fine vibration which tells of a rift, but rifts can only be transited at their very centre.'

'Then find it, Thrisdane.'

An excited mutter broke out among the waiting Archae but Thris kept his focus on the rift. 'Stop here,' he said as the vibration intensified. The rowers worked the oars expertly to keep the craft in place and Thris concentrated on the vibration. Given what he had learned since his return to Ezam, it was likely he had transited to the Bokos from this very place, but he had no memory of it.

'Is it the rift that takes us to Ezam, Thrisdane?' demanded Theros.

'No angel can be absolutely certain where a rift will exit.'

'Wait,' ordered the Archae, and briefly conferred with the Councilors. 'You will lead, Thrisdane,' he said, coming back. 'Once the Council have entered safely, I have instructed those of lesser Angellus blood to follow.'

'The rift is perilous, Archae. I ask that—'

The Archae's pale eyes flashed in the early morning light. 'You *will* lead, Thrisdane.'

Thris stepped from the craft into the rift. The iridescent walls swirled past him as usual and he was aware of the Archae strung out behind him and then, without warning, he was pitched sideways.

He managed to regain his balance but as he struggled to make sense of what had happened, the rift whipped again and he was hit by a blast of icy air and a stench so foul it brought him to his knees. The rift creaked and groaned around him, and he was horrified to discover he was alone, and then terror overtook him. He should have exited the rift by now!

Ash jerked upright as the vision of Thris faded and became aware that the Blue Helixai's sweet music had gone too, and that in its place was a beat he had never heard before. He slid from the slab and stared down in confusion as the sound echoed up through his soles, then hastened back down the tunnel to one of the opaque pools. Its surface rippled as if disturbed at regular intervals and then Ash realised what the beat was.

He sprinted to the cavern's mouth, took to the air, and sped to the Bokos The beat was thunderous there, as if the Bokos's curved walls prevented the sound's escape, and Ashdane dashed down the dim passageways to where Prime-archae Serith sat, his gaze on the sight beyond the window.

He turned and Ash hurriedly bowed and palmed. 'Kydane is at the Bokos's heart with Prime-archae Mirek,' the Prime-archae murmured, 'but what lies ahead is not the work of a Prime-archae *or* of a single angel.'

232

Ash flew, his wing-span a perfect fit for the space between the shelves, and when he saw the shadowy outlines of Prime-archae Mirek and Ky ahead, landed with a splash, shocked to find himself ankle deep in icy water!

'Ash!' cried Ky, in relief.

'I fear the rift is breached,' said Mirek as he peered up. Immense drops of water fell from the darkness above and reverberated as they joined the water on the Bokos's floor. 'It is what Senquar-archae warned us of.'

Ash followed his gaze. 'Thris is trapped there,' he panted and Ky gave an anguished cry. 'We must go to him!'

'Disturb the rift further and it might rupture,' warned Mirek. 'Ezam could be destroyed.'

'I will not abandon him,' said Ky shrilly. 'I will go alone if needs be.'

'What lies ahead is not the work of a single angel,' said Ash tremulously as understanding dawned. 'With respect, Prime-archae Mirek, you must plan for Ezam's inundation. Tell the Host to seek the Thorny Mountains or Helixai.' The Prime-archae hurried away and Ash peered up again. 'Those who disturbed the rift have gone.'

'Gone where?' demanded Ky wildly.

'Red mountains rise, red mountains fall, a home for bears and angel Halls.'

'Redice Fold! But Thris would not have shown them a rift …'

'They forced him to,' said Ash and gripped Ky's arms. 'They used love as a weapon against him,' he said urgently, 'but we can use it to heal the rift!'

'But how?' cried Ky.

'Senquar-archae, Anasdane and Paendane did it before and Senquar-archae left warnings behind.'

'*Behind* from where?' Ky all but shrieked. 'You found Senquar-archae's bones in the Green Helixai.' Ky took a shuddering breath. 'I do not want to end like that, Ash.'

'He did not end there, Ky. Had *you* visited the Green Helixai, you would have seen something different, something that *you* needed to see. The Green Helixai reminded me we are of flesh too, not just of ether; that love is not reserved for the Great Beyond but given freely *to* each other, and *for* each other.'

Ky calmed but his eyes were wide with fear. 'You will stay with me, Ash?'

'Always,' whispered Ash. They embraced and then together leapt up into the darkness.

Chapter 30

Viv watched the first barge empty, followed by the second, and the third. Thris was gone, but at least he was safe, and her *beloved* father was about to have his peace and quiet well and truly disrupted. Astraal's remaining citizens watched too, scattered in small groups along the terraces that rimmed the lake. Not many had chosen to stay, despite the city's beauty, and Astraal *was* beautiful, with its fine decorative buildings, snow-capped peak, and perfect lake.

Time to go, she decided. She reached for her pack, glanced back down at the lake, and gasped. The waters had darkened and she stared skywards, expecting storm clouds to have rolled in but the sky was clear. And then the lake's surface began to roil, throwing up white-capped waves that grew with lightning speed to mighty crests. The barges were tossed about like leaves, and spectators fled as water surged over the lower terraces. Water-spouts danced, spattering the window-glass of her prison with foam, and then Viv's breath emptied.

There was something in the water! A wing flapped like an injured bird and she flung open the door and ran. The guard yelled but there was no sound of pursuit as if he had suddenly discovered the mayhem that unfolded below. Viv wrenched off her pack and jacket as she took the stairs two at a time and when she burst from the building, tore off her boots and launched skywards.

Ataghan shouted as the elddra burst from the Halls and took to the air but she gave no sign of having heard him.

He sheltered with Baraghan under a portico as water was whipped from the lake and hurled back as hard as gravel. The storm belonged to Soaich and touched nothing but the lake

'She has wings,' gasped Baraghan. 'That's a surprise, at least to me.' Ataghan said nothing, his attention on the elddra as she wove between the water-spouts. Her wings flashed like metal as they caught the sun, but then she swooped low, oblivious to the clash waves. There was someone in the water and he yanked off his jacket, then his shirt and boots. 'You're not going in after her, are you?' cried Baraghan in alarm.

Ataghan dashed the rain from his eyes. The squalls dulled her wings, but he saw her struggle to lift someone, and then waves soared skywards, clashed in an explosion of glass-grey water, and she was gone.

Ataghan ran and Baraghan cursed and ran too, towards the wharves where there might be rope. Ataghan plunged into the lake and ploughed through the icy water. Waves broke over him, blinded him, dragged him back, tried to drag him under. He focused on where the lake had taken her, reached the spot, and dived.

She was a long way down and perilously close to a translucent maelstrom. His brain screamed at him to turn back to the world above, to flee the twisting column that threatened to devour him, but he forced himself on, caught her wrist, and dragged her back to the surface.

Her violet eyes were stark against her white skin, her gasps for air punctuated by sobs for the Angellus, and she struggled in his grip as she tried to dive again. He only had one weapon and he used it. 'Ilris! Fariye needs you! Stay with me!' Waves buffeted them, and squalls slashed like whips. 'Ilris!' He shook her. 'Fariye needs you!'

Her eyes focused on him, filled with despair, but he knew he had her, and struck out for shore, keeping a grip on her hand. She swam too but it was exhausting, the waves battering them and the fume starving them of air. And then, when he could go no further, a rope slapped onto the water beside him, he gripped it, and Baraghan hauled them in.

As soon as he could stand, Ataghan swung her into his arms, staggered up the steps, and collapsed in the portico's shelter. She had curled into him, face buried in his chest, as if she could bear the world no longer, and he tightened his arms around her. 'Ilris,' he said, and kissed the top of her head, uncaring that Baraghan saw, then rested back against a pillar and closed his eyes.

Ash gripped Ky's hand as the rift flung them from side to side. Rifts were silent, but this one roared and its sides billowed like a monstrous creature that sucked air from around it, then spat it back.

'We are going to drown!' screamed Ky above the racket.

Ash feared he was right and then Ky shrieked as the rift wall split. Water gushed in, but the rent sealed again and Thris lay gasping on the floor. He blinked up at them in shock and they cried with joy as they hauled him into their arms. The rift's violence lessened and as the roar dimmed, a calmness settled over Ash. He knew what they must do now but had neither the time nor the words to explain it.

'Hold to me,' he whispered instead, and they pressed against each other chest to chest, arms entwined, white-flecked pale gold and black wings enfolded by Ash's white wings of transcendence.

'The trinity,' murmured Ky, calm suddenly.

'The love of three friends,' said Thris simply.

'The one,' said Ash, 'with the strength of three to mend the breach.'

Together they pushed their love outwards, a potent mix of angel essence, spirit, and physical strength. They used their sweet angel breath to succour each other, but the strain was enormous and Ky the first to fail. Ash and Thris knew the moment his heart had stopped but neither faltered and the rift began to mend. Ash knew when Thris's heart fell silent too, and he cradled him as he cradled Ky, his arms under their shoulders as they fell away with wings like drifts of snow. And it was Ash alone who felt the last rainbow threads knit, and the rift become whole again.

Viv heard the sudden silence and turned her head. The lake was perfectly still with only the drenched terraces to hint at the tempest they had endured. The Syld's arms held her enclosed and Baraghan sat beside him but nobody spoke as they stared at the lake.

A ripple woke at its centre and slid in an expanding silver circle to the shore. Then a second ripple followed as a turquoise angel rose slowly from the lake, his brilliant white wings out-stretched but motionless. He cradled an angel to either side, one black-haired, one bronze-haired, both snow-winged. Thris and Ky, and even from a distance, Viv knew that they were dead.

The turquoise angel hung above the lake, his companions to either side, and then there was an explosion of stars so brilliant Viv threw up her hand against the glare. The Syld and Baraghan did too, and when she looked again, the angels had gone.

She struggled upright, her gaze on the empty water, but her legs buckled, and only the Syld's quick reaction stopped her hitting the stone. He kept his arm around her, but she shivered violently, as did he.

'Get her some dry clothes and yourself, Ataghan,' ordered Baraghan. 'And food would be good too. I image there's plenty of it lying around in Astraal Hall. I don't want to have to heal you two when I've a new home to explore,' he added with a grin. The Syld was with her as she collected her pack and cast-off clothes but she was scarcely aware of him. All she knew was that the world was empty of Thris and that she was empty too. She stepped into one of the Hall's deserted rooms and slowly replaced her wet clothes with dry ones.

The Syld waited for her when she emerged, his face purple with bruising and gashed above one eye, and she wondered why she had not noticed before. 'Feeling warmer?' he asked. 'I've found us some food. Best eat theirs and save ours for the journey back.'

'I hate them.'

'They've gone now or most of them,' he said evenly. 'And we should go too. Come and eat. Fariye's waited long enough to see you.' They settled on the Hall's steps but she was too numb to feel anything, even joy at the prospect of seeing Poss again.

Baraghan found them there as they finished their meal. He had been beaten too, she saw, and wore his arm in a sling. 'Sure you don't want to join me, Syld?' he asked. 'Plenty of opportunities here,' he added as he gazed about. Astraali had started to emerge from their compounds, many of them grey-haired, but Baraghan's head swiveled as a young auburn-haired woman hurried past.

'I have a home to go to,' said the Syld rising.

They embraced and Baraghan bowed formally to Viv. 'Farewell Violet Iris Vacia, until we meet again. You'll always be most welcome to visit.'

Viv nodded but it was beyond her to dredge up a smile. The Syld took her hand as they started down the steps, because he said she was *unsteady*, but she still felt nothing. Thris had transcended with Ky and Ash, which was what he had yearned for, what *every* angel yearned for, but what were stars? Just jagged pieces of fire, cold and remote. She wanted Thris's warmth, and smile, and scent; the feel of his arms, the sense of his strong heartbeat.

No one guarded the gate but she was glad to get through it and into the trees and sensed the Syld was too. 'We'll set camp early while it's still light,' he said. 'There's a good site close to the detritus tunnels. Then we need to decide whether to take the long or short route back to the Scinta-ril.' He still held her hand, his touch the only thing that stopped her sliding into the abyss inside. Enesha had told her to stay with the living but Thris had gone and she wanted to follow.

The camp site was hidden among the branches of a huge tree that had toppled but continued to grow. The Syld called it a *koachar*, and set a fire where its leafy branches arched over them to form a living hall. It reminded her of Erath Fold, of Syatha and Essera, but their love seemed lost to her too.

The Syld heated urrut-sa, and sliced cheese onto chunks of retsen for her, and Viv nodded her thanks. Speaking was beyond her as if the abyss inside had eaten her voice along with everything else. The Syld seemed content to eat in silence too and afterwards, to pack away the food and pitch the maark. She watched the fire burn low and knew when Horse Zadic lit the sky but did not look up.

240

'Ilris?' He was crouched in front and she started. 'Time to sleep.'

She nodded and went into the maark. He had set her sleeping-cover like last time, separated from his, and she sat on it and pulled off her boots. He followed her in, the fire's gentle light bathing him as he removed his jacket and shirt, then his boots.

He flipped the cover over himself and glanced across. 'Aren't you going to lie down?' The firelight lit the planes of his face: Rim and Sehereden's, men she had loved, and she looked away. 'I'm sorry about Thrisdane,' he said.

'It was what he wanted.'

'And what do you want, Ilris?' he asked gently.

'To listen to your heart; to know you're not dead too.' She kept her eyes on the cover, knowing how ridiculous it sounded.

He shuffled over. 'Listen away,' he said quietly. 'I'm well and truly alive.'

She lowered her head until her ear rested against his chest. His heartbeat was strong and even, his skin subtly sweet, and she lay her hand against his chest and felt its warmth. She wanted life suddenly, not death, and brought her mouth to his. He did not recoil but nor did he return the kiss.

'This is not a good time for you, Ilris. You need comfort, not—'

It was what Sehereden had once said and the rejection was the same, a knife-slash as rejection always was. 'It's not about that though, is it, Syld?' she retorted. 'You won't gift me what you gifted half the women in Esh-accom, because I'm a stinking elddra!' She scrambled from the maark and would have strode off if she'd had her boots. He burst from the maark behind her, still naked to the waist, and barefoot too. 'I'm still here, Syld,' she sneered. 'I haven't ruined your deal with Ithreya *yet*.'

He came right up to her, his face clothed in its familiar anger. 'I've wanted you a long time, Ilris, and *never* so much as now. Do you think the women who gift themselves to the *tournament champion* compare to you in *any* way at all? To your beauty? To your trueness of heart? To your selflessness in keeping my daughter alive, not once but twice?' Heat pulsed from his skin and he prowled around the fire and stopped on the other side. 'You don't know what you mean to me,' he said hoarsely. 'How much I *never* want to hurt you again. I have to be *sure* this is something you want and not just the result of seeing the Angellus you loved die today.'

Viv stared at him, too shocked to say anything. The firelight revealed the bruises that blackened his ribs and the gouge marks on his back. 'I need you,' she said thickly, 'but you might be in too much pain.'

'Elddric heal quickly.'

On the *outside* maybe, she thought, then realised it was the first time he had admitted what he was. He came back around the fire, his intensity making her heart race, and stopped in front of her, very close. His eyes caught the firelight as he smoothed the hair from her face and the backs of his fingers continued down her cheek to her neck. Viv sighed as he repeated the gesture, his fingers lingering on her ear lobes this time before stroking her neck.

He lowered his head but did not kiss her, bathing her in his breath made subtly sweet, like his skin, by his elddric blood. She ran her fingers down the ridged muscles of his torso as she savoured the sense of him and caressed the curls that thickened in a line to his groin. She craved his mouth, but he held her close as his hands slid under her jacket to circle the skin over her wing-roots and send exquisite pulses of heat deep into her body.

She wondered whether he sensed her wings' sensitivity to touch or whether the caress had been accidental, then he swung her into his arms, ducked back into the maark, and deposited her on his sleep-cover.

He lay beside her and his lips brushed hers, moved to her ear lobes again, then left an exquisite trail across her cheek while he expertly flicked open the buttons of her jacket, unknotted her shirt and eased both off. She was naked to the waist now, like him, and he paused. 'You are perfection,' he murmured.

Viv caught his face to hers, hungry for his mouth, and as the kiss deepened, clung to him, wanting him there and then. She tugged at his trousers and he smiled, as he slid her out of hers.

'I want you *now,*' she cried in frustration.

'Then you shall have me now,' he said softly, removed the rest of his clothing, and entered her. The release was exquisite and the darkness inside her ebbed but he had put her needs before his, as Sehereden had.

'You didn't ...' she stopped, not knowing the term for male *satisfaction.*

'I didn't what?' he asked, his playful tone telling her he knew exactly what she meant. His kisses prevented further speech and her skin fired under his touch again till her need of him was unbearable, and this time he ensured her ecstatic rush of pleasure was matched by his own.

Chapter 31

He did not sleep afterwards but nor did he speak. The men she had been with would roll over after sex and ignore her, and Sehereden, for all his considerateness as a lover, had quit the bed soon afterwards too. There had been no time to simply be with Thris either, not without Ky's glare.

What ya expect, Vivi? A heart to heart with the man who's hated ya since day one? The Syld's fingers played through her curls as she lay in the crook of his shoulder, but he stared at the maark's ceiling, and she felt increasingly unsure of him. No man refused sex, she reminded herself, which was exactly what she had offered him. And then there was his deal with Ithreya. The Syld's new civility was understandable given getting his hands on Sehereden's child depended on her staying at the Scinta-ril. He might even see satisfying her sexual needs as an incentive for her to stay but she wanted more than that.

She extricated herself and went back to her own sleep-cover. He watched her but still did not speak, and she flipped the cover over herself and curled up facing the maark wall. She might get her happily-ever-after with Poss, but for the first time, she wondered whether it was going to be enough.

The Syld was already at the fire when she emerged the next morning, despite it still being dark. He had heated urrut-sa and she sipped it as he toasted retsen. There was no tenderness in his face, so Viv assumed the last night's activities were not to be mentioned. Nothing new in that, she concluded cynically.

'Longer route in the light to the Scinta-ril or shorter route in the dark?' he asked.

Good morning to you too. thought Viv sourly. 'Neither, if I can find a rift.'

'I thought it was hard to tell where they went.'

Viv shrugged. 'Not as hard as I led the Astraali to believe and not as hard since my time in the Iahhel's company. The Wheel has rifts that exit *within* the fold which is convenient. It would save a hell of a lot of time to use one.'

'Not if we end up somewhere else.'

'I won't enter a rift I'm not sure of,' she said tersely. 'Besides, I'm sick of wondering if there's a knifeman behind every tree.'

The Syld's brows lowered. 'You doubt my ability to protect you?'

'I didn't mean it like that,' she said in exasperation. 'I thought you wanted to get back to the Scinta-ril as soon as possible. I certainly do so I can see Poss again,' she added.

They set off upslope, the Syld agreeing to visit nearby caves, which turned out to be rift-less, and when she finally sensed a rift, it was under some trees. 'I'm pretty sure it exits in the Leferen,' she said. 'Enda must be smiling on me.'

'Enda and Soaich are gods of *this* fold. What gods inhabit Moonsun?'

'Various ones.'

'And which do you look to for protection?'

Jimmy Wright had been a lapsed Catholic but she could not remember Lettie being anything. 'None. I don't believe in gods. If there were gods there would be no rapes or massacres or children living in fear.' Her throat tightened and she stared at the surrounding trees. 'I'm taking this rift, Syld. I want to visit the Lefer again.'

'Why?'

'One of them was kind to me.' His face still showed nothing and she wondered how long it had taken to learn to hide his feelings so completely. She forced a smile. 'You don't need to come. I'm used to travelling alone. I'll meet you at the Scinta-ril.'

'We travel together.'

'Then it's the rift,' snapped Viv, wishing she had the ability to hide her feelings too. 'You don't have any sensation of movement while you're transiting but don't be surprised if I fall on my face at the other end. It's my usual exit.'

'I won't let you fall.'

And he did not, which was pretty skilful given it was his first transit. The rift terminated where Viv had first entered The Wheel and it was just before dawn, which meant her timing was good too.

'The Lefer bring their dead here,' said the Syld, his gaze on the pods. 'It's a work of many days to weave the pods with their beaks, but they don't seem to care that they fall to the forest floor and are eaten by maragh.'

It made sense the rift was here then, thought Viv, given the dead kept rifts open. 'I want to get off the ground,' she said. 'I got chased by a maragh last time and climbed that tree. It was where I met the blue-crested Lefer, so maybe it will come back.'

He nodded. 'You go first in case you slip.'

She had not bloody well slipped last time, and she had been concussed *and* pursued by a pig-bear, but she wanted to avoid an argument. She climbed steadily to the last of the broad branches and settled with her back against the bole. 'I'm not going higher,' she said. 'The trees are brittle.'

He nodded. 'They give the Lefer some protection from wood-cutters and hunters,' he said, as he settled on a branch beside her. 'What makes you think the blue-crested Lefer will be here?'

'Nothing.'

'How long do you want to wait?'

He was obviously keen to get to the Scinta-ril and if Viv had been alone, she would have lingered a couple of days. 'I want to hear the dawn chorus again.' The Syld looked at her blankly. 'It's when the Lefer sing at sunrise,' she explained. 'Moonsun's birds sing the same way and if you're in the mountains, it's the most beautiful sound in the world. My mother used to take me, very early in the morning, and we would sit and listen, even if it rained.' She took a steadying breath. 'The Wheel's mountains, vals, and rills are very similar.'

'You'll like my sett then. It's high on the Scinta Rill.'

'I know, I saw it. But it was burned and I was running.' She stopped as her throat closed over again. *For God's sake, Vivi, get a grip.*

'It's been rebuilt and you're no longer running.'

'I—' she began, but at that moment, an explosion of birdsong heralded the dawn, and neither of them spoke as the bells and drumbeats of birdcalls built to a crescendo and then settled into a gentler wash of chirrups and fluting calls. And then, right on cue, a blue-crested Lefer crashed through the canopy and settled on the branch above.

'Is that the one?' asked the Syld softly, drawing his knife as the Lefer hopped closer.

'I'm not sure,' whispered Viv, 'but he'll do.' The Lefer chittered softly and cocked his head.

'He wants your hair. They like bright things.'

'I know, but I'm gifting him something far better.' She pulled the Waradi tryst-bracelet from her pocket, turned it so it caught the light, and tossed it to him. The Lefer snatched it from mid-air, and flapped away, cawing in triumph. 'We can go now,' she said and climbed down.

'Now all we need is another rift,' said the Syld when they reached the forest floor.

'Bingo!' said Viv and stopped. 'We can use the same one, although technically it's not the same one, given it opens on the Scinta Rill.'

'But it came from Astraal.'

'The one that was here *previously* did,' agreed Viv,

His brows drew in suspicion. 'It doesn't make sense.'

'Rifts don't *make sense*, Syld, but I want to transit before it closes. Enda seems to favour us and it's best to go before Soaich arrives.'

'You don't believe in gods.'

'I might be persuaded to if they treat me nicely,' said Viv, and stepped into the rift.

They exited beside a mountain stream but not into the clear skies they had left. Blue-black clouds boiled and the wind was knife-edged. 'The Scinta Rill,' said the Syld in relief. 'You've done well.'

'Thank Enda, not me.'

'But not Soaich for the storm he's gifted us,' he said, staring skywards. 'We're a half day's climb from the sett, but we'll head nightwise to the Soril Forest. It's safer if Soaich sends his Bolts.'

Viv followed him up the bank, keeping her head down as the wind whipped her hair around her face. He did not speak, which was nothing new, but as the temperature plummeted she would have liked to know exactly how far the forest was.

They went on through scattered stands of trees and Viv glanced nervously at the sky, reminded of when Soaich *had* sent his Bolts and scored a bull's eye. 'Not far now,' he said, without turning. He was adept at picking up her feelings and she would have blamed Taris had they been mounted.

They crossed a small ridge and she saw the dark edge of a forest stretched out below. 'We need to quicken our pace,' he said and broke into a jog. She followed, as keen as he was to reach its shelter. 'The Soril Forest is favoured by arlings and senglings,' he said when they reached the trees. 'But they won't be abroad in this weather.' It was warmer out of the wind but the branches clashed and twigs rained down. 'There is a good camp site ahead,' he clipped out.

Viv blinked at his abrupt change of tone but could tell nothing from the back of his head. 'You've camped here before?'

'Yes.'

Great; nothing like a one-word answer to get to the nub of a problem. *Well, Vivi, have a guess.* 'With Sehereden?'

'Yes.'

She jumped at a crack like rifle-fire and the canopy flashed blue. 'Run!' he ordered. They sprinted through the trees, down gullies, and up stony rises until he slewed to a stop at a massive stand of trees, grabbed her hand,

and pulled her in beside him. 'Maiwins,' he panted. 'They give good shelter but nothing's sure when Soaich hurls his Bolts. Get struck by one of those and you're dead.'

'I did get struck and I'm not dead.' The Syld looked at her sharply. 'I was with Sehereden and we got caught in a storm after we left Tahsin's sett. Sehereden found shelter but I stayed in the open.' She smiled grimly. 'I had previously been in a fold where there were multi-coloured stars and I thought the Bolts were just a pretty variation on those.' There was another crack and blue flash and Viv flinched.

'What did he do?'

'Forced air into my lungs for most the night and gave me his amé.' She gave a shaky smile. 'He saved me.'

'He saved me too,' said the Syld quietly, 'just by being here.'

The burst of heat would have been a comfort given the cold, had it not flowed from his suffering. 'Ataghan—'

'Maiwins will be insufficient shelter once the rain starts,' he said brusquely. 'Stay where you are while I pitch the maark.'

'I don't mind getting wet. It's too dangerous for—'

'Stay!' he ordered and eased himself out from the trunks.

'I'm not a bloody dog, *Syld*,' she muttered as she watched him jam the maark's struts into the ground and fasten the oiled cloth over them. And not a moment too soon, as it turned out.

'Inside,' he ordered, as a roar heralded the downpour. It was an order Viv was happier to obey but she still rankled. He pulled the sleep-covers from his pack and unrolled them, and retrieved some food. 'Bolts can linger after storms,' he said. 'We stay put until tomorrow.'

250

She nodded her thanks for the food but did not speak. 'You're angry, Ilris. Why?'

'I'm *not* one of your men and I *won't* be ordered about.'

'When you join my sett, you'll be under my authority, as are all who live there.'

'*If* I join your sett.'

Viv felt another burst of heat. 'I understood you had ended your search for your mother and wanted to be with your lein. Was I mistaken?'

'No, but that doesn't mean I'm putting myself under *any* man's power, including yours.'

His gaze was intense and she looked away. If it had not been deluging down outside she might have made her escape, in fact, she still might, except he would prevent it. He would fudge the reason as protection from Soaich's Bolts but the real reason was his need to control.

'Do they lein-tryst in Moonsun?' he asked abruptly.

'They call it *marriage*,' said Viv sneeringly. 'It's all about love and respect and only coupling with each other. My mother married Jimmy Wright and he beat her almost every night. And if you're murdered where I'm from, it will probably be by the man you married. And even where there's no violence, there's lying and cheating. Not much different to here, I suppose, given the mother of Baraghan's son is lein-trysted to another man.'

'Is that why you didn't lein-tryst with Sehereden? Because you didn't trust him?'

Viv grimaced. 'I couldn't be honest with Sehereden about what I really was *and* he believed I would have a child with him.' She stared out to where the rain sheeted down. 'Moonsun's surgeons are a hell of a lot more skilled than those here, Syld. I won't be having a child with *any* man.' She bit her lip as she considered the other things

Lady Luck had dished up. 'We didn't have enough time together either. Something always went wrong, like Eshtelin and Stelin Ridge.'

'Did you trust him?' The question of trust was obviously important to the Syld, given he kept harking on it.

'Yes. I trusted Sehereden.'

'And do you trust me?'

Shit! She felt like throwing the question back in his face. And do *you* trust *me*, Syld? And her stinking angel blood gave her no room to dissemble. She stared out at the rain searching for inspiration and found none.

'Ilris?'

'No. I don't trust you.'

Chapter 32

The silence that followed was made worse by the maark's confinement. There was nothing she could say to soften her words and she wished to God she had come up with a more obscure, more *palatable* answer. She glanced sideways at him, relieved his attention was on the rain too.

'I understand why,' he said evenly, 'but it goes back a lot further than me, doesn't it?'

'What does?'

'The betrayal.' Viv swallowed dryly and he turned, his gaze measuring. 'Your mother abandoned you; your choose-father beat you; your lover Rim abused you, as did Thrisdane, who chose transcendence. Sehereden was different, but he left too, taken by death, while I ...' He paused. 'I doubt even Rim's excesses surpassed mine.'

'How do you know these things?' she whispered.

'From what you told Fariye and Sehereden, *and* from what you *didn't* tell them; and from what you've told me *and* revealed in delirium when Soaich had his claws in you. And I know what I've inflicted on you, although not the full depth of its damage, though I can guess.'

Viv's eyes burned and she pushed a shaking hand through her hair. The Syld regarded her in silence, as if he awaited her forgiveness or condemnation, but she could offer neither. Her time in Erath was dream-like now, but Syatha's revelation of Viv's power to choose remained clear. Every instinct told her to walk away, to endure the rain and risk the Bolts, but she stayed where she was.

'My mother loved me so I think her *abandonment* was accidental,' she said slowly. 'When Thris and I first set out to find her, I imagined her as I had last seen her, and I imagined being safely back in her arms. It's taken me a long time to realise she's gone beyond my reach, and that I could spend the rest of my very long life chasing her memory through the folds. And that's all it would ever be, just a memory.

'Or I could stay here with Poss, and have something real in my arms, something loving and precious. And as for you … I know your pain, Syld. Not for Sehereden, because I've never lost a lein, but the pain deeper inside, where things are in pieces that should be whole.' She shuffled over to his side. 'You have a choice, Ataghan.' His face was a mask and she gently turned it to hers. 'You have a choice.'

His mouth came to hers with a suddenness that ignited a passion that matched his own. There was no slow love-making, just a hunger that fired and was sated, fired and was sated, until they rested at last, tangled naked in each other's arms. The rain had slowed to a pitter on the maark's roof, but the light had ebbed too. 'About time Soaich left us in peace,' she murmured. 'Maybe we should go on.'

'And maybe we should stay here.'

She propped on her elbow. 'Is that an order, Syld?' she asked ironically.

'It's a suggestion, as we're yet to reach my sett.' His expression was as gentle as when he looked at Fariye, and she savoured it as she kissed him lightly on the lips. 'Ilris.' He said the name with such tenderness it pierced her heart. He would soon be back to his usual, *closed-off* self, but she was hungry for the moment to last. It did not, he sat up and reached for his clothes. 'I'll find some dry fuel and set a fire. Then we'll eat. It's a half day's journey tomorrow, but we'll leave at first light. I need to be back in my sett.'

Viv watched the sun rise the next morning as they walked beside the Scinta Rill's bright rush. The sky was cloudless and as gold seeped over the land, the first of the bird-chimes sounded in the forests. Yep Vivi, a picture-perfect day with ya picture-perfect man. What could possibly go wrong?

'You kept the Waradi tryst-bracelet a long time, Iris. Why discard it now?'

'I no longer need it for trade,' she said evenly, her gaze on the rill. 'If living in your sett doesn't work out, I can beg a room from Baraghan in Astraal, or go back to the Kama-ril.' Her answer was true, *as far as it went*. She had initially kept the bracelet to avoid transference and later to goad the *arsehole*, a piece of grit in his oyster shell that had produced more pain than pearl. But if she *were* to share his sett, she wanted to remove as many causes of tension as possible.

'Is that the only reason?'

Shit! Yet another occasion when being able to lie would be *really* handy. 'I want to be rid of things that anger you, for Poss's sake. The last thing she needs are arguments and ill-feeling. I want her to be happy.'

'Something we share,' he said briefly, but she sensed it was not the answer he had wanted.

The val broadened as the day drew on and Viv's tension rose as a freshly constructed fence came into view and then, a while later, a group of men who worked on what looked like a barn. Her steps slowed and the Syld reached for her hand. The men downed their tools to greet them, and while Viv recognised most of them from Esh-accom,

255

it was going to take her longer to remember their names, despite the Syld's formal introductions.

'Berenth en-Scinta-ril, I present Viv en-Scinta-ril, my daughter's lein, formerly of the Kama-ril. Zeneden en-Scinta-ril, I present Viv en-Scinta-ril, my daughter's lein, formerly of the Kama-ril. Madragh en-Scinta-ril, I present Viv en-Scinta-ril, my daughter's lein, formerly of the Kama-ril.'

They went on up the slope through the sett's yards and out-buildings, the introductions repeated countless times. Men pruned retsen stands, hoed rows of some sort of green-food, weeded crops that looked like corn, cleaned stables, and came out of stone buildings, their clothes smelling of cheese and urrut-sa. Some of the men had seen the Syld tether her to the urrut caravan, others been at Esh-telin or at Stelin Ridge, still others had witnessed him strike her after Fariye's abduction, but she was something else now, her hand in his.

It was probably part of the deal he made with Ithreya, she cautioned herself, but he did not skimp on his half of the bargain. The respect he showed her, demanded his men's respect in turn, but Viv was relieved to leave them behind.

She expected him to drop her hand, but he led her on past trees and then the sett came into view and he stopped. He had used pale stone in curved walls and topped the roof with limed shingles to create a sinuous, silvery sweep. He might hate Astraal, but his angel blood hankered after its beauty

'Do you like it, Viv en-Scinta-ril?' he asked softly.

'Yes. It's lovely.'

The tension lessened in his hand and he led her on along a pathway edged with flowering bushes with stone seats to rest on, and stone dishes to trap water for birds. The plantings were recent, and the timber raw with newness, but the Syld and his men had not just rebuilt the sett, they had made a home.

The impression was strengthened by the carved wood that edged the wall and ceiling joints inside, and when they reached the hall, by the carved tables and chairs. The wood-smell reminded her of the carving-room in Esh-accom and that the Syld could do more than kill.

There were a dozen or so people seated in the hall, both men and women, and a group of noisy children playing chase beyond the window. There were still more introductions, and then Poss burst through the doorway, and threw herself shrieking into Viv's arms.

Poss's sobs soaked her jacket and Viv was powerless to stop the tears sliding down her own face. Then Poss grabbed at the Syld and pulled him closer. 'Both,' she cried, and struggled to hug them together. 'You're never going away again, are you, lein? You're staying here with me, aren't you? Aren't you?' Poss's tear-stained face turned to the Syld. 'She's staying, isn't she, da? Isn't she?'

'She's Viv en-Scinta-ril, now Fariye. She's part of my sett.'

Fariye buried her face in Viv's neck and then Drasen appeared from the passageway. There was real warmth in the way he embraced the Syld *and* his greeting of her. 'It's good to see you again, Viv, and I see Fariye's found you.' He smiled and brushed Viv's curls with his fingers. 'Longer hair really suits you.' She felt the Syld bristle, and so did he, his face showing surprise as he hastily dropped his hand.

'I came straight from Esh-accom, Syld, so I've been here a little while. Ithreya decided to come here first, instead of returning to the Verra-ril for a time, so I joined her escort. The rest of Amethen's party thank you for your sett's hospitality and have since departed.'

'The baby's well?' asked the Syld quickly.

'Very well, as Ithreya is,' said Drasen, smiling again. 'It's been a tiring journey for a woman who's newly-birthed but Ithreya's asked to speak with Viv, if *when* she arrived. I'll take you now, Viv, *with* the Syld's permission.'

The Syld nodded and Viv tried to put Fariye down but she clung on more tightly. 'No! You'll go again!' she sobbed.

Viv brought her forehead to Poss's. 'Remember how I promised never to leave without saying goodbye?' Poss nodded mutely. 'I've kept my promise, haven't I, Poss?' Again, the nod. 'I'll *never* leave you without saying goodbye, but I need to see Ithreya.' Poss reluctantly relinquished her and took the Syld's hand.

Viv followed Drasen out of the hall and down another beautifully carved passageway. He knocked on a door and when Ithreya bade them enter, politely opened the door for Viv, gave a small bow and left. Shutters blocked the morning sun, making the room dim, but Ithreya hastened forward and embraced her. 'It's so good to see you again, Viv. And your hair! It's lovely.'

'And you are well?' asked Viv thickly, undone by the warmth of Ithreya's greeting.

'I am indeed. And I have a daughter.' Ithreya opened the shutters a crack and Viv followed her to the cradle. The baby slept and Viv's throat constricted as she took in the child's face. 'She is beautiful,' she managed to say.

'And she's Sehereden's,' confirmed Ithreya. 'You know I'm gifting her to Ataghan?' Viv nodded. 'But not unconditionally. What I'm doing, I'm doing for Sehereden *and* for my daughter. You need to know that Viv, and that I'm not playing games.' Viv nodded again, and Ithreya settled back in her chair.

'Sehereden loved Ataghan as leins do, and his love kept Ataghan from the excesses that make elddric feared and despised, not that anyone ever dare utter the word *elddric* in the Syld's hearing, and Sehereden never did to me, even in our most intimate moments. But my seed-father journeyed to Astraal and spoke of those there, as you know.

'When Ataghan thought Fariye dead, only Sehereden prevented him committing even worse atrocities, and we both saw him after Sehereden's death. He had been a loving and protective father to Fariye but was prepared to abandon her.

'Sehereden would have wanted his seed-daughter to go to his lein, but I am not Sehereden and I won't risk what almost happened to Fariye, ever happening to Vivreya. So, I decided to force the issue with regards to you.'

Viv stared at her in surprise. 'Me?'

Ithreya smiled. 'I saw early on you were a good match for the Syld but his hatred of all things Astraali blinded him to it. You shared a love for Fariye, and for Sehereden, of course, and you're both fiercely protective of those you love. Your Angellus blood also gifts you a similar life-span. Together you could provide Vivreya with a safe and happy home.'

'You named her after me?'

'After *both* of us. Sehereden loved us both, so it was fitting, but I also wanted to remind the Syld of my conditions.'

'That I live at the Scinta-ril?

'Yes, and lein-tryst with him.' Viv blinked in shock.

259

'I see he hasn't shared the second condition with you. No doubt he has his reasons, but know this: if he hasn't built enough trust with you by the end of Pool Zadic for you to accept a lein-tryst, I'll take Vivreya back to the Verra-ril and gift her to someone who *is* worthy of trust.'

Viv exited the room as quietly as she could, given she would have liked to slam the door, and strode off down the passageway. The Syld was with the others in the hall but she stormed past him, too infuriated to speak. It was still fine outside, but colder, and she strode away from the sett, barely knowing where she went.

There was a path cut into the stone and she turned up it. Flowers had been planted to either side, but their blooms were spent and their yellow petals littered the ground. The steps ended at an emerald pool fed by a slender waterfall and Viv stopped. She had been here before with Poss, when the Scharii's violence had been fresh on her skin, the sett in ruins, and every shadow filled with threat.

A stone seat had been set to take in the view, but Viv was in no mood to sit. She had been suckered by some slimy bastards in her time, but the Syld took the cake. She should have known he would do *anything* to get his hands on Sehereden's child, including pretending affection, acceptance, and respect. Men had screwed her over for much smaller prizes, yet she had believed the Syld had changed, when *nothing* had changed. Even living in the sett no longer seemed possible. *No happily ever after, eh Vivi?*

There was a patter of footsteps, but she did not trust herself to turn, even when Poss's small hand slid into hers. 'Da said I would find you here, lein. The Scinta Pool's pretty, isn't it?' Viv nodded. 'I want to show you something only me and da know about. You have to keep it secret too. It's this way, lein.' Poss tugged her away and kept a firm grip on Viv's hand even as she scrambled up the slope. Frost lingered in the shadows and Viv's breath plumed. 'It's somewhere here,' said Poss, her eyes darting about.

Viv could see the sett below through a gap in the trees, but she could never be part of it, not when her place there was built on a web of lies. 'This way,' said Poss, pulling her on. She followed the little girl along a small crest, and then Poss crouched beside the remains of a massive tree, its trunk glossy with age, and gently parted the grass. 'Here,' said Poss excitedly.

A plant blossomed there with silver leaves and exquisite, star-shaped, aqua flowers. 'Only da and I know it's here,' whispered Poss, 'and Sehereden did, of course. Da brings me here every Horse Zadic 'cos he knows I don't like the cold. Sometimes the snow comes right down to the sett but Da says if we didn't have Horse and Pool Zadics, we wouldn't appreciate the other zadics as much.

'Da says the flowers remind us all things in The Wheel are beautiful. They only bloom when it's really cold, but you have to know where to look. You have to see there's not just ice and snow, but beautiful things too.' Poss carefully picked a bloom and presented it to Viv. 'It's for you, lein.'

'Thank you, Poss, but don't pick anymore. It should be left to flower.'

'That's what da says, but I wanted to welcome you to our sett.'

'Has it got a name?' asked Viv, as they made their way back.

'Yes. It's called an ilris.'

Viv said nothing until they reached the Scinta Pool. 'I think I might sit for a while, Poss, but it's cold. You should go back to the sett.'

'Da likes to sit here too,' said Poss. Her arms encircled Viv's neck and she planted a warm kiss on her cheek. 'I love you so much, lein.'

Viv sat on the stone seat and looked at the pool. It was edged with ice and she shivered, but she did not want to return to the sett, and after a while, footsteps crunched over the grass. 'Can I sit with you?'

'It's your seat in your sett.'

He sat next to her and stared at the pool. 'It's not what you think.'

'And what is it I think?'

'That my feelings for you are a lie, concocted to gain what I *really* want, namely the child of my dead lein. That anything I've offered you is part of that lie, that our coupling meant nothing to me, that it was all a pretense that would end once Sehereden's child was safely in my possession.'

'And wasn't it?'

'When Ithreya offered me Sehereden's child, the gift was so precious I was prepared to do *anything* to meet her conditions, right up to the moment you disappeared beneath the waves in Astraal's sacred lake. I thought I had lost you, Ilris. It changed everything.'

'Then why not tell me of Ithreya's demand for a lein-tryst?'

'Because I feared you would react as you have. I wanted time with you here, without threats, and fighting, and death; with Fariye, in a home I hoped you would want too. I hadn't expected Ithreya to arrive so soon.'

He pulled his amè over his head and handed it to her. 'Open it, Ilris.' The metal cylinder was a plainer version of hers, the mechanism the same. It held two locks of hair and a broken feather, and she stared at the feather in confusion. 'Fariye's hair I've had since she was gifted; Sehereden's I took before the pyre, while the feather ...' He picked it up and laid it gently in his palm. 'I found it on the feed-store floor, after you had flown from the roof, to save Fariye, as it turned out.

'For a long time, it lay forgotten in my pocket, and then I found it again as I walked in Esh-accom's rain after Sehereden's death. I crushed it and let the Vorash wash it to the cobbles. I wanted to walk away, to forget how you had come to my room, braved my knives, held and healed me, a despised elddric who had dealt you nothing but hatred and harm. But I couldn't walk away, Ilris. I put the feather in my amè to guide me in death, as precious to me as Sehereden and Fariye's love.'

She took a steadying breath and looked at him for the first time. 'What do you want, Ataghan?'

'Someone who knows what I am and loves me despite it.'

'Like Sehereden?'

'Yes, but a lein isn't a lein-tryst.' He paused. 'And what do you want, Ilris?'

'Someone who knows what I am and loves me despite it.'

'Like Thrisdane?' he asked, but the tension had gone from his voice.

'Yes, but an angel isn't elddric. Thris never understood my human part. He couldn't.' She swallowed several times. 'You've seen me at my worst.'

'And you've seen me at mine. Will you lein-tryst with me?'

'I can't give you children, Ataghan, and I won't stand in line with other women you want.'

'You've gifted me Fariye twice, and because of you, Ithreya's offered me Sehereden's child. And you've gifted me a life I never hoped to have. I want that life, Ilris, and I want it with you alone.' He offered her his hand and she took it. 'Will you lein-tryst with me, Violet Iris Vacia?' he asked formally.

His gaze was intense, but it was Syatha she thought of, and the choice the Sai had offered her between roses and thorns. 'Yes, Syld, I will lein-tryst with you.'

He closed his eyes in relief. 'I don't have a tryst-bracelet, but I'll trade for one in Esh-accom when the weather improves.'

She ran her fingers down the stubble of his jaw. 'Really, Syld. I would have kept the Waradi one had I known.' She smiled. 'I've never cared about such things.'

'It's a formal acknowledgement of our trysting which Esh-accom's Sylds will record and make public.'

'I've got something more important, Syld,' she said, and carefully extracted the ilris from her pocket. *'Da says the flowers remind us that all things in The Wheel are beautiful. They only bloom when it's really cold, but you have to know where to look. You have to see there's not just ice and cold, but beautiful things too.'*

'Fariye has a good memory,' he said thickly.

'Fariye has a good father.'

He reached for her and their kiss was long. 'Are you ready to come back to the sett, Ilris? To face those there as my lein-tryst? There will be some who will doubt, but

Fariye's squeals will drown them out. She'll give you no peace,' he warned.

'And that is as it should be,' she said, and smiled. 'Yes, Syld, I'm ready.'

This completes Viv's story in the Angel Caste series

Like to read about other wonderful female heroes in brilliant new worlds? You might enjoy Kira's story.

The Kira Chronicles 6 Book series

Book 1 The Whisper of Leaves

Amazon US - https://www.amazon.com/dp/B07D63Z91H
Amazon Australia - https://www.amazon.com.au/dp/B07D63Z91H
Amazon Canada - https://www.amazon.ca/dp/B07D63Z91H
Amazon UK - https://www.amazon.co.uk/dp/B07D63Z91H

Take a peek at Book 1

'Do you wish for aid, Healer?' asked Brem.

Kira nodded. She liked Brem, despite him once threatening to thrash her and Tresen for cracking one of the longhouse water barrels by jumping onto it from an espin. It had been a hollow threat. Every child in Allogrenia knew that violence was prasach, and the domain of the barbarous Terak Kutan, not the Tremen.

He had called her *kira-si* then, after the owlings that had yet to fledge, but now he used the formal title of *Healer*. Let's hope she deserved it, thought Kira, as she unwound the bandage, and then the stench hit her, and she reeled back. The wound was slimed and reeking, and she stared at it in shock. Not even summer carrion putrefied that quickly.

Brem was rigid, his face filled with horror. 'He was slashed first,' he said thickly.

Kira struggled to make sense of his words and gave up. There was no time for anything but ridding the wound of rot. 'Boil water,' she ordered, as she scrambled to her feet and swung on her pack. 'Then fill the wound with cloths as hot as he can bear.'

She flung on her cape and ran back to the cavern's mouth. Kest spoke to a Protector but she barged between them. 'Feseren's wound has poisoned. I must gather,' she said hurriedly.

In her head, she already sprinted towards the Barclan octad where the land was moister, but Kest's hand fastened on her arm. 'I don't know how many times we must have this conversation Healer, but—'

'I *must* have sorren now!' she said and tried to wrench herself free. 'Feseren is worsening as we speak!'

'You will remain here.'

'You have no right—' She gasped as his grip tightened, and felt another, gentler hand.

'Kira . . .'

It was Tresen, and she turned on him furiously. 'You betray your Healer-blood!'

'You need to *explain* your urgency to Protector Leader Kest.'

266

Kira's gaze jerked between them, and she gulped down air. 'Sorren is the most powerful purifier known in Allogrenia. It kills infection, but I used all I had after the attack.'

'If sorren is so powerful, why has the wound worsened?' asked Kest. 'Has journeying caused it?'

Kest's face was haggard and for a moment she was tempted to lay the blame on him. 'The journey might have made it worse, but it isn't the cause. My healing was poor.'

'I don't believe that,' interjected Tresen.

Kira kept her eyes on Kest. 'I don't ask you to risk your men, Protector Leader. I will go alone.'

Kest's face took on the expression of weary exasperation she had seen before. 'You don't seem to understand the nature of my job, Healer Kiraon. It is *you* I am bound to protect. I can't let you go.'

Kira's voice sank to a fierce whisper. 'Feseren is dying, Kest! If you want to keep me here, you had better get some rope ready, because I won't sit by and watch it happen.'

Kest's mind raced. Sarkash's orders were clear: protect the leader and his family and *protect* didn't mean binding one of their members hand and foot! And he owed his men protection as well. To lose any of them was unthinkable, but Feseren! His bondmate Misilini was heavy with their first child.

'We will go together,' he growled, and wrenched his pack back on over his wet shirt.

The Healer was already at the cave entrance, and he bawled at her to wait, then shouted orders to Penedrin. She paused for a moment but then disappeared from view, and he ran after her, the rain-edged air chill against his face as he plunged down the slope. So much for the warm meal he had promised himself, not to mention the blessedness of sleep.

The Healer leapt from stone to stone, and he copied her as best he could, to finally land with a thud in the leaf-litter at the bottom. She was already just a smudge amongst the trees and, smothering a curse, he set off after her.

I hope you enjoyed *Angel Caste* Book 5 – *Angel Blessed*.
Authors need reviews! It is how our readers find us.
I would love you to leave me an honest review on
Amazon, Goodreads, or another of your favourite reader
sites. Read on to discover my other books.

Works by K S Nikakis
Available on Amazon KDP and a range of digital
platforms.

Non Fiction

**Journey: Seeking the Sacred, Spirit and Soul in the
Australian Wilderness**

***Deadway - Finalist Best Poem
2020 Australian Shadows Awards***

When we set out into the wilderness, what is it we *really*
seek?

Do we seek new sights or do we seek new selves? And
are we *really* on one journey or on two?

Journeying fifteen thousand kilometres into Australia's
blood-red heart, Nikakis discovers that every journey is
perilous, for travellers risk carrying the clutter of their
outer lives with them; a clutter that blinds them to the
other journey they crave; that of the inner *soul-journey*
into a deeper understanding of self.

To enter Australia's vast Outback wilderness, is to enter
a place of endless horizons; a place doused with brilliant

gold dawns and dazzling sunsets; a place silvered by star-encrusted night skies and, most importantly, a place of hidden sacred places in whose deep stillness our inner journeys can at last unfold.

In the spirit of travellers like Robert Macfarlane and Scott Stillman, Nikakis asks what it is we really see, feel and understand when we follow in the steps of those who have gone before us deep into the wilderness.

Drawing on her Ph.D. in Joseph Campbell's hero myth, and using original poetry and novel extracts, Nikakis takes us on this second journey; a journey of the sacred, spirit and soul, where our inner selves finally have the time and space to gift us richer and more fully-realised lives.

Fantasy Novel Series

Angel Caste 5 Book Series – available complete in one book or as five individual books: Angel Blood, Angel Breath, Angel Bone, Angel Bound, Angel Blessed.

Angel Caste – Complete 5 Book Series - *A modern female hero on a timeless quest*

A troubled street kid, an angel guide, a binding promise . . .

Viv is on day release from jail to attend the funeral of the thug she thinks is her father, when her real father turns up, the powerful angel Archae Kald. If that is not shocking enough, Viv discovers her mother is not dead after all but lost somewhere in the tangle of worlds called the Rynth.

Determined to find the only person who ever loved her, Viv rift transits to Kald's angel world where he assigns the beautiful Thris to guide her to her mother. Thris is different to every male Viv has ever known but after a life on the streets, she finds it impossible to trust.

Thris trains her to travel the rifts, but the Rynth is a dark and dangerous place, even for angels and when Viv's angel traits emerge, disaster strikes. Lost and alone in the Rynth, Viv stumbles on a lost child in a war zone, and pledges to take the child to safety. But in the perilous worlds of the Rynth, deciding who is friend and who is foe is a deadly game of chance.

Bound by his pledge to guide Viv to her mother, Thris embarks on a desperate search for her, but a greater threat confronts them both and they must fight not just for their own lives, but for the lives of those they love.

The Kira Chronicles - 6 Book Series – available complete in one book or as six individual books: The Whisper of Leaves, The Silence of Stone, The Secrets of Stars, The Thunder of Hoofs, The Crying of Birds, The Music of Home.

The Kira Chronicles – Complete 6 Book Series – *traditional fantasy with deep forests and high stakes*

A gold-eyed Healer, a prophecy, two brothers at war.

In seasons long past, twin gold-eyed princes sundered a kingdom. Rejecting his brother Terak's warrior ways, Kasheron led his people deep into the great southern forests and established the healing settlement of Allogrenia. The Tremen flourished, upholding Kasheron's legacy of peace and healing, and protected by the vast, trackless trees.

All Tremen delight in the healing arts, but Kira is the greatest Healer of them all.

To the north of Allogrenia, drought ravages the Shargh's land, and as their suffering escalates, the chief's younger brother seizes on an ancient prophecy to snatch the chiefship for himself. The prophecy links the Shargh's doom to a gold-eyed Healer, and Kira has gold eyes.

The Shargh attack with devastating consequences and Kira must fight to save the wounded, but the Shargh wounds rot, no matter her skill, and Kira finds herself in a deadly race against time. As the slaughter continues, she makes the horrifying discovery that the Shargh hunt *her*. To halt the attacks and save her people, she sets off for the North to seek aid from her long sundered warrior kin.

But the dangers beyond the forests exceed even the Shargh attacks. The Tremen detest their warrior kin but Terak's descendants have inflicted a worse fate on the Tremen. Kira's new-found love is torn apart by ancient hostilities and when trust turns to betrayal, it risks everything she fought for.

As the battles rage on, Kira becomes increasingly sickened by the bloodshed. Desperate to end the suffering once and for all, she sets out on a quest that could cost her everything and everyone she loves.

Fantasy Novels

The Emerald Serpent – *the Celtic Fae in a fight for survival*

Book trailer: https://www.youtube.com/watch?v=bGpKxnpCEMg

Betrayal, torture, death: Etaine lives on only to destroy those who robbed her of everything she loved.

Seven years before, Etaine met fellow Ranger Cormac, the Eadar she believed was her longed-for true-mate. Emerald-eyed, white-skinned, and black-haired, the Eadar had formed into Ranger bands to fight the Fada, invading religious zealots determined to replace the Eadar's Serpent Goddess with their own gods of stone.

The pure blood of the ancient Eadar runs strong in Etaine and Cormac's veins, and their joining had the potential to open the Emerald and Serpent Ways to them, old worlds only true Eadar can enter. But their love affair goes tragically amiss, with catastrophic consequences.

Etaine flees and as the years pass, slowly rebuilds her life, but the Fada's attacks grow more ferocious, and the Eadar are forced to fight for their very existence. When the Fada mass to commit yet more bloody slaughter, and the bands join in a final, desperate effort to defeat them, Etaine comes under Cormac's command, the very last Eadar she ever wants to see again.

Together they have a weapon that can destroy the Fada, but to use it, Etaine must learn to trust again and Cormac to Remember. And time runs short: the Serpent rises.

Heart Hunter – *a female hunter on an impossible quest*

Fleet is a young Sceadu hunter: skilled, strong, and fast.
She hunts deep into the icy mountains, seeking meat
for her people, for the rains have failed and plunged the
Sceadu into hunger.

Her hunts are hard, but she has much to look forward
to. Soon she will be gifted her air-name by the Sceadu's
shaman, and then she will be a full adult, and free to
marry the man she loves.

But while Fleet is on hunt, the old shaman dies, and the
new shaman visions a very different future for her: cross
the frozen, ice-locked mountains and complete a perilous
quest or lose the man she loves forever.

In a moment of anger and frustration, Fleet commits a
terrible wrong and sets out into the frigid mountains to
atone with her life. In a journey that takes her deep into
the earth's darkest places, into strange new worlds, and
even into Death itself, she discovers that only she can
save her people. To survive, she must draw on every
shred of her hunter strength, and doing the impossible, it
turns out, is just the beginning.

The Third Moon – *science fantasy with a very human quest*

Where does the past end and the future begin?

Haunted by inherited memories of his people's dispossession and theft of their children, Warrain is just twelve years old when the nightmare repeats. But Warrain isn't living on Earth in the 21st Century, he is living on the planet Imago in the far flung future.

Five years before, Station One's Mech's got high on the opioid arrash, and in the bloodshed that followed, Warrain's scientific community were expelled from the Station, his father murdered, and his mother and unborn sibling lost to him.

The scientists carve out a rudimentary Station high in Imago's ranges, and Warrain's friends get on with their lives. Not Warrain; he climbs the Tors to stare down at Station One, dream of his mother and sibling, and plot revenge.

And then one day, everything changes. A third moon appears in the sky, one of Imago's life-forms calls him by name, and disease breaks out at Station One.

When the Mechs visit to seek help for their ill, Warrain seizes the opportunity to deal them a blow they will never forget. But the third moon brings changes that threaten them all and, to aid the life-form whose kind is being dispossessed and slaughtered, he must turn his

back on the hate that has long sustained him and find
another way to live.

Messenger – *a dystopic future filled with hope*

In a world made deaf by hatred, who will hear the messenger?

Severine's world ends the day her family is murdered. Being raised in the loving community of gay Travelers always marked her as an outsider, but being female puts her in mortal danger. Women are scarce, precious, and hunted.

When chance brings Severine face to face with the father she has never known, he assigns the son of his murdered best friend to guard her. They soon clash. Severine believes all men are violent brutes and Jeph resents his freedoms being curtailed.

An uneasy understanding grows but Jeph is glad to deliver her to the Enclaves, a sanctuary her father has carved out in the mountains for his women and children. But there is no safety in a world broken by war and sickness and when violence follows her, Severine flees to the northern city of Andhaka in search of a home amongst her mother's people. Jeph follows, bound by loyalty to her father, but the north holds terrible dangers for him.

It's been years since Andhaka has welcomed outsiders with anything but bullets, and to survive and to protect Jeph, Severine must learn to use her enemies' weapons against them. As the stakes rise, she comes to understand the horror of her mother's loss, and what drove her father north seventeen years before. His quest becomes her

quest, but she hasn't counted on the savage legacy that
war and sickness have left behind, or on falling in love.

I Heard the Wolf Call My Name – *gender-fluid shifters in search of home*

Finalist Best YA Novel – 2019 Aurealis Awards

Jax is just twelve years old and in bird-form high above his island home, when it explodes, killing everyone on it. He believes he is the only survivor until ten years later, he comes face to face with his boyhood friend, Matiu.

Matiu is military and the military need shifters for a crucial mission, but Jax refuses. Having spent ten long years burying his bizarre shifter past, he isn't about to resurrect it. But Matiu rouses other feelings too that Jax finds harder to ignore.

As the military ramps up pressure to force Jax's cooperation, he shifts to bird-form and flees to the last remaining island where he crash lands in the middle of Anahera's vision-quest. She searches for her skin-spirit animal to transform her into a protector of her people, and dreams of finding the white-wolf, but finds Jax instead. To save him she must abandon her quest but her kindness only adds to Jax's turmoil.

To decide who he truly is and where he really belongs, he must first confront his painful past, but that isn't the worst of his problems. The forces that blew Jax's island out of existence now threaten Anahera's as well, and he might just be the only shifter who can save it.
And time is running out.

Fantasy Short Stories

The Gift – A Deep Fantasy Short Story #1 – free on my website at www.ksnikakis.com

Excerpt:

Thariel sat for a long time, surveying all around her, as if she ate the world that would soon be memory. Then she took the harness from the mare, and with soft words, thanked her and bade her farewell. Her own feet she turned towards the forest, tossing her face-plate aside as she went, so that her hair fell loose to her waist, then she discarded her chest-armour, the sword and dagger, her bow and quiver.

The trees closed in and she came at last to the lake Men call Menios and stood for a while on its shore. An owl cried and a mouse shrieked, and all around her the souls of the newly dead jostled in their journey to the void. She stepped into the water and the new life inside her quivered.

'Fear not, little one,' she whispered, in her own tongue. 'We are going home.'

**The Tale of Prince Anura – A Deep Fantasy Short
Story #2** – free on my website at <u>www.ksnikakis.com</u>

Excerpt:

I should have been happy, for she was beautiful. Dark rivers of curls, skin as white as moonlight on water, breasts softer than spawn, and she loved me well. But her chamber was small, no matter the comfort of her bed, and the old feelings of entrapment rose, as persistent as gas that bubbles from rot below still waters.

I sat at the casement and listened, as I had once loitered near the watery skin of the second world and waited. The moon grew large and small many times, but it came at last, as I knew it would. The soft lament on the night-time air, the song of a soul as confined as mine. It took me a journey of many days through the depths of a massive forest to find her tower.

Stone it was and sheer, and as remote as the third world's glimmer had once been. I sang to her and she answered with sweet melodies of her own and we made love as frogs do, with our voices. And when trust had built, she let down her shining ladder of golden hair.

Glass-Heart – A Deep Fantasy Short Story #3

Finalist Best YA Short Story, Aurealis Awards, 2019.

Excerpt:

Geth moved amongst his band, exchanging quiet words while they waited. Some he had fought with since the Tallon's foul ships had first found their shores while others had come later, when the burn of cot and kin had sent them from their valleys.

Hate drove them but hate was no shield against arrow and knife. It was fighting skills that kept them hale, and Geth ensured they had them aplenty. He needed them living, not just for their own sakes and his, but for what would come later. When the Tallon's stain had been scoured away, the destroyed must be rebuilt.

Kyth sat alone and he went to her and gazed about. 'The glass-heart's fled, has it?'

'I sent her to a place of safety. She will come to me when it is over.'

'Safety was what I wanted for you!'

'And what I wanted for Nyar.' Her eyes caught the star-sheen as she looked up at him. 'But you can't always have what you want, can you, Ceannasai?'

Dragon Sprite – A Deep Fantasy Short Story #4

Excerpt:

Genn rocketed straight upwards, not just because she enjoyed seeing the limitless blue sky before her, but because a Waiwin's wing shape made vertical flight harder for them. Orin didn't try to catch her but swept in circles around her, gaining height in an ever-narrowing spiral. It was a clever tactic and one Genn didn't believe hehad thought of in the instant she had cleared the trees. He had obviously studied her strategies and developed a plan to counter them *or so he thought.*

Genn waited until the spiral narrowed to *axeel*, the minimum distance a Waiwin must keep from a Velven unless she *accepted* him, then swerved towards him, narrowing the distance between them. Orin's eyes flashed to black, shocked she *had* accepted him, but before he could act, she folded her wings and dropped.

The strength that had driven Orin's pursuit had surged to his wing-tendrils in anticipation of locking them with hers and he would struggle even to stay airborne until it flowed back.